Hell
on
Earth

Eric Andersen

Contents

Dedicated to my cousins
(Please wait to read this when you are older)

Special thanks to my family, my friends, and my many instructors for their support and having patience and faith in me.

The Stone Guardians

It was a cold, late fall evening in New York. The sun was just about to set over the horizon. A tall man in a gray trench coat was leaving a theater that just released the newest vampire movie, "Bite Knight." While other moviegoers were amazed and awed by the film and its bloodsucking protagonist, the man was frustrated and somewhat bored.

Vampires... the man thought to himself as he strode down the streets, *what's so great about them? I mean they're no better than any other creature. Hell, I can think of two better races off the top of my head.*

As soon as he finished that thought, the sound of loud chewing noises broke the man's concentration. He turned to his right and noticed a small group of people huddled together in an alleyway. With uneasy suspicion, the man moved closer to the figures. They were gnawing on what appeared to be the corpse of a homeless man. The powerful smell of blood almost left a taste of copper on his tongue. As he stepped closer, the figures all turned to face him. Although their faces were cloaked in shadow, the man could still make out the crimson gore dripping from their mouths. He could feel that there was not any trace of body heat coming from the figures as they eyed the man who interrupted their meal.

"Okay..." the man sighed as he scratched his unshaven face, "you guys are obviously not human. Regarding this, I'm going to have to ask you to leave this area or die."

The creatures cackled and starred at the tall man through bloodshot eyes. As they stepped into the light of the lampposts, the man could now clearly tell they were vampires, six total. The tallest one strutted up to the man with a huge bloodstained grin across his face.

"And what does a mortal think it can do to us?" the towering vampire asked mockingly. He was a few inches taller than the man, who stood over most people himself.

The man wasted no time to react. In what seemed to be seconds, he struck the vampire, slamming him into the back wall of the alley, creating a pile of flaming red bones that turned to black ash. After witnessing their friend's death, the other five vampires slowly turned around to face the man and starred in horror at his right arm.

From the elbow down, the man's arm seemed to have grown three inches thicker in muscle and transformed into something beastly. The thick veins on his arm intertwined together like roots from a tree. The hue of the man's true flesh was the color of ice covering rock, though it was not exactly rock that the man really consisted of, it was something far stronger. Pieces of clay that had been colored to look like human flesh fell from the converted limb as he held the tall vampire's heart, which turned into ash and blew away in the wind, revealing the huge stone claws that grew out of the man's long, thick fingers. The man's eyes shown a toxic yellow as he grinned at the vampires with jagged, ivory stone teeth. Upon seeing this, the vampires realized who the man truly was.

"Tiogra!" the vampires exclaimed in fright. Even mentioning the man's real name made them shudder, let alone the fact that he was a gargoyle.

Watching the vampires begin to scatter, Tiogra lunged at another vampire and completely obliterated him with a stone punch to the skull. The other vampires eyed their comrade in terror as they saw Tiogra's stone fist turn completely solid before he hit their friend in the head, a hereditary reflex all gargoyles possessed. While the other vampires crawled away, Tiogra grabbed one by the leg and slammed him against a dumpster, which tore the vampire in half. As Tiogra watched his victims slowly turn to ash, he looked up in time to see the others make a clean escape onto the rooftops.

"Crap," Tiogra muttered at his rotten luck, "this is going on my record."

The gargoyle quickly transformed his other arm, leaving a pile of beige clay on the ground, along with fragments of a torn, leather sleeve. He then dug his claws into the wall and climbed up after his prey.

"Lets see how long this takes me." Tiogra challenged himself as he dashed after the vampires.

First, the vampires struggled to leap over a ten-foot wide gap between the buildings in front of them. Tiogra however, leapt across it with ease.

I really don't see the big deal with these guys, Tiogra thought as he ran after the vampires, *my race is faster, stronger, and we have more experience. We have honor and respect for life... well most of it anyway. Plus we know the arts of combat better than anyone else.*

As Tiogra pursued his prey, he listened to the sound of his heavy footsteps upon the rooftops and compared them to the softer sounding sprint of his quarry. This gave Tiogra an uncoordinated feeling of amusement. During the first few weeks of their training, gargoyles were taught not to make such loud noises while in hostile situations. Nonetheless, Tiogra had to admit that he was being careless on purpose, mainly to make his victims scarred enough to become unfocused. It was shamefully amusing for any gargoyle to see an unorganized opponent.

Two of the vampires spun around and gestured at Tiogra, summoning a flock of pigeons that swooped down and pecked at the gargoyle's head. Tiogra quickly swatted the pigeons away and regained pursuit of the vampires.

Within moments, Tiogra caught up with the vampires, leapt over one and snapped the running vampire's neck, smiling as he felt his trench coat flowing behind him as he leapt.

Tiogra had many things in his life that he loved, one of which was the feel of a trench coat in his human disguise. The coat itself gave him a sense of importance and a sensation of intimidation towards his enemies. The way the coat flowed behind him was as if it were a second pair of wings. It was also useful in the fact that if Tiogra ever found himself in a situation that he recognized as hard to get out of, he could throw his coat over his opponents like a net.

Continuing the chase, Tiogra caught another vampire in his right hand and came to a halt, holding the vampire off the ground to keep him from running away. The pressure from Tiogra's grip made the vampire suffocate and unable to move. As he starred into the vampire's bleeding eyes, Tiogra started to squeeze his prey's neck until his head popped off his severely crushed throat, which turned to ash within Tiogra's grasp.

"Pigeons…" Tiogra scoffed as he walked away from the vampire's decomposing corpse.

After slaying his fifth victim of the night, Tiogra continued chasing after the remaining vampire. After being followed over a few more leaps and jumps, the vampire stopped and spun around, revealing a gun in his hand, much to Tiogra's surprise. Though taken back with shock to see an urban vampire with a firearm, Tiogra ducked behind a wall for cover. Simultaneously, the vampire began to shoot at the wall as if the bullets would pass through and hit their target.

As Tiogra crouched behind the wall, he wondered why a civic vampire would be carrying a gun. Usually, vampires were too arrogant to want to carry guns, thinking that they were far too powerful to need firearms in the first place.

Maybe they're finally getting smart. Tiogra thought to himself as bullets kept hitting the wall he was sitting behind.

Then it occurred to him, he was so deep in thought that he forgot to count the shots being fired. Tiogra could have sworn he heard six shots, yet was not sure if the gun the vampire held was a revolver or a semi-automatic pistol. Regardless of the gun's nature, he had to react fast before the vampire could get away.

As he leapt over the wall towards his victim, the vampire fired another shot, which hit Tiogra in the shoulder. The gargoyle warrior grunted in pain as the bullet pierced his flesh. As he knelt down and clenched his shoulder, Tiogra used his claws to brush off the clay pieces and pick out the bullet as green blood flowed from the wound. This was no time to feel pain, however. He had a vampire to catch, who was currently running away. The wounded gargoyle transformed his shoulder into stone so that the bleeding would stop and pursued his quarry.

After a few more obstacles and gaps, the vampire stopped at another gap that was too wide for him to jump. Tiogra saw the vampire's

3

predicament and took off his coat, leaving it on the rooftop behind him. Traffic buzzed below the vampire while Tiogra walked directly behind him as if to taunt him.

"C'mon, lets see you make it…if you can." Tiogra teased with a grin.

The vampire glanced at Tiogra, whimpering in fear. Seeing no other option, the vampire jumped, but only made it ten feet through the gap. Tiogra reacted quickly and sprouted stone wings, which tore through his black, ash-stained shirt, flew over the vampire, grabbed him by his leather jacket, and flew up into the sky. There, still frustrated about being shot, Tiogra hovered above the buildings and punched the vampire in the sternum, hard enough to smash a steel door. The vampire coughed up the blood from his earlier victim and wheezed from the impact of the blow. Starring into the eyes of his prey, Tiogra grinned menacingly at his victim, showing off his ivory stone teeth once more.

"What're you going to do?" the vampire asked, frightened and in pain.

Tiogra raised an eyebrow in response to the vampire's question, thinking it was obvious enough that he intended to kill his prey.

He grabbed the vampire by his leg and dangled him over the streets of the city that was now fifty feet below. Smiling with satisfaction even he thought was twisted, Tiogra dropped the screaming vampire and watched him travel downwards. The punch Tiogra had delivered to his victim's chest made the vampire slowly turn to ash until his remains hit the ground and completely disintegrated, without leaving any notable hint of his existence.

After retrieving his coat, Tiogra flew off into the night sky toward a nearby church, where he perched onto a ledge next to one of its gargoyles. The gargoyle Tiogra sat next to was much larger than any of the other gargoyles that sat around it. It's eyes were hidden in shadow from under it's enormous, horned, hairless brows, which were a common feature most gargoyles shared. A thick flap of skin sat across the bridge of it's short, thick nose and drooped down to it's jaw line. A beard of scales formed on the gargoyle's strong chin, giving off the appearance of facial hair. It's mighty, rippled ears were pushed close to it's head where the tips curved towards it's face as if they were horns. These features gave the gargoyle an expression of exaggerated unhappiness, which gave it's strong frame an impression of powerful melancholy. As Tiogra examined at the gargoyle's eyes from underneath it's brows, the gargoyle had the appearance as if it were sleeping.

"You shouldn't sleep on the job, Ghin." Tiogra said.

Instantly, the gargoyle sprang to life, startled by Tiogra's sudden appearance. His color changed from granite to maroon and bronze as he jumped from the ledge. As he looked at Tiogra, he sat back down and resumed a disgusted look on his face.

"Ah, Tiogra. Never could give your buddy Ghin a chance to rest could ya?" the gargoyle asked as he straightened his posture.

"Just making sure you don't give the grandmaster a reason to make you clean the castle." Tiogra said, "Besides, they call it watch duty not sleep duty."

Ghin chuckled as Tiogra mentioned the grandmaster, the leader of the gargoyle nation. The title of grandmaster was chosen for the gargoyle leader since he was the one who taught every gargoyle their way of life from the beginning of their race. This naturally made the gargoyles the grandmaster's students as well as his subjects. However, the grandmaster preferred to call the gargoyles his "pupils" since he personally saw the word "subjects" as degrading.

"I feel like I could sleep for the rest of my immortal life." Ghin said, looking down at the city, "I haven't had any sleep in…"

"Days?" Tiogra asked, interrupting his friend.

Ghin looked at Tiogra in a slightly exasperated manner. "Please, Tiogra," he said, "I could handle days. It's weeks I can't stand."

"C'mon, Ghin, you know the rules." Tiogra reminded, "The grandmaster says you need to divide the year into three sections. You should spend seventeen weeks on guard duty, at least seventeen on scouting and watching, and you get to divide seventeen weeks of sleep and free time between each duty your assigned."

"Yeah, yeah I know." Ghin muttered in acknowledgement as he looked down at the streets below. "It makes you wonder why no one ever suspects why one gargoyle would be bigger than the crude parodies on the rest of the church." He noted.

Tiogra chuckled at what uncanny sense his friend's comment made. "Good thing they have their egos to keep them occupied." He jeered.

Ghin chuckled at his friend's quip.

"Speaking of responsibility," Ghin began to ask, "What happened on your job this week?"

"Well," Tiogra began, "I did kill a group of suck heads a few moments ago. Found them feasting on a homeless guy. Oh, and apparently they carry guns now."

Ghin eyed Tiogra with suspicion and noticed the bullet wound on his friend's shoulder.

"Apparently…" Ghin said, "like that's 'apparently' a bullet wound."

Tiogra laughed at his friend's sarcasm. If there was anything Ghin was known for, it was his dark sense of humor.

"But in all seriousness, do you think they're getting wise on us?" asked Ghin.

"Yeah," Tiogra responded, "they're probably starting to realize they aren't as high on the food chain as they think they are."

"Probably... I don't suppose you were discreet about killing them, were you?" Ghin asked.

"Of course not." replied Tiogra.

"Figures." Ghin muttered.

Tiogra looked at his friend and smiled. "Look, maybe this way if people found out that vampires were living among them they'd start to fight them, you know? Fend for themselves."

"No, they are too weak, impulsive and uninformed." Ghin said, sternly.

Tiogra looked at his friend with pity. "You shouldn't be so judgmental, Ghin." Tiogra said, reminding Ghin of the grandmaster's teachings.

Ghin grunted at his friend's statement. It was bad enough he had an uneasy temper, but despite being thankful, Ghin hated when Tiogra would address his mistakes so abruptly.

"My point is," Ghin started to explain, "you shouldn't assume strength in people who obviously aren't ready for certain challenges. If humans ever found out that vampires exist, every human with a fetish for the narcissistic suck heads is going to want to become one. They'll start seeking out vampires just to get turned in hopes that they'll become sexy or something. In the end, we all wind up with the lycanthropes getting pissed off and hating us even more. The other races are going to get angry. The grandmaster surely won't be pleased..."

Ghin stopped to stare intensely into Tiogra's eyes.

"...And we'll wind up with a cesspool of a planet filled with beings allergic to the sun. A full-scale war would be inevitable, and life as we know it may cease to exist."

"Hmm, I never thought of it that way." Tiogra said.

"Probably for the best." Ghin muttered, "Pessimism is a real pain."

Tiogra smiled at his friend's dark humor. Yet as he thought about Ghin's negativity, he was mournful at the fact that Ghin had personal demons from his past that he could not overcome easily.

Centuries ago, Ghin was a rebellious young gargoyle who was always searching for action wherever he could find it. He was cheerful and outgoing and spent the majority of his days at parties thrown by other gargoyles. Though his carefree lifestyle was somewhat frowned upon by the grandmaster, Ghin was allowed to enjoy himself with little consequence.

To top off his amazing life, Ghin had a wife, Rejan, who had known him since they were both children, beginning their training within the gargoyle nation. His charm, masculine looks and humor were enough for Rejan to consider him for a spouse over the years. Within time, Ghin and Rejan had gotten married, making them the happiest gargoyles in the world. They were a match that was as impossibly perfect as "a diamond made from rain clouds" as Tiogra would say.

Years with Rejan made Ghin seek a humble existence with her. To ensure this, Ghin built a cottage in the Thuringian Forest in Germany, where he had taken work as a blacksmith. The skills Ghin had learned from master Boragen, the chief blacksmith of the gargoyles, were enough to provide a comfortable life for Rejan and himself. Humans from all the corners of Germany wanted to purchase the strong and exquisite iron works that Ghin produced. To secure their identities, Ghin and Rejan disguised themselves in flesh colored clay, using the techniques the grandmaster had taught them during their years of training.

The process was long and agonizingly dull, but thankfully, gargoyles were taught how to retract most of their beastly features so they only had to cover their arms and faces with clay. Wings and horns usually had to be hidden under clothing and accessories while the clay could easily make rock hard flesh look like callused skin and birth defects. Even the fur on their bodies could be used to mimic human hair. The most tedious part was that the gargoyles had to return to the castle in France, where the grandmaster resided, to retrieve more clay to hide their features. Luckily, Ghin and Rejan were able to maintain their secrecy well enough that no one would have guessed who they truly were.

For the longest time, everything was peaceful for Ghin and Rejan, until the night Ghin's life changed forever.

On that fateful night, Ghin was out late collecting firewood for the winter while Rejan stayed at the cottage. When Ghin was only a mile away from home after a long and tedious trip, he dropped the logs in horror at the sight of his house set ablaze by a group of bandits. As Ghin dashed toward his house, his eyes turned from shock to anger as he noticed Rejan was outside in the snow, doing her best to fight off the bandits in her gargoyle form. With a roar loud enough to frighten lions, Ghin reverted into his true form and lunged in the direction of the assailants. As he came closer, Ghin could see the light of the moon glisten off of the smiles of the bandits, revealing smooth, ivory fangs and showing him that these were, in fact, vampires. Observing the situation, the young gargoyle noted that there were seventeen vampire soldiers total. It suddenly became clear to Ghin that these vampires were not looking for money or valuable items, but that they were simply there to kill Rejan and himself. How their secret was revealed made no difference then, what mattered was making sure that Rejan was safe and that the vampires paid dearly for destroying the gargoyle couple's home.

Noticing Ghin, six of the vampire assailants leapt in his direction with their German broadswords drawn and aimed at the gargoyle's chest.

Using the stone fingers of his wings, Ghin parried the swords and cut three of the vampires through the chest, reducing them to ashes. On instinct, Ghin leapt over to another vampire and lacerated her head off her shoulders with his hands. As the other two vampires lunged at their target, Ghin used his powerful tail to decapitate the attackers as soon as they were within range for the counter attack.

Rushing towards Rejan and the remaining vampires, Ghin's anger rose as he witnessed the assailants punch and kick at his wife. In a fit of rage, Ghin's hands sparked and burst into flame.

Since gargoyles were born from the earth, each gargoyle was attuned to it's natural elements. Modern day gargoyles could use only fire and water, either as martial techniques or methods of healing. Similar to human perspiration, fire and water came from the gargoyles' pores and could be emitted at will. However, there were not any gargoyles who were privileged to be able to use both elements, excluding the grandmaster.

As Ghin's hands blazed, he repeatedly thrust is hands forward, sending streams of flame in the direction of the vampires. Most of the assassins dove out of the way and charged at Ghin while three others were incinerated by the flames.

In a blinding rage, Ghin hit the vampires who charged at him with near perfect accuracy. Unfortunately, the young gargoyle was too angry to be cautious and was struck hard in the back of the head by an unnoticed figure. As he fell into the snow, the last thing Ghin saw was Rejan, covering her attackers in water and freezing them in their place before being overwhelmed by more vampires, who had come out of hiding.

When he awoke, Ghin was in his gargoyle form and freezing in the snow. Remembering what he had seen before his unconsciousness, he sprang up in hopes that Rejan had survived the onslaught. Yet when he looked up, disbelief and uncontainable sadness came to his eyes. Displayed in front of the gargoyle was a large pyre made from what was once his home and the charred stone corpse of a young female gargoyle, formerly known as Rejan.

The obvious knowledge that Rejan could control water and the fact that the vampires burned her alive until she could no longer produce hydration made Ghin dizzy from anguish. Above Rejan's remains was a sign that read "Broken Guardian," which was written in her blood. Wondering why Rejan had not crumbled apart like every gargoyle did when they died, Ghin's eyed widened in horror from realization. The vampires had crudely stuck the rocks of Rejan's body back together so that Ghin could see her terrible expression as she screamed from the flames.

Feeling overwhelmed by guilt, Ghin roared out into the sky, loud enough that it echoed through the forest. He cursed himself relentlessly for being too weak to protect his wife. After moments of grief, the gargoyle widower took Rejan's remains back to the castle where the gargoyle nation held a token funeral in her memory. Many tears were shed at the loss of their deceased friend. Even the grandmaster felt overwhelming sadness from the misfortune of his students. It was not just a dark day for Ghin, but for the entire nation as well. This day was a realization that gargoyles were not as powerful as they had believed themselves to be. Not only were Ghin and Rejan the first gargoyles who had tried to live outside the castle, they were also the last. From that point forward, Ghin's soul retreated to the darkest place within himself and there was nothing anyone could do to bring him back.

"Yeah, it's been a long, rough ride. Right Ghin?" Tiogra asked, sighing as he came back from the memory.

"Psh, you're telling me." Ghin stated, "Hey, I'm thirsty, got any water on you?"

"Sure," Tiogra confirmed, "One second."

Tiogra then began to fully revert into his gargoyle form. As Tiogra's beastly features expanded out of his human disguise, Ghin moved away to give his friend some room.

There were some details Tiogra had that were distinct features of a gargoyle with power over water. Unlike Ghin, Tiogra's hunched, animalistic frame was larger and muscular. Another trait was that Tiogra had moss on his chin instead of scales like Ghin, a vary distinctive difference between water and fire gargoyles. As Tiogra's triple clawed gargoyle feet burst out of their shoes, Ghin winced when he saw his friend crack the knuckles of the retractable thumbs within the heels of his feet, a feature Ghin was personally glad his smaller, double clawed feet did not share.

In all the decades he had been alive, Ghin had never seen a water gargoyle run in their true form before. He imagined that due to the retractable thumbs in their feet, if they tried to run they would cause severe damage to their joints. Despite this inability, the thumbs were useful when both hands were occupied and the larger feet overall were useful for swimming.

Just like all gargoyles, both Ghin and Tiogra's bodies had the appearance of rocks covered by thick, short furred flesh with strong wings and powerful tails. Almost all gargoyles had at least one pair of short, thick horns that rested on different parts of their heads. Unless they were identical twins, no two gargoyles had a set of horns that were the same texture, length, width and curved in the same direction. Every gargoyle had one unique feature about themselves like the flap of skin that lay across Ghin's nose. For Tiogra, it was that his rough and narrow stone face had an out worldly nose with a small hole in the bridge, along with the stone plates that folded over Tiogra's neck the helmet of a Chinese warlord.

Once Tiogra was done transforming, he untucked his tail from the gargoyle tailored slacks that he was wearing underneath his human clothes and laid it across the ledge, away from Ghin. Tiogra then pulled two water canisters out of the pockets of his trench coat and turned his head to stone. Holding the canisters under his head, sanitary drinking water started to fall out of Tiogra's mouth until the canisters were full. Tiogra's head then converted back into flesh as he handed one of the canisters to Ghin.

"Thanks." Ghin said as he and Tiogra drank from the canisters, "Are you gonna need more clay for later?"

"Nah," Tiogra said reassuringly, "The grandmaster said he wanted to see me later, so I need to go back to the castle anyway."

"Ok." Ghin said as he took another swig.

"Mmm!" Tiogra began with a mouth full of water, "Speaking of which, I gotta go. I'll catch ya later, Ghin man!"

"See you later...Tiogra." Ghin responded.

Tiogra laughed as he grabbed his coat and flew off into the distance while Ghin resumed his position on his ledge and reverted back into a statue.

Within seconds, Tiogra was flying through Queens, looking for his destination.

"Nope, nope, nope... Ah hah!" Tiogra exclaimed as he finally found the opening to the sewers he was looking for. Luckily, the street was currently clear of human bystanders. Noting this, Tiogra fell right out of the sky, quickly opened the manhole and jumped inside, closing the entryway as he leapt.

The sewers reeked with the smell of waste. To anyone else, this would be a problem, but to Tiogra, it was a natural smell, considering he spent quite some time scouting the sewers for lycanthropes. As he flew through the pipelines, he remembered one of the many important instructions the grandmaster gave to all his novices from years ago that followed the tragic event with Ghin.

Remember, if there is any problem you can't handle or you need to get to the castle right away, fly to the nearest concealed location. There, you will always find the right and safe passage home.

As the grandmaster's calm voice passed through Tiogra's mind, he observed the tunnels until he found a hole on the upper left side of the pipeline. Tiogra flew straight into the hole and downward into the black abyss.

Good thing gargoyles can see in the dark, Tiogra thought, *Otherwise, I'd be helpless.*

Once Tiogra neared the end of the tunnel, a room with three gargoyle engineers who were working on machinery, was waiting on the other side. The machinery looked like it was from the early industrial age of human civilization. Any human would have assumed that it was from the earliest days of the sewer system. This machinery, which was used to make portals around the world, was known as a "window maker." It was the quickest method the gargoyles had for traveling and was also the kind of machinery only gargoyles could use without being completely destroyed by the portals. One of the gargoyles noticed Tiogra flying down the tunnel and immediately pulled a lever attached to the gateway.

"We've got one coming in, Charlie B." The gargoyle said into his microphone.

The other gargoyles ran about the machine, pulling levers and pushing buttons until the gateway spun, clicked and whirled, opening a portal in the center.

"Thanks guys!" Tiogra yelled as he flew into the portal.

Hot steam shot out of the mechanism as the portal closed behind him, making uneasy sounds of malfunction.

"We've seriously got to cut down to just three jumps a day, Bok." One gargoyle said to the other.

The portal took Tiogra all the way to the gargoyle castle in Normandy, France. This castle was a safe haven for gargoyles built around an enormous mountain by the grandmaster himself, centuries ago. At first glance, no one would guess that not only was the castle a structure outside the mountain, but that the inside of the mountain was hollowed out and housed thousands of gargoyles.

Deep within the mountain, gigantic caverns twisted and networked miles beneath the surface. They were caves that many other races would call "magic," simply because the caves became larger every year. This was because everyday, the caverns dug themselves. They would eat away at the earth and produce large rocks in the shapes of serrated stone eggs, which developed the gargoyle children within their shells.

Thankfully, the gargoyle nation was able to keep curious human minds and affairs out of their lives by anonymously paying the French government with the help of the wealth and treasures they had accumulated from raids on vampire churches and lycanthrope garrisons. This was not seen as stealing as much as the simple rights of war.

At the very top of the mountain on the castle's northern tower was an immense landing pad. Instead of aircrafts however, the pad was used to support window makers that lined up near the edges of the pad, which were assigned to a specific capital of particular cities throughout the world.

As soon as Tiogra reached the other side of the window maker he had entered, twelve gargoyles dressed in ragged gray robes were waiting for him.

"Welcome, master Tiogra." One of the robed gargoyles said, "The grandmaster has been expecting you."

Tiogra brushed off the grimy residue from the sewers and followed his comrades into the castle. As Tiogra and the robbed gargoyles approached the castle entrance, he gazed at the gargoyle glyph imprinted on the large wooden doors in the stone archway.

The gargoyle glyph was a blue image of a triangle pointing downwards, with a line passing through it from left to right. The triangle was imprinted on the head of a lamb within a square.

Each of these imprints represented a characteristic of the gargoyle nation. The triangle represented the earth, the foundation of the gargoyles' flesh. The lamb represented spring, the first season the star of the gargoyles shown brightly in the sky. The square represented the souls of the earth's inhabitants and the four influences upon each one. Those influences were human, angelic, divine and diabolic.

Once Tiogra and the robed gargoyles stepped through the doorway, they ascended down a long, dark, spiraling flight of stairs into a well-lit hallway that led into a tavern. There, hundreds of other gargoyles were climbing on the walls, resting on the ceiling, or drinking at the tables within the pub. The whole tavern smelled of ale and meats as well as steamed vegetables and spices. Further into the castle, down the ivory, marble main stairwell that led into the core of the mountain, even more gargoyles were found crawling across the ceiling and walls or gliding down the center of the stairwell.

When they reached the bottom of the fifth section of stairs, Tiogra and his comrades proceeded into a room where forty or so other gargoyles were waiting for them. It was one of the castle's shrine rooms, which was used for remembering friends and family who had died in battle. The room had somewhat of a dark, Celtic tone to it, giving it a morbid yet serene feeling, along with the pictures of deceased gargoyles. In the back of the room was a small man wearing a blue hooded robe, who was lighting candles that smelled of cherry blossoms to honor the deceased comrades of the gargoyle nation.

The small man turned around to face Tiogra and pulled back his hood to show his face, revealing that he was the grandmaster in what other gargoyles called his "diminished" form. The gargoyle scholars bowed when the grandmaster removed his hood. He had unadulterated gray skin and torn webbed ears, which complemented his aging, inhuman face. His hair had three, small, white marble horns sticking out of the silver weave that went into his ponytail. Though short in appearance, the gargoyles knew that the grandmaster had retracted his beastly features simply to move about the castle freely without getting stuck anywhere. The grandmaster smiled as he greeted his students.

"Rise, my pupils." The grandmaster calmly commanded.

When Tiogra rose, the grandmaster greeted him with a bear hug.

The other gargoyles flinched when they heard Tiogra's spine crack as he was hugged. The bullet wound in his shoulder did not help the soreness either as it reopened from the pressure.

"Tiogra!" the grandmaster exclaimed happily, "Long time no see! How are you?"

"I-I'm good sir." Tiogra said, wincing in pain.

As Tiogra snapped his spine back into place, the grandmaster's smile faded as he noticed the wound in Tiogra's shoulder.

"What happened to you?" the grandmaster asked, looking at the bullet wound.

"Oh, just a run in with some vampires, sir." Tiogra said humbly as he covered the wound back up with stone.

The grandmaster was stunned upon hearing this information. "They carry guns now?" he asked.

"It would seem so sir." Tiogra said, rubbing his shoulder.

The grandmaster shook his head. "It's just as well." he muttered sarcastically, "We've only been at war with them since the dawn of man. Very well, starting today all gargoyles from ages ten and up are to be trained against guns in the urban field."

The gargoyles nodded and made a mental note to spread the news before the grandmaster made the official broadcast. The grandmaster then turned around to face the candles in the room.

"Anyway… I suppose you know why I called you back here?" the grandmaster asked.

"Actually sir, I have no idea." Tiogra responded.

"Well, as you may hopefully remember in the future," the grandmaster replied, "today is the day when the caverns produce more gargoyle children."

Tiogra lowered his head in embarrassment for forgetting the date of the arrival of gargoyle children, yet raised his head back up to hear the grandmaster's words.

"What I want you to do," the grandmaster continued, "is to help the other gargoyles retrieve the newborns from the cave and take them to the nearest nursery."

"Yes, grandmaster." Tiogra said.

The grandmaster turned around to face his student. "You will be searching in tunnel three of the thirty-fifth level." The grandmaster stated, "You will be notified as soon as the area has been cleared for retrieval. You are dismissed"

"Thank you, grandmaster." Tiogra said as he bowed, and flew out of the room, eager to relax a bit before his newest assignment.

The grandmaster looked out the door with a smile at his student's discipline, thankful that the other gargoyles had Tiogra's example to follow.

Responsibility

As Tiogra flew into the tavern that was a few flights of stairs below the shrine room, he noticed a gargoyle playing with the flames in the fireplace to his left. This gargoyle, who was slightly taller than Tiogra, had a face that resembled a diminished European dragon with golden skin and a coat of grey fur on his back. Though the gargoyle's body was covered in scales, his overall figure was elegant and smooth along with his angular, soft face. There were not any exaggerated brows, an oversized underbite or anything uniquely grotesque about this gargoyle, except for the five horns that circled his face in the shape of a star. The horns covered his tiny ears, which were already hidden behind a mane of short, brown hair. This gargoyle's name was Yemz, one of the master gargoyles of the gargoyle nation.

Tiogra flew around the room and landed right next to his comrade.

"Yemz!" Tiogra exclaimed, extending his arms.

"Tiogra, old friend!" Yemz answered, extending his arms as well.

The two comrades embraced each other in a hug, slapping each other on the back as hard as they could. Yemz's tightened his red gargoyle slacks and the two walked over to the bar as they laughed, past some gargoyles who were singing, drinking and having a friendly exchange of fisticuffs over a comment one made about the other's wife.

There was no doubt that Yemz was a stunning gargoyle, everyone within the gargoyle nation knew this much to be true. During the Middle Ages, whenever he would turn to stone to disguise himself as a statue of a church, humans would admire the "craftsmanship" of Yemz's handsome features. His dragon like characteristics mixed with his humanoid figure made human women swoon over him as if he were a creature from a romantic story. Much to his dismay, gargoyles saw the human standards of beauty unpleasant. Even though Yemz's features were too animalistic to retract into a human disguise, this did not change the fact that his appearance was radiant.

The gargoyle nation had always considered what humans called "ugly" features of warriors. To the gargoyles, hideousness was a sign of fearlessness and masculinity. Even the gargoyle women had terrifying features of their own, only for them their features were considered the traits of strong women who would raise even stronger offspring. Though considered "softer" than the gargoyle men both physically and emotionally, the gargoyle women still were expected to live up to their reputations as warriors.

Despite his handsome features that could be looked past, the gargoyles disliked Yemz for other reasons. One reason was that Yemz was an enormous flirt. If he was lucky enough that they would flirt back with him, Yemz did not shy away from trying his luck with the women of his race. The only problem with this, aside from when he took his flirting too far, was that some of the gargoyle females he trifled with were already married and that Yemz, himself, was in a marital bond to a quiet gargoyle woman named Chem.

Another reason Yemz was disliked was his disrespect for those around him. Though no one was sure if he realized it or not, Yemz seemed to talk down to everyone he came across. It was as if he felt vanity was a normal feeling that everyone had not mastered as well as he did. There was even an instance where Yemz had kicked a child out of his way while walking down the streets of the gargoyle cities. Though the master gargoyle was heavily punished for his mistreatment of the child, many gargoyles were tempted to beat Yemz further for his disruptive behavior, yet Tiogra stood in the way between their fists and Yemz's face.

No one understood why Tiogra would bother himself with someone like Yemz, let alone why they were friends. Only Tiogra knew that he felt like there was some part of Yemz that was good and wanted to do what was best for his nation. This was due to an experience long ago, when Tiogra had found himself up to his throat in lycanthropes. It seemed to Tiogra that he would die on that very day when suddenly, Yemz dove into the crowd and set the lycanthropes ablaze, driving the survivors back into hiding. The abuse of his power sent Yemz into a coma. Tiogra was the one who returned Yemz to the castle and set him in a medical center to heal. Afterwards, the two became friends, but the thread that held the friendship was getting thinner with every century.

Once Tiogra and Yemz arrived at the bar, they immediately took the seats of two gargoyles that punched each other in the face and knocked themselves off of the stools.

"Bartender!" Tiogra yelled, "Two whiskeys, over here!"

The bartender slid the beverages over to the master gargoyles, who inhaled their drinks upon receiving them.

"So what brings you to France?" asked Yemz, "and what the hell happened to your shoulder?"

"The grandmaster wanted to see me," Tiogra said with a smile, "more gargoyle children are being born and he wants me to help retrieve them from the caverns. As for my shoulder, I had a run in with some vampires. Evidently, they got smart and are carrying guns now."

Yemz grinned at the first half of the news. "Well, it'll be nice to have some more members." He noted, "I just hope they'll be good additions to our race."

Tiogra looked back at his friend with a half smile. "They will be," he said, "They always are."

"It doesn't surprise me as far as your shoulder wound is

concerned," Yemz stated, "They had to catch on sooner or later."

"Yeah," Tiogra said, "But hey, it's not like anything will dramatically change."

"True, true." Yemz said laughing.

As the immortal friends paused in conversation, two more whiskeys slid down to them. The friends drank these beverages with a single swig as well.

"You know what I was thinking about a little bit ago?" Yemz asked Tiogra, who looked back at his friend with a raised eyebrow.

"The first battle we had as a nation," Yemz said with a slightly solemn look.

"What about it?" Tiogra asked, somberly.

"Well," Yemz began, "it was our very first battle with the vampire race. They outnumbered us one thousand to one. Almost every one of them died and we only suffered a little over twenty casualties."

Tiogra listened closely to his friend's words, drinking his third beverage in sips this time.

"You know that we're probably the most powerful race on the planet," Yemz explained. "I mean, we're not as strong as the tortasapiens and we're not as quick as some of the rattus, but we're an equal combination of strength, speed and power. With all these traits, plus our elemental control over water and fire, we're almost unstoppable."

"That, and the fact that we're derived from the earth itself." Tiogra added with a chuckle.

"I guess I just think it's weird that it's been over five hundred years and I'm still envious of humans." Yemz said.

Tiogra felt confusion for his friend as Yemz shared his beliefs. "...Why?" he asked, as if the question consisted of alien words.

"Well for one thing, they admire beauty." Yemz explained, "If I were human, I wouldn't have to be ashamed of my handsome looks and I could probably be happier."

Tiogra looked at Yemz with slight disgust for his friend's narcissism. "I wish I could feel your pain, Yemz." Tiogra chuckled, "But honestly, I can't."

Tiogra then dramatically slammed his fist down on the bar. "I love being a gargoyle! It's the greatest thing in existence!"

The lightheaded gargoyle then leapt up onto the counter to get everyone else's attention, much to Yemz's embarrassment.

"We were born into a world filled with guts, glory and adventure beyond our wildest dreams!" Tiogra shouted to the whole room, "We're the greatest warriors the world has ever known and the nastiest warriors the world won't dare remember! There isn't a single immortal, damned or saved, that doesn't fear us! We don't move heaven, we raise hell! WE ARE GARGOYLES!"

The room roared with intoxicated excitement at Tiogra's speech. Then returned to their drinking, fighting and singing.

As Tiogra sat back down, Yemz lifted his head up from his hand, trying to conceal a smile.

"You see?" Tiogra asked his friend. "Who would want to give this up? Not to mention your woman."

Yemz looked at his friend with a confused expression at the reference to Chem. "What about my woman?" he asked, grinning with concern.

"Well, think about it." Tiogra started to explain, "If you were never a gargoyle, you would've never met her. What's insane is how dedicated she is to you."

Yemz punched Tiogra in the arm and the two uneasy friends laughed at Tiogra's jibe.

A few more hours and drinks passed and Tiogra and Yemz were still at the bar, sharing conversation and laughs as Tiogra waited to hear back from the grandmaster about his mission. The tavern was almost completely empty, due to the other gargoyles being sent off on missions and some going home to their wives, husbands and children.

Just then, Yemz looked at Tiogra with a depressed expression. "Ey, Tiogra…" he said, "Do you think the vampires will ever stop multiplying?"

"Well," Tiogra began, "Ghin thinks that they'll only stop once the human race dies out, and who knows how long that will take."

Yemz looked into his glass at what remained of his drink with a sorrowful expression.

"If only humans weren't so obsessed with lust. Maybe then they'd stop letting the suck heads bite them so easily." Yemz said, "I swear if I didn't find it so amusing I'd be disgusted."

Tiogra chuckled. "Humans can't help who they are." He said with a smile, "They think their purpose is to grow and populate the earth as much as they can."

Yemz looked at his older peer with a slightly surprised face. "And what do you think they're here for?" he asked.

Tiogra finished his drink as he tried to retrieve his answer from memories of past conversations. "I believe we're all here for a much greater purpose than to procreate." He explained, "I think we're here for a reason beyond anything anyone under the stars can comprehend, and as far as I'm concerned we'll never know."

Yemz looked back down at his glass, finished his drink and then looked back at Tiogra. "So do you think we're bound by the same guidelines as the humans?" Yemz asked.

"What do you mean?" Tiogra asked, slightly drunk after the swig of his twenty-second drink.

"Oh you know," Yemz began to elaborate, "the ten commandments and things like that."

Tiogra stopped drinking to answer his friend's question with a straight face. "Well," he began, "the grandmaster says we have to stay vigilant of rules that are similar, and I feel that sin is a disgusting thing within itself. And as much as I don't like vampires, killing them is still technically murder."

Yemz took another confused expression. "How so?" he asked.

Tiogra looked at his reflection in the mirror behind the drinks at the bar. "Because they were human once." He stated, "And we're supposed to protect humans."

Yemz nodded his head and continued to drink his alcoholic beverage.

Just then, a gargoyle dressed in gray robes ran up to the two drinking comrades to address Tiogra.

"Master Tiogra," the gargoyle said, "the eggs are ready."

Tiogra nodded to the gargoyle, downed his whiskey and rose off his seat as easily as he got on.

"Well, my friend," Tiogra said, "it was a good drink, we shall have to do it again some time."

"My thoughts exactly." Yemz said smiling as the two friends shook hands.

Tiogra smiled as he flew out of the room and journeyed towards the center of the mountain, where his mission would take place.

As Tiogra traveled down into the caverns within the castle, the effects of his beverage were fading away as fast as he flew. There were forty-seven levels within the mountain, each one was large enough to house entire neighborhoods of gargoyles, thanks to the number of caverns each level had. There was no way to tell how many caverns would be on a certain level since the tunnels had a mind of their own. It was not a big problem since the grandmaster knew when each tunnel would expand and gave accurate instructions to his students beforehand to prepare. This was because of the grandmaster's psychic link to the mountain the gargoyles resided in.

When the caves were done producing children in a certain area, the gargoyles would build homes, medical centers, taverns, nurseries and other buildings within the cavern walls from whatever minerals were left behind. The gargoyle buildings were built along the walls and the ceilings of the caves, leaving the cavern floors completely cleared for easy transportation. The homes gargoyles lived in were built similarly to human apartments in the fact that they were small and supported all of the residents' basic needs. The majority of the homes consisted of three bedrooms, a living room, two bathrooms, and a kitchen. The interior of the homes were built with hardwood and tiled floors and had stone brick walls that consisted of lamps filled with molten electricity for light sources, an invention by the grandmaster that was similar to the window makers. There were also numbers carved into the wooden front doors to each home for individual addresses.

There was a specific residence within the twenty-second level in its second tunnel that was home to Tiogra and his wife, Mojhyn. The young couple had met when Mojhyn was graduating from her tenth term of combat training and Tiogra was beginning his training for a master status. This was around the same time Ghin was considering moving away to Germany with Rejan. Even though he was a master gargoyle, Tiogra's living arrangements were no different than any other gargoyle home. This was a common quality all the master gargoyles displayed to show humility towards their peers. The grandmaster himself had no designated quarters since the entire castle was considered to be his home. There was not a single place within the mountain the grandmaster did not visit regularly and as far as anyone else could tell, he never slept enough to need private accommodations anyway.

As he flew down towards the thirty-fifth level, Tiogra had to tilt his body left and right to avoid crashing into the cavern floors and walls. He flew directly through the center of the tunnels so that he would not collide with the homes on the ceiling or the gargoyles walking below him. Thankfully, gargoyles that were off duty made it a habit to crawl along the walls and fly through the tunnels only when they knew it was safe to do so. This way, if gargoyles that were currently on missions were passing through the tunnels, they would not have to take as much caution to avoid oncoming crowds and could get to their destination faster. Thankfully, Tiogra had lived within the castle walls long enough to know exactly where everything was without any surprises.

Once he arrived at the thirty-fifth floor, Tiogra flew to his right until he came to a tunnel with a large number three imprinted on the top of the cavern entrance. Inside the cavern, Tiogra could see that the homes had already been evacuated, incase any eggs emerged out of the walls they were built into. A wall of neon green tape that had the words "egg-collecting" imprinted on it, crisscrossed at the entrance of the cavern to warn other gargoyles that eggs were being collected in this area. Many gargoyles who lived within the thirty-fifth floor were inside the cavern searching for any eggs they could find. Any gargoyle who was not currently searching for eggs was on the cavern floor meditating.

Meditation played a very strong part within the gargoyle's lives. Through centuries of training, the grandmaster had shown his pupils how to calm themselves in their violent lives of being guardians and how to use their energy to help them complete objectives and spiritually strengthen themselves. During the training process, the grandmaster taught the gargoyles that since their power originated from the earth, they could sense everything on the planet within a thirty mile radius of themselves by either using their energy like a radar or transmitting their spiritual essence out of their bodies and finding whatever it was they were looking for, almost as if they were specters. This training also helped gargoyles develop a "meditative vision," which allowed them to sense the aura of nearby living entities.

After Tiogra flew past the wall of tape, he laded on the cavern floor, knelt on one knee next to his peers and began meditating. With the help of his meditative vision, Tiogra could see the light green auras of the gargoyle eggs, pulsing with the heartbeats of the babies currently residing within the stone shells. The gargoyles who were currently present had already collected the majority of the eggs from the back of the cavern. Despite this accomplishment, there were still hundreds of eggs that needed to be retrieved from the walls of the cave.

With his meditative vision still active, Tiogra flew towards a large patch of eggs to his left and carefully landed next to them so he did not crush any of the other eggs nearby. Regardless of their seemingly durable shells, the gargoyles had to be careful when moving the eggs out of the cave, so they were not damaged or broken. After all, these were the new members of the gargoyle nation and had to be shown excellent care before they hatched. The eggs were large enough that Tiogra could only fit three in his arms at a time. The fact that each egg weighed roughly fifteen pounds each did not help the collecting process. To help take his mind off the weight, Tiogra thought about what fine new warriors these eggs would produce. Being as careful as he could be, Tiogra flew the eggs over to the gargoyle nurses at the end of the cavern and handed the eggs into their custody. The white robed nurses would then fly the eggs to the nearest nursery, where the eggs would reside until they hatched. Afterwards, the gargoyle infants would be assigned either to an adult gargoyle couple or a single gargoyle adult to watch over the babies and help them develop into strong, proud members of the gargoyle nation.

The collecting took over three hours of labor, but eventually, there were only a handful of eggs left to collect at the entrance of the cavern. As the remaining eggs were collected, Tiogra thought to himself of how thankful he was that there were never any gargoyle eggs that grew from the ceiling of the caverns. If that were possible, the eggs would have to be caught immediately before they hit the ground and smashed apart. As he finished the morbid thought, Tiogra suddenly froze with shock. Out of the corners of his eyes, Tiogra saw a faint green pulse emit from the ceiling of the cavern. Jolting is head up, Tiogra saw a gargoyle egg develop out of some loose rocks in the ceiling and start to fall towards the floor. Flying as fast as he could, Tiogra managed to catch the egg just as it was a few feet from the ceiling. As his own pulse calmed back to a normal gargoyle heart rate, Tiogra hovered back towards the cavern floor with the egg safely in his arms.

Much to Tiogra's shock, the egg began to hatch after he landed. At first, Tiogra thought he had damaged the egg until he saw a tiny gargoyle hand punch it's way out of the shell. There was never and instance when a gargoyle egg had hatched before it was taken to a nursery. Within seconds, the egg in Tiogra's arms had hatched into a tiny, gray, baby gargoyle.

Though his features were small, the gargoyle infant was nothing short of a wonder. His forearms were thicker than a normal gargoyle newborn and the bumps on his elbows, shoulders and knees were not as pointed, but a tad broader than regular infant ridges. This gave Tiogra an idea of what the child's spikes would look like when they were fully developed. The child's torso was still plump and as soft as an average gargoyle infant's, yet the rest of his features were still hard to identify. From what Tiogra could tell, the three claws on the child's feet resembled a water gargoyle, but the fact that the outer claws curved inwards like a hoof represented a fire gargoyle. Then there was the fact that this child had two retractable thumbs on each foot instead of one.

There were many features about this child that struck Tiogra as the strangest. After the child hatched, roots from his backside had coiled themselves together and formed stone flesh over themselves to make a serrated tail. The child's wings were typical stone gargoyle wings and were as gray as the rest of his body, yet pulsated with green energy three times before the baby tucked them behind his back. Tiogra could also feel three rows of small bumps running down the child's back through a coat of short, black fur.

The child's face seemed to be a mix of animalistic and humanoid features. His heavy baby brows had three bumps each that sat directly along the tops of the brows in rows, pointing back towards the top of his head. Though the baby's brows were heavy, his sizable emerald eyes were not sunken so far into it's face that Tiogra could not feel his stone heart melt when he looked into them. The feature that surprised Tiogra the most were the baby's ears. They were not rippled or exaggerated, but the pointed tips that curved back towards the baby's spine were covered in stone.

As Tiogra looked over the baby, a surge of what felt like electricity unexpectedly shot through the infant and into Tiogra's hand.

As the current flowed through Tiogra's arm and into his mind, images of his fellow gargoyles flashed before his eyes. Visions of vampires and lycanthropes beating the other three races into pulp blazed as if they were physically in front of the stone warrior. It seemed like the end of the world until suddenly, out of the flames and chaos, stepped a figure cloaked in shadow. A blue light that shown behind the figure, burned the vampires and lycanthropes away in seconds. As he gazed at the figure, Tiogra could distinguish a strong gargoyle frame as well as magnificent wings that unfolded as the figure walked forward. Tiogra could also see that it's eyes shown like incredible emeralds and that it's skin resembled gargoyle flesh, yet was composed of something even stronger. This gargoyle had short frills resting along the tops of it's brows, which complimented it's powerful ears. The last image Tiogra saw was a vision of the entire gargoyle nation bowing in respect to the new green-eyed gargoyle.

A confused expression fell onto Tiogra's face as he awoke back in reality. Despite the strangeness, there was no time to think about the oddity of the images. With the gargoyle infant already asleep in his arms, Tiogra flew as fast as he could towards the cavern entrance to the first nurse he could find. As he passed the child over to the nurse, Tiogra gently grabbed the nurse's shoulder to give her specific instructions.

"Inform the grandmaster that I wish to speak with him." Tiogra said to the nurse, "There's something strange about this child."

The nurse nodded and flew back towards the nursery with the baby wrapped in a red blanket in her arms. As Tiogra watched the nurse return to the nursery, he could hear the gargoyle child cry as he realized he had left Tiogra's custody.

Looking back at the cavern with his meditative vision, Tiogra could see that there were not any more eggs to collect. Signaling to the supervising gargoyle that the area was clear, the master gargoyle flew out of the cavern towards the nearest tavern within the thirty-fifth floor.

The taverns within the mountain were built with a variety of architecture, mostly inspired from European human buildings, most of which had hardwood floors and cobblestone walls. Other gargoyle taverns simply kept the cavern theme, but still had a bar, a kitchen and a fireplace. The only qualities that remained the same in every gargoyle tavern were the stone tables carved from the stalagmites and stalactites in the caves and the booths carved into the ceilings and walls.

Tiogra approached the bar and asked for a cup of "Xong-Zox's Black Tea." It was a herbal beverage that was made from a recipe that the grandmaster's niece, Xong-Zox, had fabricated herself. The tea had proven to be beneficial to gargoyle genetics, making their bones stronger and improved their digestive systems, all while giving them enough energy to complete their tasks. The tea also had a sweet extract added into it to make it taste like honey and vanilla. It was one of Xong-Zox's greatest masterpieces and proved that her immortal hobby of tea blending had paid off exceedingly.

As he nursed his beverage, Tiogra contemplated the strangeness of the last baby he had found in the cavern. The baby felt as though he contained enough vitality to be the earth itself. However, this made no sense since the only creature on earth that could have this much energy was Trog, the original gargoyle, and he had passed on thousands of years ago. Another thought was the child's cry as it left Tiogra's arms. Though it had never happened before, Tiogra felt a faint sense of dejection as the baby was carried off to the nursery.

As the master gargoyle starred at his beverage, deep in thought, Ghin had flown into the tavern and sat next to Tiogra.

"Hey," Ghin addressed his close friend, "what's up with you?"

"I had the strangest thing happen today..." Tiogra said as he began to explain the event to his life-long friend.

Just then, another gargoyle dressed in gray robes ran towards the bar to the two master gargoyles.

"Master Tiogra!" the gargoyle exclaimed, "The grandmaster wants to see you urgently! It's about the baby you found in tunnel three. He is in the main training hall."

Hearing the grandmaster's summons, Tiogra jumped to his feet and finished his tea.

"Sorry Ghin, I've got to go. I'll talk to you later ok?" Tiogra said reassuringly.

"Alright." Ghin confirmed in a weary tone, sad that he could not talk with his friend.

Without hesitation, Tiogra flew off towards the castle's prime dojo to answer the grandmaster's summons.

The Prophecy

Once Tiogra arrived in the main training hall, which was located close to the core of the mountain's pinnacle, he could see the grandmaster was waiting for him near the entrance.

"Grandmaster..." Tiogra said as he bowed, "I received news that you summoned me."

"Ah yes, Tiogra!" the grandmaster exclaimed, "Right this way. No time to lose!"

The training hall was enormous, large enough to fit twelve tractor-trailers inside. To save time, the grandmaster and Tiogra flew to the end.

Tiogra could not help but notice that this was the first time he had ever seen the grandmaster fly. His wings seemed like they belonged to a much bigger creature that was covered in burgundy moss and had what appeared to be hands on the first fingers of his wings. Tiogra could only guess what the grandmaster's true gargoyle form looked like if his wings were so magnificent. What was even more amazing was the grandmaster's ability to retract his vast wings into his comparatively small body.

When they reached the end of the training hall near the shrine at the back of the room, the grandmaster took the picture of the gargoyle glyph off the table surrounded by the candles, causing a secret door to open behind it. The door led them to a stone stairway, which spiraled downwards into a secret part of the mountain. The grandmaster led the way with Tiogra following closely behind. As the stone warriors made their way through the staircase, Tiogra carefully observed the walls of the structure. The whole construct was surprisingly clean, considering it was a secret passage that even Tiogra had never seen, without a single sign of moss or tarnish to be found anywhere.

Once they reached the bottom of the stairs, they entered a candle lit room filled with books. This was the gargoyle's principal library. Every gargoyle knew this room existed within the castle, yet no one was allowed to venture into the library without permission from the grandmaster. Even when someone was granted access, the grandmaster had to accompany him or her into the library through one of its many entrances located throughout the castle.

It was understandable why the grandmaster took such careful precaution with the library, considering the gargoyle nation's most important documents and secrets were resting on the bookshelves. There were genuine records regarding the history of past battles and strategies along with original books regarding the sciences and culture that went into the nation within the mountain. If any of this knowledge fell into the wrong hands, it could be the gargoyle nation's undoing.

There were five gargoyles dressed in amber monk robes that resided in this part of the castle, who were assigned the positions of caretakers for the room. There was a rumor among the gargoyle nation that these five gargoyles were once the grandmaster's elite students, until a horrible attack from a team of lycanthropes crippled them for the rest of their immortal lives. The robed gargoyles only came out of the library when they were hungry or when the grandmaster had summoned them. They never spoke a word to anyone except the grandmaster and that usually only happened behind closed doors. It was not that the grandmaster ordered them to do so, it was that they simply preferred these methods. These were habits that were considered strange, even to the other gargoyles.

The robed gargoyles immediately unsheathed their swords once they heard the grandmaster and Tiogra approaching. The swords these gargoyles used were unnaturally bright. So bright, in fact, that Tiogra had to shield his eyes from their glare.

"It's ok kids," the grandmaster said, holding his hands up as a sign that he meant no harm. "It's just me and a student. We'll only be a moment."

When the light dimmed, Tiogra looked around at the robed gargoyles and noticed that along with their bald flesh and missing wings, they were blind, due to two of them having trouble finding their scabbards. Tiogra could see that their swords were of original gargoyle craft. Thick, rough and short double-edged swords with wooden grips made from the trees that grew on the mountain. The wood was stronger than oak and was as beautiful as rosewood. Each sword weighed no less than twenty pounds, but with some additions. The fullers of the blades were hollowed out and filled with a kind of glowing gel, which gave them the ability to shine the way they did.

"What's…" Tiogra began.

"That glowing gel is an old invention of mine." The grandmaster explained, "I made it specifically for these gargoyles since they can't see. The gel temporarily restores their sight, but also blinds their opponents."

It was a wonder how the grandmaster was able to come up with such amazing inventions such as the window makers, the molten lamps and the glowing gel. The grandmaster picked a red leather book up from the shelf at the end of the room and placed it on the maroon, antique Chinese table, sitting across from it.

"But my imagination isn't why I summoned you here." The grandmaster explained as he flipped through the pages of the book.

The grandmaster motioned for Tiogra to come look at the page he had turned to. Before Tiogra could even glimpse at the page, the grandmaster held the book shut with his finger, marking the page he had flipped to.

"The child you asked me to examine…" the grandmaster began, "you received visions once you held him?"

"Yes, grandmaster." Tiogra replied, wondering how the grandmaster knew about the visions.

The grandmaster's fingers skimmed through the pages until he came across the section he had been looking for. The tattered, ancient page displayed a picture of what appeared to be a giant creature, constructed from numerous elements of the earth. Beneath the picture was the gargoyle glyph, which was a subtle hint that the picture was portraying Trog, the first gargoyle.

Tiogra looked at his master with confusion as to what the page had to do with the child he had retrieved from the cavern.

"When I held the child…" the grandmaster began, "I too, received visions of what the future held and what the child's role in the war was."

The grandmaster held the book up to Tiogra and pointed at the picture on the page. "This page speaks of a prophecy of the return of the first gargoyle." The grandmaster explained, "I believe the visions you saw were telling you about Trog's reincarnation."

Tiogra was taken back by surprise. This was wonderful news. The rebirth of Trog meant that the gargoyles had a greater chance of winning the war between the vampires and lycanthropes. However, Tiogra could not fully comprehend what Trog's divine plan was, let alone what purpose the child served.

"I'm afraid I don't understand, grandmaster." Tiogra said.

"The meaning behind the child is something I've known for quite some time, actually." The grandmaster unashamedly admitted, "A few centuries ago, when the vampires and werewolves were increasing their numbers by the day, I was going through a crisis of faith. With all the humans the two races were consuming, I was almost certain that the world would fall into unending darkness. Then, in the midst of my agony, Trog gave me a vision. He told me that in time, a green-eyed savior would be born within one of the mountain's caverns. This child would have to be watched over and trained until it was ready to fend for itself. That child is the one you sent to me."

Tiogra nodded his head in understanding. He remembered the event the grandmaster spoke about when the vampires and the lycanthropes erratically increased their numbers. Many gargoyles had died in those years and all hope seemed lost. Tiogra now further understood that the reason the gargoyle nation pulled through was because through Trog's reassurance, the grandmaster was able to remain calm and lead the gargoyle nation with a cool head to put the world back into relative safety.

"I will need some time to examine the child further." The grandmaster said as he closed the book and placed it back on its shelf. "I need you to stay here in the castle until I can figure out what the next step in Trog's plan with the child is."

"Of course, sir." Tiogra responded as he bowed in respect.

"Good," the grandmaster said as he walked towards the ascending spiral of stairs, "I will contact you soon."

Tiogra nodded and followed the grandmaster back into the dojo. When they left the training hall, the grandmaster returned to the nursery while Tiogra went to the castle's rock garden to meditate.

The castle's rock garden was in the second tallest tower of the castle's northern zone. The tower itself was constructed out of steel and glass, giving it an artistic sense of tranquility and attunement with the outside world. This was a place the grandmaster had built so that gargoyles would have an area of quiet reflection and peace if needed and was large enough that thirty gargoyles could meditate within it, undisturbed. Every afternoon, several gargoyles were chosen to take time from their shifts to rake the sand within the garden as well as clean the windows and polish the surroundings for good feng shui. The act of cleaning the castle in general was considered a good method for the gargoyles to show others, as well as themselves, that they cared for their home and displayed discipline.

Tiogra flew from the entrance to the rock garden and landed on a giant boulder located near the bamboo pond as the automatic sliding door closed behind him. There, Tiogra folded his legs in the gargoyle seated meditative position, closed his eyes and reflected on the history of the gargoyle nation.

In the beginning, before war and conflict were even a thought, there was Trog, the first gargoyle. The grandmaster had told his students that Trog was not only the first gargoyle, but that he was also the only pure elemental creature ever to walk the earth. The grandmaster had described Trog as a creature that stood as tall as a mountain that would walk similarly to a sauropod with apelike arms. Huge, magnificent trees covered Trog's back. Their roots grew through his body and wrapped around the rocks of his torso. Wild, yet small, constantly burning fires made up the eyes within Trog's enormous, ancient, calm stone face. The grandmaster had also stated that when Trog spoke, either water flowed from his mouth like a waterfall or calm winds blew from between his teeth. Whenever the grandmaster and his nephews and niece were calm, they could hear Trog's words within the falling water and gentle air. Thick, seemingly endless vegetation dragged behind the prime gargoyle like a tail when he strode through the forests of the world. He was the very spirit of the earth.

It always amused the gargoyles how enthusiastic the grandmaster was about telling Trog's story. It gave them satisfaction in thinking that

Trog was to the grandmaster as he was to them. What amazed them the most was that every time the grandmaster told this story, he always kept the details the same. There was never an over or under exaggeration of Trog's features and the story itself never changed.

Along with Trog, there were the other two races. There were the rattus, a humanoid rat race led by Scadge, and the tortasapiens, the mystical, gigantic turtle people led by their three mysterious elders, whom were never seen by anyone. The tortasapiens had always respected Trog in the fact that they lived off of the earth. The rattus, however, attacked Trog the first time they saw him out of confusion and savagery. It took time and brutality, but eventually, they were able to form an alliance with the prime gargoyle.

One day, the first primitive men started to appear into the world. Trog's initial reaction was curiosity and he decided to keep a watchful eye on the newest additions to the earth. Eventually, the primates started to show signs of intelligence. Soon, they began to take the rocks and twigs from the earth and used them in ways that even surprised the other races. This made Trog become fascinated towards the apes and their creative ways. What amazed him the most was that the early form of humans had no help from magic or elemental channeling of any kind to assist themselves in their daily tasks. Regardless of their initial reaction towards the other creatures of the earth, the primitive humans had shown Trog their ability to be good-natured and were able to live in peace with the gentle creature.

Despite Trog's peace with the humans, the other races did not see them the way that he did. The grandmaster had said that the tortasapiens did not care for humans for unknown reasons and the rattus were too paranoid to make peace with a race that they considered narcissistic and close-minded. Much to Trog's dismay, the rattus were right. Scadge tried to introduce his people to the humans, but the humans treated the rattus as if they were abominations.

A small war broke out between the two ancient races. Before the rattus could be completely exterminated, however, Trog rushed in to save them. He then commanded the humans to retreat from the rattus' location and, knowing their difficulties with other people, told the rattus to find a place where they could not be bothered by other races. The rattus obeyed and went into hiding underground. To this day, no other race knew where it was the rattus had escaped to.

Although he was disgusted with the way humans treated the rattus, Trog felt that they should be given a second chance. He saw that even when the humans showed anger and contempt, they were still capable of good and beautiful things. With the conflict of human negativity still in mind, Trog took three rocks from his own body and formed three creatures from them, giving them characteristics of his own image and from his imagination. He then placed life into the statues using two elements for each one. Those statues became his sons, Dorgran, Jung and the grandmaster.

Along with the fact that they were made out of the strongest rocks Trog could create, the grandmaster and his brothers were given control over the elements that were used to bring them to life. The grandmaster was given life by the elements of fire and water, Jung was given life from wood and lightning, and Dorgran was brought to life by the elements of wind and metal. With their unique abilities, the three brothers were given specific commands to watch over the humans in secret, since Trog decided that it would be best if their presence were kept hidden. He sensed that the humans unjustly did not trust him because he defended the rattus against their wrathful intentions.

The grandmaster, along with his brothers and Trog, lived in relative peace and watched over the humans for many decades. Over time, Jung and Dorgran created their own guardians, similarly to the way Trog had created them. There was Xong-Zox, Aro, Durin, and Tun-Taig. Xong-Zox and Tun-Taig were Jung's daughter and son, while Aro and Durin were Dorgran's sons. They were the grandmaster's niece and nephews as well as the first of his pupils.

For the next forty years, Trog spent time with his sons and their children, helping them master their abilities and teaching them effective ways to protect themselves and the human race. These techniques would later be passed down through generations as gargoyle martial arts. Aro had once asked why there was a need to learn to fight at all if he and the other gargoyles already controlled the elements of the earth. The grandmaster had stated that whenever Aro would ask this question, Trog would respond by saying that he could not completely explain and that Aro had to show patience and trust his judgment for the moment. Being reminded of his skepticism, Aro would humbly nod his head and continue practicing.

Little did Aro and the others know that Trog's lessons would come in handy soon. During the later years of their training, Trog had been receiving sharp pains within his head. The grandmaster and his brothers had inspected their father's skull to discover that the pain was coming from small quakes generating from within his temples. The grandmaster had said that the most unnerving part was watching the rocks in Trog's head crack apart with red energy as he suffered from the migraines.

One winter, after the twenty-sixth year of headaches, Trog gently instructed his sons and grandchildren to stay away from his location for a few hours. While most of the prime gargoyle's descendants did as they were instructed, the grandmaster disobeyed and stayed behind incase Trog would need help. As he hid behind a cluster of rocks that were out of Trog's view, the grandmaster witnessed an event that would haunt him for the rest of eternity. As Trog lay on the ground, he suddenly began to twitch violently in pain. Doing his best to not shake the earth from his aggressive movements, Trog's head swayed back and forth as he tried to adjust to his physical torment. Before the grandmaster could step in to help his father, a blast of red light burst from the cracks in Trog's temples.

Trog collapsed onto the ground roaring in pain as the energy shot out of his head and into the sky. Violet flames followed the red energy as it leapt out of the prime gargoyle's head. These flames twisted and lashed out of the light, creating disturbing images of maggots, bats and wolves as they flowed towards the sky. One of the flames shot out of Trog's head and struck the grandmaster in the face, knocking him to the ground. Ungodly images of the human race committing terrible sins against each other and damaging the earth ran through the grandmaster's mind. Suddenly, upon receiving the images, a violent current of fire coursed through the grandmaster's head and transmitted a voice that rang through his skull. This voice, whose tone was like the sound of burning flesh, threatened the grandmaster as he clutched his head in pain. The grandmaster had described the pain like a cold liquid that flowed through the veins in his head and stung like tiny needles. The voice told the grandmaster that it was going to warp the world into it's own likeness and twist the earth to it's satisfaction. Images of humans being transformed into abominations and the rattus and tortasapiens being slaughtered, flashed before the grandmaster's eyes before the pain disappeared without a trace.

After the flames and red light vanished into the sky, Trog rose off the ground and walked over to the grandmaster, who looked up at his father in guilt for disobeying his command. After looking the grandmaster over to see if he was ok, Trog reassured the grandmaster that everything was fine, but to never disobey him again. It was later explained to the grandmaster that the creature the voice belonged to was Egn, currently known as the god of the vampires and lycanthropes. Trog explained that Egn was a dark being of unnatural origins that even he did not fully understand. Since Trog was the spirit of the earth, he could see everything that would happen regarding the future of the planet, which was why he had the grandmaster, his brothers and their offspring practice the ways of combat to prepare for the future events.

After explaining what had happened to his sons and grandchildren, Trog gave specific instructions that they would have to move as far away from their current location as possible to a place that would later be known as Normandy, France. Without question, the gargoyles followed Trog all the way to their destination. Once they arrived in a forest where Trog had stopped, the prime gargoyle told his sons and grandchildren to prepare themselves for a battle in the near future. Egn would be sending his forces to their location and Trog had to prepare himself for the moment when his spirit would pass from his gargoyle form into the earth.

Confused, the grandmaster and his brothers asked what exactly was going on. Trog responded by telling his sons that in time, humanity would continue to populate and cover the majority of the planet. Egn's diabolical scheme to reshape the earth in his image involved transforming the humans into sinister beings of unbearable destructive ability. Trog had predicted that Egn's despicable plan would even go far enough to spread to other planets within the universe. The mad god had threatened Trog, saying he would not stop until everything was brought under his fiery, maggot covered fist. To ensure the planet's protection, Trog had to completely become one with the earth by spiritually leaving his gargoyle form. He would become stronger and more powerful, but he would sacrifice the privileges that came with his gargoyle form. Trog reassured his sons that this was a necessary sacrifice that would have to be done for the greater good of the universe and that they, along with their children, would have to protect the humans to keep Egn from becoming too powerful to stop.

Tears were shed at the response of this sad news, but Trog reassured his kin that he would always be with them through telepathic contact with the earth. He also stated that he was not dying, but simply moving his soul from one body to another.

After his comforting words, Trog told his descendants that they needed to protect him from Egn's forces while he transferred his soul into the earth. The grandmaster, his brothers and their children nodded and assumed their fighting stances around Trog as he had instructed them to, keeping their eyes out for anything strange or threatening. Trog sat in his meditative position with his tail curled around his body, starred up into the night sky and began the transfer process.

Soon enough, Dorgran had spotted shadowy figures off in the distance. They looked like the primitive men he and his family were used to seeing, yet something was amiss about them. Their eyes were bloodshot and burned with an emotion Dorgran could only describe as mindless hatred. The humans' teeth had grown and mutated into fangs while they had grown claws on their fingers. Their muscle mass had also increased, as if they had become more like beasts than human beings.

Before he could further comprehend what creatures these were, the mutated humans darted towards Dorgran, growling and snarling as they leapt through the trees. Dorgran slammed his spiked fists into the ground, making geysers of wind shoot out of the soil and launched the misshapen humans into the sky. Once they were airborne, Dorgran slammed his fists into the ground again, extracting iron ore from the dirt. Using his power over metal, Dorgran made the ore form into sharp projectiles, which he launched at the human parodies. The impact of the metal reduced the mutant humans to ashes. Though as strange as the sight of his attackers turning to ash was, Dorgran did not deter from his position and continued to defend Trog from the attackers.

Jung was the next to be assaulted. As a horde of the deformed humans dove at him from different sections of the forest, Jung thrust his claws forward and shot a thick bolt of lighting from his hands. When the lightning struck the attackers, it reduced them to ash on impact. This puzzled Jung since he had never seen a creature turn to ash whenever it was struck by lighting, yet he continued to fend off the attackers as they continued their assault.

The grandmaster's niece and nephews wanted to desperately help their fathers in their struggles, but remained in their positions to keep Trog protected. The grandmaster could sense his father's spirit slowly fade into the earth as his brothers fought. Using his meditative vision, the grandmaster could see that Trog's spiritual essence had sunken slightly past his shoulders by now and was moving like sand passing through an enormous hourglass.

Then it was the grandmaster's turn to receive opponents. A large group of the mutated humans sprang out of the trees and lunged at the youngest gargoyle brother. The grandmaster bellowed, emitting a pillar of fire from his mouth as he roared. The human parodies were set ablaze as the grandmaster's flames showered over them, leaving no hint of their existence behind.

Aro could feel the intense heat from the grandmaster's flames as his uncle obliterated the mutants with ease. To Aro's right was Xong-Zox, who felt the earth shake from Dorgran's powerful attacks. Pretty soon, the cousins were attacked by another group of deformed humans, who charged viciously through the trees towards Trog. The gills on Xong-Zox's pale blue forehead buzzed and fanned rapidly as she channeled her power over wood through her finned feet to create spiked logs that shot up out of the ground and shattered the chests of the vile creatures. Reacting as fast as he could, Aro used his inherited power over metal to cover his crimson wings and horned tail with liquid steel that flowed from his pores. As the metal hardened, he then leapt into the crowd of mutants, creating a pile of ash as he hacked and slashed his way across the horde.

Tun-Taig had positioned himself between Jung and Dorgran, facing towards the south of Trog's position. The splinters from his father's wooden projectiles and the sparks from Dorgran's metal blades impaired the young gargoyle's vision, yet he remained focused. Sure enough, another horde of the demonic humans charged forward from the forest. Smiling with relief from boredom, Tun-Taig's black eyes shown white as bursts of lighting flashed from his dark yellow, quadrilateral eye sockets and destroyed the creatures before him. To destroy even more of the crude parodies, Tun-Taig made electricity shoot from his hands and annihilated the hordes within his range of vision.

Despite the ruckus his family made, the mute gargoyle, Durin, stood patently, waiting for any attackers who dared face him. Almost as expected, a small group of demonic humans rushed towards Durin with their claws barred. Without a hint of emotion on his pale, nose-less, stone face, Durin calmly gestured his hands forward. The smooth bones which intertwined through the silent gargoyle's white forearms suddenly shrieked and shot powerful gusts of wind at the mutants, tearing them apart as their ashes were swept away.

The gargoyle family continued to successfully fight off the demonic horde for forty-five minutes before Trog's spirit was at the base of the talons on his knees. Before his spirit could ascend any lower, the deformed humans, who were fighting the grandmaster, leapt away towards Aro and Durin. Startled by this change in attack, the grandmaster held his breath in an attempt to kill the demonic humans before they could get to his family. Before he could shoot another blast of fire, a painful pulse was sent through the grandmaster's head, similar to the pain he felt when Egn spoke to him.

The grandmaster roared out in pain, which made Jung and Dorgran direct their attention towards him. Using this distraction to their advantage, the demonic humans tackled Dorgran to the ground and clawed at his body, chiseling chunks of stone out of his frame.

Hearing his brother roar out in pain, Jung turned his attention to Dorgran. Before he could make a complete turn, one of the demonic humans scratched at Jung's throat, which made him collapse to the ground in a puddle of his own blood. Seeing their fathers in trouble, Xong-Zox, Aro, Tun-Taig and Durin leapt to their rescue after completely obliterating the mutated humans in front of them. When his head had cleared, the grandmaster sprang up and concentrated all the energy he could muster into his hands. Blasts of fire and water shot out of the grandmaster's hands, burning and freezing the demonic horde where they stood.

The trees around the gargoyle family had been completely demolished as Trog's soul had nearly sunk completely into the earth. Before it could be completely drained, a sad hum emitted from the prime gargoyle's giant feet as his entire body turned to solid stone.

The grandmaster rushed over to his brothers to see that Jung's body had crumbled apart and that Xong-Zox and Tun-Taig were beside themselves with despair. Looking back to Dorgran, the grandmaster could see that his oldest brother was still breathing. The grandmaster carefully knelt beside his dying brother and grabbed his blood-covered hand in an attempt to see if Dorgran had enough life left.

"It is too late for me." Dorgran had said in his deep, gentle voice, "The damage made to my body is too great to repair."

The grandmaster cursed himself for diverting his brothers' attention away from their battles.

"Do not blame yourself." Dorgran said calmly, "We were concerned for your safety like brothers should be for one another. Trog's spirit is safe, as well as you and our children. If anything, I can die knowing that you will be fine. Have faith… Jung, Trog and I will always be watching over you… little brother."

As the sun rose over the horizon, Dorgran's body hardened and crumbled in the grandmaster's hands. Watching his brother die, the grandmaster wept with his niece and nephews for the loss of their loved ones.

Once they were ready, the gargoyle family placed Jung and Dorgran's bodies at the bottom of a nearby lake, so that the water would wear away at the stones of their bodies. An hour of silence passed before the gargoyle family returned to the forest, weary and depressed from the event.

After the funeral, the grandmaster was telepathically summoned by Trog, who told the grandmaster that although he too was sad for the deaths of his sons, their spirits resided with him inside the earth. It was reassurance for the grandmaster to not worry too much about the demise of his brothers. Trog had also said that Jung and Dorgran's deaths could not have been prevented. Egn possessed the ability to stunt Trog's foresight, giving the evil entity an opportunity to rob the prime gargoyle's sons of their lives.

The grandmaster was consumed by skepticism. He wondered how he could protect the earth if Egn possessed such power. Trog told his youngest son that all hope was not completely lost and instructed the grandmaster to return to his old body. The grandmaster, accompanied by his nephews and niece, traveled back to Trog's body to see that inside his mountainous remains, a cave had formed where the prime gargoyle's throat had once been. The grandmaster ventured inside the cave and discovered that the cavern walls and floor pulsed with green energy, which was coming from jagged stones that looked like large eggs.

Trog told the grandmaster that these were new gargoyles, born from the foundations of the earth. Since the grandmaster was the only brother left alive, these new gargoyles would posses the power over fire and water. Over the years, the new gargoyles would become fearsome warriors, who would aid the grandmaster in his struggle to protect the earth. Until they were ready, the grandmaster was left with the responsibility to look after the baby gargoyles and train them to use their abilities and the ways of combat. Upon hearing this, the grandmaster promised that he would fulfill Trog's wish and began to watch over the gargoyle infants with the help of his niece and nephews. To add to his humility, the grandmaster stopped using his name as a symbol that who he was would be laid to rest with his brothers and father. The grandmaster had ascended from the status of "little brother" to the leader of a nation.

As the years passed, the grandmaster had built a castle around Trog's body to house the gargoyles as they slowly unfolded into a nation. The grandmaster's natural immortality gave him time to learn specific skills to help improve the gargoyle nation such as engineering, cooking, construction, blacksmithing, art and the medical sciences. These skills, along with daily training, gave the gargoyle nation discipline, education and humility.

During the time the gargoyle nation was being formed, the grandmaster could sense Trog's spiritual presence in a blue star that shined in the night skies of the spring and fall seasons. The grandmaster was told by Trog that the star marked whenever new infants would be born into the gargoyle nation. The caverns within Trog's body also produced the clay that the gargoyles would use to help blend in with the constantly expanding populace of humans. The grandmaster taught the gargoyles that the star and clay were gifts from Trog and in return, they should help preserve the mountain and care for it as it cared for them.

Unknown to the gargoyles, somewhere in Transylvania, one of the mutated humans had escaped the reach of the grandmaster and his family. This creature was found by Egn and was evolved by the evil god's power, becoming Dracula, the first of the vampires. Dracula was given instructions to transform any humans he came across into vampires through a bite to the throat. Within weeks, the prime vampire had created a country from the humans who gave into his temptation. Soon, the gargoyle nation became aware of this new country as well as the havoc it wreaked upon the world and the two nations engulfed themselves in war with each other.

Around the 1100's, while the gargoyle nation was at war with the vampire country, the grandmaster had received news that a young woman in Germany had been found dead behind a house from unnatural and possibly supernatural causes. A team of gargoyles was ordered to retrieve the corpse so the grandmaster could evaluate what happened in the bizarre incident. The woman's body appeared to have been nine months pregnant and was torn apart from the inside by what the grandmaster could conclude were claws of some sort of beast. The grandmaster meditated next to the corpse, allowing Trog to see the body through the grandmaster's eyes. Trog confirmed that this was the work of Egn, giving the grandmaster reason to believe that Egn hid himself in the guise of a man with beastly features and seduced the young woman. Nine months later, Aldalfrid, the first werewolf, was born and immediately began to populate the lycanthrope kingdom. Since then, the human race was always kept under extremely careful watch from the gargoyles in their attempt to keep order and balance within the world from the two demonic nations that threatened to throw the planet into complete disorder and damnation.

As Tiogra returned from his meditative state, he cracked his neck and stood up on the rock he had placed himself on. Tiogra personally never liked the last part of the nation's history regarding Egn. To him, any supernatural being that would stoop low enough to destroy a human life in such a manner was the symbol of scum.

Suddenly, another gargoyle dressed in gray robes entered the rock garden and addressed Tiogra.

"Sorry to disturb you, master Tiogra." The robed gargoyle apologized, "The grandmaster has requested your presence again."

"It's alright." Tiogra said reassuringly, "I will be there shortly."

Tiogra flew off the rock and exited the garden with the robed gargoyle, who went in another direction to tend to another duty. Tiogra flew to the nursery the prophesized child was taken to, where the grandmaster was waiting for him.

"Tiogra!" the grandmaster exclaimed as he noticed his student, "I have another task for you."

Tiogra eyed the grandmaster in suspicion for the abruptness in the request. "What can I do for you, sir?" he asked.

"I spoke to Trog when I inspected the child for the second time." The grandmaster said, "He told me that the child you brought to me needs a family to care for him, so that he may feel like any other member of the gargoyle nation. He also told me that he had a specific gargoyle in mind for caring for this child. That gargoyle was you, Tiogra."

Tiogra's eyes widened in surprise from hearing the news. He could hardly believe that Trog himself had chosen him for the honorable mission of caring for the prophesized child.

"I assume you are up to the task?" the grandmaster asked, calmly.

Tiogra's eyes lit up. Mojhyn would be overjoyed. She and Tiogra had always wanted a child to love and raise. Such a responsibility was too much of an opportunity to pass up.

"Yes!" Tiogra exclaimed.

The grandmaster starred at Tiogra with a raised eyebrow.

"I-I mean, yes sir." Tiogra said as he calmed down.

The grandmaster smiled at his student's excitement. "Your child is waiting for you inside." He said.

"Thank you, master!" Tiogra exclaimed as he jumped up and flew into the nursery as quickly as he could to receive his son and tell his wife the good news.

When he arrived at his home on the twenty-second level, Tiogra opened and shut the door as fast as he could with the baby in his arms. He ran right past Mojhyn, who was in the living room reading on their couch. Doubling back, he stopped in front of his wife.

"Hey, pretty lady!" Tiogra said as he tried to calm down.

"Hey, honey." Mojhyn said, giggling at her husband's silliness, "What's going on? Why do you have a baby?"

"Honey," Tiogra said handing Mojhyn the baby, "this is our son. The grandmaster asked if we could raise him."

Slowly, upon realizing the news, tears of joy came to Mojhyn's eyes. She took the baby and held it close to her chest without hesitation. As the baby looked up and smiled at Mojhyn, it felt as if a tiny angel that was composed of overwhelming bliss outstretched it's wings from within her chest. The feeling was slightly interrupted when Mojhyn noticed the bullet wound in Tiogra's shoulder as he leaned over the couch.

"What happened to you?" she asked in surprise, yet still focused on the baby.

"Its no big deal," Tiogra said, "just a run in with some vampires."

Mojhyn was concerned after hearing that vampires now carried guns, but her focus remained on the gargoyle infant. Tiogra told Mojhyn about the prophecy and of the responsibility that resided with the child he had brought to their home. Mojhyn acknowledged her husband's words and assured him that she was fine in knowing the purpose the newborn carried with him. She was still fixated on the child and the warm emotions that flowed within the room.

"Isn't he beautiful?" Mojhyn asked Tiogra, "We finally have a son! Trog be praised!"

"It's amazing." Tiogra said happily, "Now only one question remains."

Mojhyn looked up at Tiogra in curiosity.

"What will his name be?" Tiogra asked.

"I like the name Jhonig." Mojhyn said, after some thought.

"Jhonig..." Tiogra repeated the name to himself. It was a rare name that he recognized in the gargoyle language, which translated to "Stone of Justice."

"I think it fits him perfectly." He said with a smile.

As the new couple looked at the cooing baby, emotions of happiness and warmth filled their faces while the infant began to chew on his blanket.

"Welcome to our home..." Mojhyn said softly, "...Jhonig."

The Vampire Estate

In a hidden region of Transylvania, Romania, there was an enormous, arcanely exotic, black castle, hidden from the world by a cloaking field, which protected over twenty thousand inhabitants from the natural light emitting from the sun as well as attention from wandering human and gargoyle eyes. The residents themselves were servants to the inheritor of the castle, who had "baptized" every one of them with a bite on the throat. Through this mark, he copied his genetics into his victims as well as draining them of blood, making them slaves to his bidding. Over hundreds of years ago, this man had made names for himself such as "Son of the Impaler" and "The Slaughter Dragon." He was hated and feared by his subjects and enemies from the dark image he projected onto them. Women would swoon over him like blankets of snow over a large field through his hypnotic gaze and he ruled his people with a cruel blood-coated fist. This ungodly tyrant was none other than Vlad Tepes, the current vampire monarch.

It was twelve o'clock in the afternoon. Most vampires were fast asleep, hanging from the decorated ceilings of the castle. Others were off having carnal affairs either with fellow vampires or with humans in the numerous bedrooms within the structure. Some were at the castle social lounge, having drink after drink in an attempt to save themselves from boredom. Very few were in the estate's gym, training to fight against their gargoyle adversaries. However, one vampire was roaming the enormous, dark, arched halls, looking for her master.

She had been wandering around the castle since ten o'clock in the morning. Looking everywhere and finding no hint of her lord. Having exhausted all the usual places, the vampire climbed the narrow spiral stairs of the castle to the tallest tower. Once she reached the top, she opened the slot in the door to look outside. She dared not step completely outside since the tower she had climbed was the only one not completely covered by the cloaking field and direct sunlight could provide a problem. There, at the edge of the tower was Vlad, standing directly in the sunlight without any show of flint or ash on his tan complexion. His orange cloak flickered in the wind like licks of flame. His power kept him alive in the sun, yet he was still weakened as the rays of light washed over his body. This was the only place he could be alone, away from the "fools" he had taken in to serve him. Currently, the vampire lord was reflecting on how his father had named him after one of his own aliases, simply for the name to have more meaning.

"Master!" the vampire girl yelled through the door slot, "I request an audience with you!"

Vlad turned around and raised an eyebrow at his servant. Seeing who it was, he then retreated from his solitude, back into the castle.

"I have urgent news from the outside world, sir." The young vampire said as she followed her lord down the spiral staircase.

"What is it?" Vlad asked impatiently.

"The vampire population has recently suffered a massive decrease." She explained, "This is mainly due to the number of humans that are being sucked dry instead of turned."

Vlad snorted in her direction. "Any good news, Trang?" Vlad asked as the vampire woman's name hissed past his lips.

"None so far." Trang said sheepishly as her confidence sank back into her stomach, "But I must note that we've lost exactly six hundred, seventy three vampires in only a few weeks. Not just to the gargoyles but to the tortasapiens as well."

"Your point?" Vlad asked in an ill-mannered tone.

"My point is that you need to keep a better eye on your troops if we are to survive in this world." Trang commented, "Not only that, but it would be nice if you disciplined them a bit more."

"And what's wrong with the way I discipline my subjects?" Vlad asked as he scowled at his underling.

"I passed by the gym today." Trang began, "I only saw ten, maybe less vampires training and they weren't even doing that good of a job. They fought each other like super human children would. Not to mention everyone else is either drinking, sleeping or fornicating."

Vlad rolled his eyes in disgust at his lackey's report.

"Tortasapiens should not be able to kill our people." Trang said with revulsion, "That's pretty pathetic."

"I swear Trang, can you ever bring any good news?" Vlad asked.

"It would appear not." Trang snapped back.

Vlad stopped suddenly and raised an arm in Trang's direction. He hated sarcasm and wanted to strike the young vampire's head off her shoulders, but restrained himself.

"If you were not my daughter, I would kill you with such ecstasy." Vlad growled.

The two continued to walk down the hallway until they reached the throne room, where Vlad slumped on his seat of power with a finger pushing against his thin brow in annoyance.

"Fine." Vlad said, "Starting tomorrow, training will increase ten fold. Anything else you wish to tell me, encumbrance?"

"Yes." Trang responded with a slight hint of a sneer, "Last night, Jonnen, one of our elite agents, went on a feeding spree with five other vampires. We found his ashes in an alley next to a hole in a wall he was no doubt slammed against."

Vlad's eyes widened with shock. Jonnen was one of the vampire lord's favorite bio-engineered successes. The elite vampire was genetically altered to have three times the strength of a normal vampire as well as twice the endurance. With him dead, the gargoyles stood a heavier chance against the plan Vlad had been working on for over fifty years.

"UNBELIEVEABLE!" Vlad yelled angrily as he quickly rose from his seat. His yell echoed through the throne room, causing the sleeping vampires to fall from the ceiling, startled at their master's frustration.

"Another biological failure! He was the perfect soldier! There was no way the gargoyles could have killed him so easily!" Vlad yelled as he slammed his hand down, leaving a dent in the throne's armrest. "Now I will have to wait for another Egn-knows-how-many years until I can create another vampire of the exact caliber! This is ludicrous!"

When Vlad cried out, the other vampires stood shaking with fear from the booms of his voice. As the vampire lord's breathing calmed down, he returned to his throne, straightened his back and then slumped in the chair.

"Any new orders, father?" Trang asked calmly, terrified of her father's anger but showing no signs of fret.

Vlad glared at his daughter. "Yes," he replied, "as a matter of fact there is. Did you find the rattus?"

"Yes." Trang replied.

Vlad smirked from hearing this tiny shred of good news. "How many are there?" he asked.

"Our reports say less than five hundred." Trang said, trying her best to remember.

"Good." Vlad sneered, "Gather any troops you can find and wipe them out, at least that'll be one race out of the way."

Vlad typed in a code on the keyboard located on the right arm of his throne and instantly, a holographic image of Egn's symbol appeared before his eyes.

The symbol of Egn was similar to the gargoyle glyph in the sense that the two images mirrored each other. Egn's symbol consisted of a salamander biting it's tail in a circle. Inside the circle was a flame that spread out in separate directions, which represented torment and destruction. The salamander represented the season of winter in the ancient belief that a salamander's body was cold enough to extinguish flames. Winter was also one of the seasons when Egn's star shown brightly in the sky, along with the summer. The circle formed with the salamander's body represented never ending might in the fact that the circle never stopped at any angles to complete it's shape.

"As for the rest of you..." Vlad said to the vampires, who were milling about, "try to find as many humans as you can and turn them. We're going to need as many men as we can. And this time, make sure you're discreet about it!"

"Yes sir!" the vampires exclaimed with shaken voices as they flew out the door.

"And Trang…" Vlad began, as his daughter was leaving the room. "Make sure you do something about Tiogra. With him out of the way we might stand a chance of winning this war."

"Yes… sir." Trang scoffed.

Once the room cleared, Vlad ignored his daughter's tone and entered another combination on the keyboard. This time, a holographic computer screen appeared in front of his face.

On the holographic screen was a report from a vampire agent about the geological site in Egypt that Vlad was funding. It said that the workers had found an airway coming up from the ground that was calculated to lead twenty miles into the earth.

Vlad then typed in another command and clicked on the screen. An image of vampires digging near the site popped up on the computer. Vlad then pressed the command "talk."

"How are things coming along, Vincent?" Vlad asked the supervising vampire on the screen.

"Things are going well, father." The vampire replied.

"They better be," Vlad sneered, "I'm putting well over an unhealthy amount of money into the dig. There should be no other reports than good ones."

"Y-yes, father." Vincent sheepishly responded.

"How far are you?" Vlad asked, scowling at his son through his brows.

"We're nearing the mantle of the earth, sir," Vincent replied, "We've found over a thousand preserved vampire bodies along the way. They all have stakes through their hearts, which bear Egn's glyph on them."

Vincent entered a code from his side of the conversation. A picture of a stake shoved into a mummified vampire's chest appeared on the lower right corner of the screen. Vlad zoomed in on the image and saw the symbol of Egn imprinted on the top of the stake. The symbol of his god made the vampire lord smile from ear to ear. To him, this was the only news worth considering good he had received all day.

"Carefully have each body sent to the castle." Vlad ordered. "Make sure they are protected and in excellent shape. I don't have to remind you what punishment will be dealt if you fail me."

"Yes, father." Vincent responded.

"Good," Vlad said, "carry on."

As the screen shut down, Vlad rose out of his throne, walked towards a lever near the left side of the room and pulled it down. An elevator door appeared to the left of the lever, which the vampire lord took to the basement level where his lab was housed.

Inside the lab were many experiments, weapons, and test subjects. Most of the test subjects were humans while few of them were of other species. One empty rack had a sign under it that read "gargoyle." Vlad tried his best to ignore his failure to capture a specimen for the empty rack as he ventured further down the lab toward the central computer, which took up a whole wall of the lab. There was one occasion when Vlad's soldiers had managed to capture a gargoyle child for their lord's experiments. Unfortunately, one gargoyle child was hardly considered a catch compared to an adult gargoyle. Luckily for him, Vlad managed to collect enough data from the infant's DNA before it died under the stress of the research, in turn, allowing the vampire lord to create the successful cloaking field for his castle. As he proceeded towards the computer, the vampire lord gazed over all the personal accomplishments he had achieved in life.

To his right was a sword he was engineering in hopes to have an ultimate weapon against the other races. The bodies of prisoners Vlad had captured hung on the racks he had chained them to. They were also test subjects in the various experiments Vlad had subjected them to in order to make a new weapon against his enemies. Each one of them had died from the overwhelming pain or the stress that was put into them through the many needles and knives Vlad had kept on the surgical trays, which nearly crowded the area he experimented in.

To his left were pictures of women he had known and possessed over the years. Each one had interpreted the vampire lord's advances as love. In truth, they were meals to feed Vlad's hunger for ecstasy. It was not the experience as much as it was the fact that each woman hated him for deceiving them that gave him a rush of power.

The most prized trophy of all was Vlad's central computer. This machine kept a reading of Vlad's physical, mental, and financial power and how it was progressing everyday. It even gave him details of how high he could jump, what objects he could lift, what elements he could either destroy or survive through, and so on.

Vlad had stolen the computer from a remote military base in Iraq long ago. It was said that the soldiers in Iraq were going to use this computer to test new weapons. However, they had never gotten a chance to do so since the day it "disappeared" unexpectedly from their lab.

Vlad typed his password into the computer and opened the file titled "Project: Godhood" once he arrived at the keyboard. The file displayed a diabolical scheme that would combine genetics from different species from all over the world. Such a monstrosity would have the speed and agility of the rattus, the invulnerability of the tortasapiens, the brute strength of a lycanthrope and the raw martial power and guarded immortality of the gargoyles. These elements, mixed with a vampire's genetic structure, would prove to be most destructive.

Vlad smirked at his progress. The bar under the data collection read eighty percent complete, but the other twenty percent was yet to be captured. Vlad's smug smile disappeared quickly back into his gaunt face once he saw the missing twenty percent. He exited the file and pulled up another that was titled "stone catcher." Inside was a picture of the sword he was engineering. The fuller of the sword appeared to be filled with nets that sparked with electricity. The way the sword worked was that by throwing the nets within its fuller, Vlad could capture and stun anything he caught within the nets.

As Vlad looked over the sword he began to fantasize about destroying the other races that populated the earth. He pictured himself standing over a mound of bodies that consisted of everything that stood in his path. The races that opposed him were helpless against his might as he slaughtered thousands of creatures with every blow, laughing as the carnage spread over the world.

When Vlad finished daydreaming about his victory over the earth, he shut down his computer and walked away, breathing a heavy sigh of disappointment. His dreams would have to wait, for now he had to work at turning his goals into reality.

The Strange Woman

Three months had gone by since Tiogra had found baby Jhonig. In that period of time, Tiogra's shoulder had fully healed and he was ready to assume his regular duties again. The grandmaster had requested to see Jhonig once every few weeks for meditative study. This process consisted of Jhonig sleeping in his crib while the grandmaster sat next to him, trying to figure out the gargoyle infant's potential strengths and weaknesses. Through this, Jhonig had shown signs of what weapons he was best with, the kind of combative personality he had, and being able to use both fire and water.

The grandmaster had also stated that through meditation with Jhonig, he had seen an image of what could only be described as a tree of light in the center of a pit of demolished concrete. The image was strange enough to make the grandmaster want to study the gargoyle child further over time.

Jhonig was a very productive baby. Whether it was playing with blocks, climbing onto the shelves, or making tiny ice balls in his fists and then melting them with his flames. He had also started crawling a week before average gargoyle children could.

There were a few instances though, when Jhonig showed signs of being destructive. One instance was when Mojhyn and Tiogra decided to go on a vampire hunt for the evening and had left Ghin and Mojhyn's friend Celan in charge of the apartment to watch over Jhonig. It had been nearly two hours after Celan and Ghin had put the gargoyle infant to bed when suddenly, smoke began billowing out of his nursery. They rushed into Jhonig's room to make sure he was all right. Instead of screams however, all they heard was the baby's giggling.

Celan doused the crib with water to submit the flames while Ghin made sure that the fire she missed managed to stay within the room by absorbing the flames into his pores and reducing them to steam. The process was slightly painful since the flames he absorbed were from another gargoyle and were not his own.

Cooing and charcoaled, Jhonig looked innocently up at the babysitters with no sign of pain. Just then, another burst of flame shot up out of the crib, engulfing the entire room in fire. Thankfully, Ghin and Celan managed to put out the flames and cleared the gas from the fire in time before Tiogra and Mojhyn arrived home.

The new parents had arrived at their residence to find their home mostly scorched and the neighborhood within the tunnel inspecting the commotion. The sight of a gargoyle baby resting in the center of the wreckage with two tired babysitters made Tiogra chuckle. Mojhyn however, was less than amused. Instead of punishing Jhonig, Tiogra insisted that they only gently scold him and put him to bed. He also promised Mojhyn that within the month he would repair their home. Thankfully, with the help of a few neighbors, the apartment was fixed and looked even better than before.

To Mojhyn's disappointment, however, Ghin and Celan never had any kind of connection other than friendship. Her plan was to have Tiogra ask Ghin to help Celan watch over Jhonig in hopes that he could move on from his past relationship. The subject of dating had come up once or twice in conversation, but Ghin always seemed to direct the discussion onto other subjects.

For five years following the event, Tiogra and Mojhyn watched their child grow into a lively young gargoyle. In school, Jhonig was at the top of his class, excelling in everything except for when it came to being spiritually attuned through meditation. It was not that Jhonig did not understand the spiritual practices so much as he could not organize his mind enough to complete the process. A minor problem, since the classes for five-year-old gargoyles consisted mainly of using the elemental powers that they possessed. Since Jhonig was a bi-elemental like the grandmaster, he had to take both fire and water classes. However, due to an eruption of lightning that had shocked the teacher of the water class, Jhonig was sent to study with the grandmaster and his nephew, Tun-Taig, for further analysis and to exercise the young gargoyle's power.

This greatly surprised Mojhyn and Tiogra when they found out that their child could conjure lightning from his hands. Jhonig even surprised the grandmaster again and again with what he was capable of. There seemed to be no limit to Jhonig's imagination when it came to using his powers, which was an impressive feat for any five-year-old.

One day, an unpleasant event had taken place in the first-time parents' home. Yemz had stopped by the apartment for a random visit where he, Tiogra and Mojhyn spoke about current events and Jhonig's production as a gargoyle. During the conversation, Yemz jokingly asked Mojhyn to prepare some refreshments and food for him and her husband. Mojhyn was less than thrilled with Yemz's request.

"I was only kidding." Yemz said, shrugging his shoulders.

"If you were kidding we'd both be laughing." Mojhyn responded with a sarcastic smile.

Tiogra got up out of his chair, walked over to his wife and massaged her shoulders. "No need to worry, dear." He said calmly, "We both know that Yemz lacks grace in the social skills department."

He and Yemz laughed as Mojhyn remained seated in her chair, her false smile still fresh on her face. Luckily for Tiogra, Mojhyn knew when her husband was trying to elude unnecessary problems. This kept her from acting recklessly for both their sakes as well as Jhonig. Tiogra then retrieved three glasses of refreshments from the kitchen and gave one glass of scotch to Yemz, one glass of red wine for Mojhyn, and one glass of rum to himself.

"See?" Tiogra said smiling as he sat back down, "No need for conflict."

Yemz looked into his scotch and swirled the glass in his hands to make the ice cubes spin in the goblet. Suddenly, Jhonig entered the room with a winged toy monster, holding it up in the air and pretending it was flying around the room. Yemz grinned as he saw his friend's adopted son play with his toy. At this point, Mojhyn knew about Yemz's inability to be censored in front of children, got up from her seat and ushered Jhonig out of the room. Yemz stopped stirring his drink by the time Mojhyn got back and had helped himself to a box of chocolates that was sitting on the table.

"You know I've seen Jhonig's reports…" Yemz commented, "He's becoming quite a young warrior."

"Yes, we're certainly proud of him." Mojhyn said looking into her glass, trying to keep herself for speaking about how she felt regarding her husband's loose friend.

"Have you considered what occupation he'll have?" Yemz asked.

"No." Tiogra dully answered.

"Well," Yemz continued, "If I were you, I'd get to it. Before you know it, the little tike will be seven."

"Yes, Yemz, we are aware." Mojhyn said.

Tiogra could see the tension building in the room between his wife and unsteady friend. He knew Mojhyn had never been fond of Yemz and had to do something before all hell broke loose in an argument between the two. After all, he did not want his child to have to deal with drama at such an early age.

"Well, it's getting late." Tiogra finally said, winking at Mojhyn in a way so that Yemz could not see, "We'd better get some rest for work tomorrow."

"Really?" Yemz asked, "When was the last time you slept?"

"About two months ago." Mojhyn said immediately, catching onto her husband's plan.

"Oh… ok." Yemz said as he grabbed his coat, trying to remember when the last time Tiogra and Mojhyn had gotten sleep was. "Well, get some rest, don't let me keep you from your sleep."

"Ok, Yemz, thank you." Tiogra said smiling, holding the door open for the master gargoyle.

Yemz was still baffled, but walked out the door despite his impulsive intentions to stay. "Take care, alright guys?"

"Thanks, Yemz." Mojhyn said, smiling sarcastically.

"You too!" Tiogra yelled as Yemz leapt off into the tunnels.

As soon as Tiogra closed the door, Mojhyn dashed to the window to see if Yemz had gotten far enough away for them to talk. Once Yemz was out of sight, Mojhyn sighed and slumped in a huge leathery chair near the window she was looking out. Tiogra went over to the window and pulled the curtains closed, then went over to the matching couch in the room and collapsed in it. Mojhyn got up from her seat and slumped next to her spouse so they could hold each other.

"I cannot believe that man." Mojhyn said in a tired monotone voice as she ran her fingers through the short, thick fur on Tiogra's hand.

Tiogra sighed as he gently held his wife's spikey elbow. "I know." He replied. "I sometimes wonder how we became friends."

"I believe it was when he 'saved' you from a lycanthrope raid." Mojhyn said, looking up at her consort.

Tiogra chuckled at the memory. "Yeah." He said grinning in remembrance of the event.

"I still think he was only doing it for publicity." Mojhyn said skeptically, moving the middle claw on Tiogra's left foot between the two curved claws on her smaller, fire based foot.

"Even if he did, at least I'm here with you now instead of hanging on a wall in the lycanthrope kingdom." Tiogra responded.

Mojhyn smiled and hugged Tiogra for half an hour before she finally got up and beckoned him to follow her to their bedroom.

"One of these days," Mojhyn began as her husband got up and followed behind her, "That man is going to be the death of you."

Tiogra then stopped her and kissed her smooth, marble lips reassuringly. "I don't think we have anything to worry about." He said calmly.

Mojhyn smiled as she closed the door behind them. Despite what they had told Yemz, as far as she could tell, she and her spouse were overdue for sleep.

Not long after the obnoxious visit, the grandmaster called upon Tiogra yet again for another task while the master gargoyle was in England, trying to gather information on the whereabouts and events with the lycanthropes. Tiogra hurried to the main training hall as the grandmaster instructed. There, he sat and waited patiently for the mission to be bestowed upon him. After less than three minutes, the doors to the dojo creaked open.

"Tiogra! Walk with me." the grandmaster instructed as his student rose to meet him.

Tiogra bowed in respect to the grandmaster and the two walked down the dojo back into the principal library as they did five years ago.

"I must say, Tiogra," the grandmaster began with his hands folded behind his back, "your boy has shown promising results in his classes. He might even succeed to become a master himself someday."

"Thank you, grandmaster." Tiogra said respectfully.

"It's only the truth in what I observe." The grandmaster responded modestly.

As they neared the end of the room, the grandmaster turned to his right and pulled a book slightly out of the shelf until it clicked. Then the bookcase turned, revealing a secret entrance to a hidden room, where the grandmaster beckoned Tiogra to follow.

As they walked through the opening, the bookcase slowly closed behind them. Instead of darkness however, Tiogra saw a bright blue light emitting from the back of the room, which was coming from a wall of computer screens. An enormous screen appeared in the center, with the gargoyle glyph horizontally spinning on its screensaver.

These computers were used to keep track of information regarding the window makers located around the world. Now and then, with the grandmaster's instructions, gargoyle engineers would venture down into this room of the castle and study the readings of the window makers on the screen for any unusual activity or problems that could occur. The window maker's were shown as black dots on an image of the Earth, each one pulsing with radar signals that covered sixty thousand miles around themselves. These readings told whether or not there were any supernatural beings within the surrounding areas, allowing the gargoyles to protect the world a bit more effectively.

The grandmaster proceeded to the back of the room, sat down and typed a password into the large curved keyboard placed in front of the screen. Instantly, the rotating image of the Earth appeared. The grandmaster eyed the screen, and then calmly turned his head towards Tiogra.

"As you're probably already aware," the grandmaster began, "We've managed to eliminate over fifteen thousand vampires within the past four years, yet more and more still appear on our global surveillance system."

As he typed in another code, thousands of orange dots appeared on the picture of the Earth. These dots represented vampires.

"Have we suffered any severe casualties?" Tiogra asked.

"Every casualty is severe." The grandmaster stated, "Each life within this mountain is precious. But comparatively speaking, we haven't lost nearly as many people as the vampires have."

The grandmaster typed a third code into the computer, which then displayed a single orange dot in Beijing.

"What's wrong with this picture?" the grandmaster asked.

Tiogra looked up at the clock in the room that was connected to the time in France, which read eleven fifty-seven in the evening.

"It's daytime in China." Tiogra responded, confused as to why there was a vampire in broad daylight.

"Precisely," the grandmaster confirmed, "Tiogra, in all my years I have discovered that there is a reason behind everything, no matter how uncanny it is. That is what your mission consists of, find out who that vampire is."

Tiogra looked at the screen with confusion. "Could it be Vlad?" he asked.

"I doubt it," the grandmaster stated, "Vlad hasn't come out of his castle in centuries. It'd be incredibly risky for him to do so now, especially with all the gargoyles around nowadays."

"What about a glitch in the system?" Tiogra asked.

"Kiddo, these computers are made with technology the human world doesn't even have yet." The grandmaster said in a tone he used only when stating facts he thought were blindingly obvious. "It would be impossible to get any kind of virus in the system."

"Right, forgive me, grandmaster." Tiogra said bowing.

The grandmaster smiled, realizing he lost his peaceful complexion for a moment and placed his hand on Tiogra's head.

"It's fine." The grandmaster reassured his student, "You have shown to be one of the most respectful souls within these castle walls. You have nothing to worry about."

Tiogra nodded in return as he straightened his back. "To China then?" he asked.

The grandmaster nodded in response. Tiogra flew out of the room, eager to complete the mission with a perfect personal record, or at least a near perfect one.

After he retracted his beastly features, applied a coat of Caucasian, flesh colored clay to his body and dressed himself in human clothes to take on a mortal disguise, Tiogra traveled through the window maker to his destination. Within minutes of arriving, Tiogra realized that it had been years since the last time he was in China. To readjust himself, the master gargoyle began jumping off of buildings, flipping off of walls, and scaling alleyways as if he were back in New York, unnoticed by the humans below. After he readapted himself, Tiogra resumed the mission before he got carried away with too much fun.

Hours went by as Tiogra flew from rooftop to rooftop, looking for the daytime vampire. Still, nothing seemed to come up, not even when he meditated. Just then, Tiogra received a call on his cell phone from the grandmaster.

"How is the mission coming along?" the grandmaster asked.

"It's coming, sir," Tiogra said with a sigh, starring off into the city from the rooftop he stood on. "Not much action though. At least I've gotten the hang of the city again. If the vampire tries to run, I should have no problem catching him."

"The computer still says the vampire is in the area. I can't seem to pinpoint where he is though. Try meditating again." The grandmaster instructed.

"Yes sir." Tiogra confirmed as he hung up his phone.

As he knelt in his meditative position, the image of the world changed into negative hues within Tiogra's vision. His mind stretched out of his body and into the crowd below, moving from person to person, looking for the vampire's aura. It took twenty minutes until Tiogra found his target. It was a vampire female dressed in black and indigo leather. She seemed very young with an Asian complexion, and she seemed to be looking right back at him!

A woman? Tiogra thought, *How interesting, but how can she see me?*

As Tiogra's mind traveled back to his body, he noticed five gray auras approaching the vampire.

Lycanthropes! Tiogra thought, *They must be after her as well. I'll need to beat them to the punch if I want to complete this mission successfully.*

Once Tiogra awoke back from his out of body transition, he immediately ran after the vampire woman.

Flipping off the building and into an alleyway, Tiogra proceeded to blend into the surrounding crowd. He could see the lycanthropes close by, pushing people out of their way to get close to the vampire woman.

Nudging people out of his way, Tiogra made his way through the crowd. Unfortunately, the lycanthropes were getting closer to the vampire woman than he was.

Tiogra kept up the pursuit until he was inches away from the vampire damsel. Once it seemed like he almost had her, she vanished without leaving any kind of hint that she was there.

Whoever she is, she's incredibly good. Tiogra thought.

Looking back at the lycanthropes, Tiogra could see that they were just as confused as he was. Suddenly, a faint scent of ash filled the air. Tiogra looked up to the rooftop where the scent was coming from. On the roof of the building was the vampire woman, who had cut open one of her fingers to get a scent to him.

Why? Tiogra thought, *why would she want me to follow her?*

Then the master gargoyle remembered; if he could follow a scent of vampire ash, the lycanthropes could as well. He looked behind to see where the pack had gone. In a distant alleyway, Tiogra saw that the werewolves had already started to climb up the walls.

He sighed and proceeded to a building on the other side of the street. Once he was behind the building and away from the public eye, Tiogra jumped up the wall in three swift bounds.

When he landed on the top of the building, Tiogra could see the vampire running faster than any normal vampire could, keeping the lycanthropes behind her for more than twelve feet.

Making a note of the vampire's skill, Tiogra smiled and pursued her and her half-wolf assailants. Leaping from building to building, he watched closely as the vampire mistress created obstacles for her pursuers by throwing flocks of pigeons and swarms of rats at them as well as bricks she had smashed off of walls along the way. Tiogra was especially impressed when the vampire turned into mist to move through a wall that was in her path. As he looked into the sky, Tiogra noticed that the sun was setting over the horizon.

I should probably end this now. He thought.

Tiogra leapt the gap between the buildings and chased after the lycanthropes, forming blades of ice in his hands as he ran. He then threw the blades into the backs of the werewolves to get their attention, making the lycanthropes cry out in pain. One blade decapitated a werewolf, turning him into steam and fur.

"It's Tiogra!" one of the lycanthropes yelled before an icy blade took his jaw clan off his face. The lycanthrope then felt cold, stone hands snap his neck off his shoulders before he could react to the pain.

The lycanthropes' eyes widened in fear after witnessing their friend's death. They had heard stories of Tiogra, the "Tombstone Bogeyman," when they were children. A gargoyle who slaughtered lycanthropes and vampires without showing any signs of remorse.

The half-wolf soldiers were frozen in their tracks. Tiogra kicked one out from under his legs, then stomped on his chest and crushed the lycanthrope's skull by falling onto his stone knee.

The last two lycanthropes quickly transformed into their beast forms in reaction to the death of their comrades. Tiogra only scoffed and lunged forward, grabbing one by the snout, flipping over him and slamming the lycanthrope soldier onto the roof in front of him. The master gargoyle then proceeded to stand on the lycanthrope's shoulders, bent over and quickly tore his head off. The last lycanthrope had managed to scratch Tiogra across the stomach and face, but then had the courtesy of getting his spine pulled out of his back and decapitated with his own frozen backbone.

When the carnage was over, Tiogra shook the blood and pieces of broken clay from his hands and walked over to a nearby wall. He looked down at the scratches on his stomach that were already starting to heal. As he turned to look out at the crowds below, Tiogra brushed the shattered clay pieces from his stomach, so that the wounds would not heal over them.

"How long have you been watching?" Tiogra asked the vampire woman, who was leaning against another wall, watching the carnage from a distance.

"Since you crushed the one flea-bag with your knee." The vampire said, eyeing the pile of steamy fur on the concrete roof. "I must say, you certainly live up to the stories…Bogeyman."

Tiogra turned to face the vampire woman and glared at her through patches of fur that had been uncovered by the scratches.

"Who are you?" Tiogra asked.

"I am Trang," she said smiling, "daughter of Vlad."

Tiogra raised his brows in surprise. If this were truly Vlad's daughter, the gargoyle nation could capture her and hold her for ransom to end the war. Then again, Vlad never cared for anyone other than himself, why would he care for his own daughter? Even so, capturing the young vampire would not be honorable at all. Tiogra figured he could beat himself up over the thought later. Right now he needed answers.

"What does the daughter of the vampire lord want with a humble gargoyle like me?" Tiogra asked, mockingly.

Trang scoffed at the gargoyle's question. "I'd hardly call you humble." She sneered. "How can a murderer of Trog's children be humble?"

Tiogra's eyes widened for a moment. "What business do you have speaking our forefather's name?" he asked sternly.

"You're not the only one whose had a history lesson." Trang said smirking, "Unlike other vampires, I actually give a damn about the history of the world and surviving."

Tiogra looked at Trang with a plain expression to hide his impressed consciousness.

"Still," Trang said with a sigh, "I digress. The reason I lured you here wasn't just coincidence. I need your help."

Tiogra's expression changed yet again into confusion.

"Give me one good reason why I should help you." Tiogra slowly growled.

"Because I want to dethrone my father just as much as you do." Trang responded, "He hasn't just been a nuisance to your kind, you know. Ever since I was born he's treated me like I was lower than dirt. To make matters worse, he doesn't even seem to care about our survival. All the other vampires do is drink, sleep, and screw. However, there are a few things I thought I should bring to your attention."

Tiogra abandoned his hostile stance and assumed a relaxed position against the wall. "Go on." He urged.

Trang smiled. "My father's been financing a dig in Egypt." she said, "So far they've uncovered one thousand or so preserved vampires sleeping with stakes in their hearts. Each stake has a symbol on the top."

Trang stopped to pull a photograph of Egn's glyph out of her coat pocket. "Are you familiar with this?"

Tiogra took a moment to search his memory. He did recall such a symbol. These were not any regular vampires. They were personal servants to the cult of Egn.

They were the closest things the human race had ever personally witnessed as supernatural. However, like all things the human race did not want to remember, the cult had disappeared from human history. The cult of Egn would terrorize cities, feeding off of women and children while the men would be used for sacrifices. In time, it was explained to the gargoyles by a rattus survivor of a cult raid that the cultists believed the souls of the men would be used by Egn to make stronger soldiers in his realm.

The gargoyles suffered terrible losses when they fought the cult. Many gargoyles died the day the cult was erased from the world. Dracula had taught them diabolical magic through Egn's profane messages, making them formidable foes. They could punch through the thickest walls, survive inside the harshest climates, and their reflexes were unrivaled.

The thought of having to fight the cult of Egn again sent a chill up Tiogra's stone spine. This time, the gargoyle casualties would probably be in the hundreds or worse. Who knew? Maybe in death, Egn had taught his followers more magic for preparation when the day came that they would be resurrected. Being a god, it was not so hard to believe that Egn could know the events of the human world throughout time, especially since he originated from Trog's head.

As the master gargoyle jumped back into reality from his memories, Trang looked up at her stone adversary, studying his expressions as he recalled his old opponents.

"Yes," he said, "I have heard of this cult."

Trang's eyes relaxed as Tiogra spoke. "The cult of Egn." She said. Tiogra nodded his head.

"Here is what I will do," Trang said, "I will do my best to stall my father's work. You must alert your people of this catastrophe. Here is my number so we can keep in contact."

Tiogra accepted the piece of paper that was handed to him. After the vampire princess handed him her number, Tiogra figured it would be wise to let her have his as well. If the vampire princess were a true ally, she could use his number to keep him updated on events happening on her corner of the supernatural world. If anything, Tiogra had given Trang his number for the purpose of a test of trust.

As Trang was about to jump off the building to leave, she was stopped by an ice blade that struck an inch away from her foot.

"A word of warning, vampire." Tiogra said sternly, "Should I catch you doing anything suspicious, my people WILL kill you without hesitation."

"I would expect nothing less." Trang said smiling as she leapt off the roof into the crowd below.

After he was sure she had left, Tiogra pulled his cell phone from his pocket and placed it to his ear.

"Did you get all that?" Tiogra asked.

"Yes." The grandmaster said from the other line, "Whatever Vlad's planning, we need to make sure we can stop it."

"What about the vampire girl?" Tiogra asked.

"We will keep her leash short for now." The grandmaster said, "We will be ready before she tries anything. You should return to the castle until I have a sturdy plan to work off of."

"Yes sir." Tiogra responded.

As he placed the cell phone back into his pocket, Tiogra checked himself for tracking devices. Seeing that he was free of tracers, Tiogra's wings shot out of his back, tearing through his shirt, and he flew off into the night toward the portal.

Extermination

It was three o'clock in the morning in Queens, New York. Several vampires had gathered around a manhole on Pidgeon Meadow Rd. after putting up signs for construction around the street. One of the vampires opened a manhole and signaled for three other vampires to climb through. As two of the vampires searched through the sewage, the third signaled up to their comrades above. The vampires on the street then proceeded to grab huge oil drums that they had placed next to the manholes and dumped them into the sewers, filling the sewage with oil and gasoline.

This action also occurred on, Utopia Pkwy, 46th Ave, 164th St., and Booth Memorial Ave. All orchestrated by vampires.

Five minutes after the gasoline and oil was spilled, a vampire from each group was ordered to go to the vans they arrived in and retrieved the flamethrowers and four strange canisters they had brought with them. As the vampires brought their supplies back to the manhole, they carelessly threw the canisters into the sewers.

Meanwhile, under the city streets, a civilization of beings the extramundane world knew as the rattus were living out their lives the only way they knew how, in secrecy, from under Flushing Cemetery to Kissena Park Golf Course. For centuries, the rattus were living peacefully, away from the problems the rest of the world would throw at them, calmly allowing the disease that plagued them for the last four hundred years to eat away at their population, until today.

Scadge, the rattus monarch, who was strolling around the sewage pipelines at the time, was the first to notice the flammable liquids and canisters flowing into his underground town. He watched as the canisters broke open, emitting an orange gas that filled the tunnel. The elderly rattus squinted his eyes to observe the strange vapor that seemed to crawl towards him. He had seen this strange behaving color before, but could not make any sense of it.

Then, Scadge's eyes widened with shock. He remembered exactly where he had seen this color before. It was the aura of the vampires of the cult of Egn! The vampires had dug up the remains of the cult and somehow made weapons out of the magical essence that remained in their bodies. As soon as he sensed the vampiric essence, he immediately hobbled as fast as he could to the center of the rattus town to get to the speaker and warn his people of the threat. Due to his limp however, he could not get very far.

Sadik, Scadge's only son, saw that his father was in trouble and ran to help him. However, he too smelled the vampiric gas.

"R-r-run..." Scadge yelled as he fell into the sewage, "Get the people to safety."

Sadik looked at his father with sadness in his eyes. He knew that his father would die if he did not get him out of danger and he did not want to leave Scadge to die, but he knew that if he failed to save the people he and his father swore to protect, both their lives would be forfeit.

Looking at his father for the last time, Sadik ran as fast as he could to the announcement tower in the center of the rattus town. On his way, he alerted what little soldiers his people had to guard the tunnels to prepare for an attack outside of the underground village.

As soon as Sadik reached the speaker, he stopped, frozen with fear. He could see the gas flowing down the sewage into the town. Before he could yell to take cover, he saw the fires ignite in the distance.

Explosion after explosion occurred as the rattus screamed and ran for their loved ones and belongings. Most of them were burned to death as they stood their ground and accepted the fate that lay before them out of decades of depression. Sadik managed to escape with a few survivors, but as for the rest of the civilization, all was lost. It was total eradication of the underground settlement his people had called home.

The vampires watched with glee from a distance as the flames rose up out of the streets. Some danced while others cheered and threw alcoholic beverages into the fires. After the flames died down, they waited to slaughter any rattus who survived. Halton, the current elite vampire team leader and Vlad's commanding assassin, smiled as he heard the screams of women and children dying in the flames. For years, he had waited to have some sort of victory over one of the vampire nation's enemies, feeling slight pity it had to be the weakest one.

Unbeknownst to the vampires, behind them, manholes were being uncovered, revealing incredibly angry rat-human hybrids. Each one was thirsty for blood and every ounce of their bodies wanted revenge. Some drew guns while others unsheathed swords. Hadwin, captain of the rattus guard, signaled for his men to wait until they could all attack at once. Unfortunately for them, Halton noticed them before they got within inches of their assailant's throats.

"Now!" Hadwin shouted. The rattus fired their 9mm's at the vampires, only to have a few of the bullets actually hit their targets in the heart. Even then, the bullets were not strong enough to penetrate into the elite vampires' flesh. It was three to one and the vampires outnumbered the rattus by fourteen men. Even though the rattus were faster, the vampires bested them in martial skill.

Within seconds, the vampires had eliminated half of the rattus soldiers. Sadik had managed to escape the commotion from another manhole with the three survivors he had taken with him, a baby rattus girl and her parents. Watching the combat from a distance, Sadik ran south to another destination, remembering the words his father had told him about the rattus treaty with the other races as he ran.

We have finally made peace with the rest of the world, Scadge had said, *they will leave us alone if we do not interfere with their affairs. However, if any race breaks this treaty, go to either the gargoyles or the tortasapiens, one of them is guaranteed to help us for their own beliefs and codes.* For all Sadik knew, this was the only way he and the remaining rattus would have a chance of surviving.

While Sadik and the survivors were escaping the commotion, three vampires noticed them and immediately pursued. Carrying the baby in his arms, Sadik pulled a 9mm out of his unwashed coat pocket and fired at the vampires until the gun was out of bullets. Two of the vampires were shot in the head, giving them mortal injuries, but not until after they fired bullets from their vampire-altered Desert Eagles, killing the baby's mother.

As Sadik and the infant's father ran from their attackers, the rattus prince reloaded his gun and fired round after round, hoping that the bullets would kill the unaffected vampire. This one was swift however, and managed to doge every bullet that came his way.

The father, realizing that the rattus prince probably had little chance of escaping, pulled his knives from his greasy belt and ran toward the vampire assailant. Sadik yelled for the civilian to stop, but it had been too late. The father had leapt onto the vampire assassin and stabbed him in the throat, killing him. Before he could get up to fend off the other attackers, the vampires who Sadik had wounded earlier shot at the father and killed him where he stood. Rage burned in the eyes of the vampire assassins as they clutched their injuries and chased after the rattus prince. Sadik continued to run for cover, in hopes that the assassins would lose him, but the vampires continued to fire upon the prince, determined to kill him. Bullets that were modeled to look like fangs flew by Sadik's head as he ran towards a nearby building for cover.

Sadik leapt onto the wall and quickly ran up the side of the building, onto the rooftop. As Sadik continued his escape, he noticed something horrific, the baby was not crying anymore. When Sadik looked down at the infant, he noticed a burning vampire bullet lodged between her eyes. A tear rolled down Sadik's fur covered face as he saw the infant's horrible expression. He wanted to bury the baby, but had to run from the vampires. He painfully pulled out the steaming bullet, laid the infant's corpse behind a wall on the rooftop and ran as fast as he could with one of the vampires following closely behind. Building to building they ran, with Sadik gaining more and more speed. Just then, one of the vampire's arms transformed into enormous bat wings and began to fly after the prince.

With the elite vampire gaining, Sadik finally stopped running and turned to face the assassin. With feelings of hate and sadness coursing through his body, Sadik made a great leap into the air and managed to strike the vampire in the throat with the knives he carried in his grimy, torn shoes. The vampire shrieked and turned to ash within seconds, but not after cutting Sadik across the belly with a claw as the two creatures fell to the ground. Stumbling to his feet from the impact and fatal wound, Sadik regained his breath and held his now bleeding stomach as he continued south.

Regardless of this victory, one vampire assailant still remained. Luckily, a nearby police officer had arrived and was watching with curiosity as to why he could see fires in the distance. Sadik lunged at the policeman and grabbed his gun from the holster. He then ran towards the vampire and shot the gun out of the assassin's hands. The rattus prince leapt onto the vampire, pinning him to the ground and pressed the firearm into the wound he had made earlier, pulling the trigger three times so that one of the bullets would go into the vampire's brain and watched as the assassin turned into ash from the wound. With his attackers dead, Sadik ventured farther down Queens.

As he ran past the policeman, Sadik was prepared to fight off another potential problem. Luckily, the officer was too stupefied by the event to try to stop him.

Running through the borough, many people, who had come outside to investigate what they had heard, saw Sadik and instantly viewed him as a monster. They initially ran in the opposite direction and threw garbage at him, but Sadik, nevertheless, did not care. This was only a reminder of what it was like for him for the majority of his life, back when he fought humans as a child all those centuries ago.

Searching from manhole to manhole, Sadik looked for the one place where he would find the portal known as a "window" his father spoke of.

Apparently, this portal was what the gargoyles used to quickly move around the world. If Sadik could find this window, he could warn the gargoyles of the vampire's violation against the rattus pact. Even though the vampires and lycanthropes were hostile races, the rattus managed to make a personal treaty with the two countries so that they would be left alone in exchange for keeping their existence a secret from the world forever. So it was agreed that none of the races were allowed to throw another into extinction. Even if the rattus could manage to attain enough power to kill off the vampires or werewolves, they would only use that power to protect themselves and remain secluded from the world as they always had.

Just then, a loud explosion was heard in the distance. Sadik spun around and saw a cloud of fire where the rattus' lair once was. The vampires obviously wanted it so there would be no trace of what happened there that night. More tears rolled down Sadik's furry face as he watched his home burst into flames.

Whoever those vampires were, Vlad must have trained them himself, Sadik thought, *which explains the vampire with the wings.*

After Sadik was done with his thoughts, he continued his search until he finally found the right manhole. There, Sadik plopped in out of exhaustion, and headed farther south.

Once you reach the manhole, look for a hole in the top of the sewers. There, you must go down a large tunnel and you will find three of the gargoyles guarding the window.

Thinking about his father's words, Sadik continued his journey down the sewers until he came to the hole in the top of the pipeline. Climbing into the hole, Sadik saw a dark tunnel with light at the end. As he crawled through the tunnel, he could hear the voices of the gargoyles working around a machine, along with the rattling and clanging sounds that came from around the contraption as they tried to fix its malfunction.

As Sadik dropped into the room, he caught the attention of Bok, who was tightening the circuitry on the top of the window maker.

"In the name of Trog!" Bok exclaimed as he leapt down to inspect the rattus prince, who was bleeding to death on the floor panel, "What happened?"

Bok immediately recognized who the bleeding stranger was and took a step back in shock. Then, remembering the honor code the grandmaster promised to the rattus years ago and assuming that this was the case, Bok threw Sadik over his shoulder and carried him over to the window, where another gargoyle was at the top, tightening some metric hex bolts with a wrench.

"Ey, Riyhn!" Bok yelled, "Hurry up with the window, I've got a rattus here in need of help!"

"A rattus?" Riyhn yelled back, "Why'd you bring a rattus here?"

"I didn't!" Bok replied, "He fell through the hole!"

Riyhn held a blank expression on his dry face. "How the hell did he find this place?" he asked.

"Never mind that!" Bok yelled, "I've got to get him to the castle!"

"Why?" Riyhn yelled back.

"Because he's bleeding to death, that's why!" Bok replied.

"Oh," Riyhn said, "Why didn't you say so?"

Bok shook his head as Riyhn slammed his wrench against the machine. The mechanism clinked and whirled until a window opened.

"Listen!" Bok yelled to Sadik over the noise of the portal, "The window was only meant for gargoyles, alone you'd be torn to shreds! Hold on tight and close your eyes!"

Sadik did as instructed and held onto Bok's gargoyle tailored A-shirt. Before Bok jumped into the window, he wrapped his wings around Sadik and shifted them into a cocoon of stone.

It took ten long seconds, but the two made it through unharmed.

Once they arrived, several gargoyles, who were guarding the outside of the castle, rushed to see why there was a gargoyle returning from his post so early.

"I need a medic, now!" Bok yelled.

The other gargoyles quickly flew to the closest medical center of the castle to alert a medical team while others gathered around Sadik and tried to help him as best they could. As carefully as they could, the gargoyles managed to fly Sadik to the emergency room, without injuring him any further.

Once he was hooked up to the life support systems, Sadik requested to speak with Tiogra.

"How do you know about Tiogra?" asked Bok.

"Everyone knows Tiogra." Sadik replied through his heavy breathing, "He's the Tombstone Bogeyman."

The gargoyles smiled at their colleague's reputation. Considering Tiogra was the most outgoing and had more time to build up such a title, this was not hard to believe. If anything, the other gargoyles were proud of their friend and the image he gave their nation.

Once Tiogra arrived at the castle, he was immediately informed of the rattus prince's quandary. He hurried as quickly as he could to the side of the bed his comrades had hooked Sadik up to. A smile slowly stretched across the prince's face as soon as he saw Tiogra.

"I have heard stories of you, master Tiogra." Sadik said through his wheezing.

"You have?" Tiogra asked, truthfully surprised.

"Yes." Sadik replied, "You are the champion of the gargoyles, no?"

"I'm not a champion." Tiogra said humbly, "I simply wish to do my part as a gargoyle."

The other gargoyles smiled at their friend's humility.

"Nonetheless," Sadik said coughing, "I am honored to speak with you."

Tiogra smiled in return, then glanced at the bandages around Sadik's stomach.

"Who did this to you?" Tiogra asked, "Where are your people?"

"My people… are dead." Sadik wheezed, "I am what's left of the rattus and our legacy, soon to be history. The vampires did this to me."

The other gargoyles tried not to scowl at the mention of their most hated enemy. The fact that the vampires would break a treaty with a race that the gargoyles knew to be as harmless as mice was even worse.

"They arrived unexpectedly." Sadik said, "We were surrounded with gasoline and explosives. They set our underground town on fire. With no way out, my people and my father were left to perish. Only I, a few of the guards, and some survivors made it out alive. Hadwin, our head guard, told me to take the survivors to safety, while he and his troops distracted the vampires."

Sadik took a pause to cough.

"But these were no ordinary vampires..." Sadik began again, "They had reflexes and power like I had never seen! Vlad must have trained them himself. Three of them saw that the survivors and I were trying to escape and chased us. I tried to fend them off..."

Sadik then began to cry heavily. A mournful look moved across Tiogra's face, as it did the rest of the gargoyles in the room.

"There was a child with us!" Sadik cried, "An innocent child!"

Tiogra told Sadik to take deep breaths and to take his time to calm down. It was a short while until Sadik could speak again.

"So when I ran from the last two vampires," Sadik continued, "One of them grew wings out of his arms and flew after me."

Tiogra's expression changed into concern. If the vampires could shape shift like that, this was a bigger problem than the gargoyles had expected.

"I managed to kill him though." Sadik assured Tiogra, "That's when I was cut across my stomach. After I killed the last attacker, I proceeded south and an explosion came from where our town once was. We were totally obliterated. The vampires didn't want to show any evidence of them being there. Then I proceeded here, until I found the window machine and Bok brought me here."

Tiogra placed his hand on Sadik's shoulder. "Bok is a good man." He told Sadik, "Just rest here. You should be fine in a couple of days."

As Tiogra's hand left Sadik's shoulder, the rattus prince caught the gargoyle's grasp before it was out of his reach. He then pulled Tiogra closer to speak once more.

"It's too late for me, Tiogra." Sadik said crying, "I can feel my heart failing as we speak. I cannot avenge my people, so I'll ask of you one thing."

Tiogra looked into Sadik's large black eyes as tears rolled down the rattus prince's face.

"Please, Tiogra," Sadik pleaded, "Avenge my family and friends for me. Kill Vlad, slaughter his accursed people! Save the world from the vampire menace!"

Tiogra placed his hand on top of Sadik's. "If it will bring you peace in death, friend." Tiogra said calmly.

Sadik nodded and drew his last breath. His grip on Tiogra loosened, the sound of a flat line rang out of the life support systems, and the last member of the rattus was no more.

Later that night, a funeral was held in honor of the rattus nation. The gargoyles placed Sadik's body on a bed of hay and set it on fire. As the smoke rose into the air, the gargoyles hummed their ritualistic burial songs and beat their funeral drums in mourning for the secluded, peaceful fallen race. Though the two races were loosely acquainted, the gargoyles could still show respect.

Afterwards, Tiogra retired to the grandmaster's shrine to Trog, where he prayed for Sadik's safety in the afterlife. On both sides of the picture of the gargoyle glyph were portraits of Jung and Dorgran's faces that the grandmaster had painted from memory.

The picture of Jung displayed a gargoyle with significant aquatic features. Jung's dark azure, scaled skin complimented the overall calm image the picture presented. The strong, curved, stone bones that covered Jung's powerful jaw was one of the only features that gave him a form of masculinity. Jung's face had two short horns on his cheekbones and another two short horns above his gilled, hairless eyebrows, which curved towards the back of his head. Two frills that ran over Jung's head and downwards towards his spine, covered a short black mane that grew down towards the deceased gargoyle's shoulders. The frills almost gave the appearance of a broken egg trying to contain the hair within its shell. The stones that covered the back of Jung's throat lay over each other similarly to the stones on the back of Tiogra's head. However, instead of smooth edges, the stones that covered the back of Jung's neck were serrated. From what the picture displayed, Jung did not have any ears. Instead, there were two holes on both sides of Jung's head covered with flesh, similar to the webbing found on a frog's foot. Jung's huge, black fish eyes and lack of a nose completed the dead gargoyle's saurian tone.

Dorgran's picture was a completely different story than Jung's portrait. The copper face of Dorgran was old and ridged, almost as if it were made of tiny broken glass shards and concrete. The oldest gargoyle brother had small horns, completely covering his eyebrows like gravel paving a road. A patch of long scales covered Dorgran's chin and upper lip like a beard. His massive, horned cheekbones and eyebrows made his dark, glowing red eyes look as if they were hidden in the backs of two caves. Four thick horns ran above the dead gargoyle's brow line, curving towards each other like an exotic crown. A dark crimson mane ran down Dorgran's head and over his shoulders. Tiny horns ran down the bridge of the dead gargoyle's broad nose like an armored brace. A small chunk of Dorgran's nose was missing in the picture. The grandmaster had said that it was from a sparring match Dorgran and Jung had when they were still children. Despite these brutal features, Dorgran was shown smiling gently with cherry blossoms in the background. Tiogra guessed that this was the grandmaster's favorite memory of his brother, a beastly creature at peace with the world around him.

The grandmaster walked into the room and stood next to Tiogra as the two gargoyles starred at the pictures of the grandmaster's deceased family, surrounded by white candles.

"I heard everything Sadik said." The grandmaster told Tiogra, "Do you know what this means?"

"Yes." Tiogra said. "It means we need to stop them before anyone else gets hurt."

Tiogra pulled a picture of Vlad out of his coat pocket. The picture had Vlad posing with six other vampires. These vampires were his brothers, Radu and Desmond, his mother, Rasha, his two stepmothers, Xaing and Dara, and his father, Dracula. All were vampires either killed by gargoyles or by Vlad himself. Tiogra then tossed the picture into the air, and then threw an ice blade at it, pinning it to the wall. The target was small, but the blade landed exactly on Vlad's heart.

Young Jhonig

It had been another year since Jhonig's last training report. It was difficult to find time for gargoyle children to learn, due to the extermination of the rattus. Most of the teachers were busy on missions trying to collect information on the vampires and whatever schemes they were plotting. Nevertheless, Jhonig was still able to continue his training and move along with the rest of the gargoyles his age.

During that year, Jhonig had passed his minor sword lessons and was ready for five more combat techniques. He had passed the beginner's fire classes faster then the water classes, making his teachers believe he was more of a rigid martial artist than a calm one. Apart from his success, Jhonig's teachers were still wondering what to do about the lightning he could conjure from himself.

The grandmaster had informed Tiogra that Jhonig was also showing signs of being able to use the earth around him to an advantage as well. This was discovered when Jhonig and the grandmaster were sparring one day and the young gargoyle had seemingly absorbed physical strength from the ground to gain an advantage, an ability that was surprising even to the grandmaster.

Jhonig's teachers were not the only ones pleased with his progress. His classmates smiled upon him and encouraged him as well. Whenever Jhonig was having a bad day, there was always someone to lift his spirits. It was wonderful news to Mojhyn that her son had no rivals in his learning experiences.

Some young gargoyles even made friendships that went into the core of Jhonig's heart. There was Beihdah, a shy child who had introduced herself to Jhonig at lunch in the youth dinning hall when they were both four.

One day, Beihdah noticed Jhonig was sitting alone with his lunch that was packed by Tiogra. In the gargoyle community, the fathers were supposed to make sure their children grew healthy and strong and provided the meals for their sons and daughters. Everyday, Jhonig had brought the same thing to lunch. Some apple slices, a tiny roast beef sandwich, a juice box, and a stick of cheese. Beihdah, not knowing that the cheese was for the sandwich, thought that it was out of the question that Jhonig did not have anything to go with it. One day she grabbed her lunch, walked over to the other side of the youth dining hall, and offered him her crackers. Beihdah explained to Jhonig that her father had taught her that it tasted better when food was sometimes mixed together. Jhonig then proceeded to stick half of the cheese into the chocolate pudding Tiogra had packed him for a dessert. After his expression of disgust,

Beihdah laughed and told him that things mixed, but you needed to know what to mix them with. After that day, the two became close friends and spent every lunch session together.

Another friend of Jhonig's was a young gargoyle named Lokk, the son of Bok. Jhonig and Lokk had started their friendship as rivals at first. Lokk was relatively big for a gargoyle his age as well as wide. He also had the idea that whoever was the biggest was the best at fighting. He was proven wrong when he challenged Jhonig to a fight one afternoon on the castle's training field. Jhonig accepted and wound up punching Lokk with enough force to leave a permanent crack in his jaw. After a hefty amount of tears, Lokk had then seen the error of his ways and asked Jhonig to forgive him. Jhonig, who was still depressed from the lecture his teacher gave him on unnecessary fights, accepted Lokk's apology and they became good friends ever since.

After school, every Wednesday and Friday, Tiogra would take Jhonig out on patrol when he was not busy helping prepare for the upcoming battles with the vampires, figuring this would help to give Jhonig a better view of the world. When he was six, Jhonig witnessed Tiogra kill a lycanthrope, who was attempting an attack on a group of human teenagers. Being a child, Jhonig was scarred at first. Usually, gargoyles would not learn to take lives until they were eleven years of age. The gargoyle child's adrenaline was coursing through his body so much from witnessing Tiogra kill another living being that he was shaking. Tiogra tried to comfort his adopted son by explaining to him why gargoyles killed creatures like lycanthropes and vampires.

"We are stronger than most beings in this world." Tiogra explained to Jhonig, "The strong are meant to protect the weak, something that vampires and lycanthropes don't understand. They feel as if humans are mere objects that they can toss around however they like. Therefore, it's the job of a gargoyle to protect humans from threats."

Tiogra also explained that over many decades, the gargoyle nation had seen the human race commit terrible crimes against the earth by destroying the wildlife and creatures that dwelled within it, as well as tearing up the ground to produce ways to support their cities and fuel their vehicles. This made the gargoyles ask the grandmaster why they would bother protecting such a vile race. The grandmaster responded by explaining that humans could be just as destructive with themselves as they were to the planet and other species. It would take decades of bloodshed and pain for humans to eventually fully understand how the world worked and become peaceful beings. The grandmaster also said if the gargoyle nation was to expect peace within the human race, they must find peace within themselves first.

Jhonig soon calmed down after Tiogra explained the lifelong situation the gargoyles had.

"Why don't we see any tortasapiens like we do lycanthropes and vampires, dad?" Jhonig asked.

"Well," Tiogra began, a bit confused at the haphazard question, "The tortasapiens live up somewhere in the mountains of China. Plus, we haven't really ever gotten a report on them in over five hundred years now. I'd be surprised if they had an army waiting to be unleashed into the world."

"Dad?" Jhonig asked, eager for another question to be answered, "Where did the vampires and lycanthropes come from?"

A blank expression crossed over Tiogra's face.

"I'm not really sure." Tiogra responded, "The grandmaster never said anything about them being Trog's creations. They just sort of showed up I guess."

Thinking back on the actual history of the world. Tiogra thought it was best that he would not over burden his son with knowledge he did not need to know until later in his life.

A look of confusion rested on Jhonig's face.

"Look kiddo," Tiogra said, "this world has a funny way of working. I'm sure there's an explanation for them, we just haven't found it yet."

Jhonig looked down from the ledge of the building he and his father had perched on, with a look that was neither concerned nor sad or happy. Tiogra felt as though his son was still confused. Either that, or he thought that his response made Jhonig sad.

"What's wrong son?" Tiogra asked.

Jhonig looked up at his dad and then out over the rooftops into the night. "I have too many questions." Jhonig said, "but only three are on my mind right now."

Tiogra smiled at his son's curiosity. "You can ask me anything." Tiogra said.

"What am I exactly?" Jhonig asked, "Why was I born this way? And why am I here?"

Tiogra waited a few seconds to answer Jhonig's questions.

"You are here because the world needs protectors like yourself..." Tiogra finally said, "You were born this way because Trog saw that our nation would need a warrior specifically like you one day, and to answer your last question..."

Jhonig waited anxiously to hear his father's answer.

"You're a gargoyle." Tiogra said putting an arm around his son and hugging him, "Just like me, just like your mother, and just like the grandmaster. Simple as that."

Jhonig responded with a smile and a hug. As Tiogra hugged Jhonig back, he felt a slight sense of sadness and reassurance. The sadness was from the fact that he used to think, due to his inability to have children, he would never have the joy of having his own offspring. The reassurance was the fact that Tiogra now had a son who he was very thankful for. A child who he felt he would forfeit anything for.

Tiogra scooped Jhonig up and placed him on his back to carry him home.

"Ok." Tiogra said smiling, "Let's go home, I know someone who's missed you all day."

Jhonig smiled and laughed happily in return. He knew Mojhyn was waiting for them with dinner and dessert that she had made herself.

As the father and son duo ventured home, Jhonig noticed three figures in the shadows following them, yet pretended not to notice them.

"Watch out." Jhonig whispered to Tiogra as his grip loosened around his father's throat.

"I know, kiddo." Tiogra whispered back.

Just then, six vampires leaped out of the shadows. Jhonig immediately hopped off Tiogra's back and landed in his fighting position. One vampire tried to front flip towards Tiogra, but Tiogra managed to kick the vampire through his spine before he could make it halfway through the flip. Another vampire tried to maneuver an air based kick onto Tiogra's head. The master gargoyle countered this by grabbing the vampire's leg and slamming her into the ground.

The next three vampires charged at Tiogra from three different angles while the last vampire lunged at Jhonig. Before they could take out their firearms, Tiogra leapt up into the air and kicked two of the vampires, hard enough that their chests were completely crushed from the impact. Tiogra then grabbed another vampire by the head and simply squeezed it open with his claws.

As the vampires turned to ash around Tiogra, he turned to see how Jhonig was doing with his own attacker. The young gargoyle leapt all around his opponent, trying to confuse the vampire as he shot blindly at the gargoyle child. One by one, Jhonig broke the bones of the assailant. First in the right arm, taking away the vampire's firing arm, then the legs and then the left arm. However, this vampire was stronger than his comrades and his regeneration abilities were starting to take effect. Jhonig reacted without thinking and punched the vampire in his head, hard enough to push his nose into his brain completely. Dazed from the punch, the vampire collapsed in front of Jhonig and slowly turned to ash.

Jhonig felt unusual as the vampire turned to ash in front of him. Usually, his adrenaline would be shaking him uncontrollably. His heart would be beating incredibly fast and he would come unusually close to blacking out from the energy. This time however, he felt unnaturally calm, as if this was a natural feeling for him. Jhonig had taken his first life, and yet he did not feel any kind of paralyzing emotions.

Tiogra walked over to Jhonig and placed his hand on his son's shoulder.

"It's ok, Jhonig." Tiogra said, "It was in self defense, you did nothing wrong."

Jhonig looked at Tiogra with a blank expression.

"Can we go home now?" he asked.

"Of course." Tiogra responded.

Once the two arrived back at their home in the mountain. Mojhyn was waiting for them with the food she had prepared. After seeing the look on Jhonig's face, her happiness turned into concern and she asked what was wrong. Tiogra told her that he would explain what happened after dinner.

The feast was fabulous. There was roast turkey, mashed potatoes, rolls with butter, stuffing and large broccoli. It was everything Tiogra and Jhonig loved in a meal. However, Jhonig suddenly lost his appetite and asked to be excused from the table early. Mojhyn and Tiogra excused him and watched him walk out of the dinning room to his bedroom. After the door to Jhonig's room closed, Tiogra wrapped the leftovers and placed them in the refrigerator while Mojhyn sat on the couch with her hand on her metamorphic forehead.

"What happened?" she asked as Tiogra sat down in his enormous padded chair.

"He took his first life today, Mojhyn." Tiogra explained, calmly.

Mojhyn's dark yellow eyebrows raised in shock from hearing the news.

"But it's too soon!" she exclaimed, almost in tears, "He's only six! You're supposed to wait until you're eleven to make your first kill!"

"I know, honey." Tiogra said, holding his wife's hand as it shook, "But the good news is he didn't cry or overreact. He already knows the spiritual rules on taking a life from his classes and he seemed to act like anyone else would on their first kill."

Mojhyn stopped shaking and calmed down. "Well, at least he'll be a good warrior." She reassured herself.

"Or a castle guardian." Tiogra said with a smile.

Mojhyn smiled back and sighed. It was still stressful that her adopted son had killed someone at the age of six, but it was reassuring that he would at least have a good role to play in the gargoyle nation.

"Can I ask you something?" Mojhyn asked Tiogra.

"What?" Tiogra asked in return.

"What kind of being was it?" she asked.

"It was a vampire, dear." Tiogra responded.

Mojhyn breathed a sigh of satisfaction. It was not bigotry that was the cause of Mojhyn's hatred for vampires. It was the fact that Dracula himself had killed her father centuries ago.

Not many people knew this, but since Egn had evolved Dracula into the tyrant that he was, his genetic code was written into each vampire with every bite he made in the throats of his victims. Therefore, with each passing generation, a fraction of Dracula's mentality, strength and personality were copied into every living creature he bit.

Mojhyn had witnessed Dracula's evil firsthand when her father, a gargoyle named Jegen, encountered the vampire lord in the thirteenth century. Jegen had taken Mojhyn with him to a raid on a vampire church in Ireland, with similar intentions that Tiogra had when Jhonig accompanied him on patrol. After the vampire church was burnt to the ground, Jegen and the other gargoyles of his team were busy collecting the treasures from the church's cellar while Mojhyn was occupying herself with a plush gargoyle doll her father had bought for her after her mother died from reasons that were not fully explained.

Watching his daughter play with her toy in the sunny Irish field gave Jegen a feeling of warmth and happiness that he was her father. Unexpectedly, one of the gargoyles fell dead to the ground as he was bringing gold up the stairs. Jegen and the other gargoyles rushed over to see what had happened and noticed that there was a thick arrow sticking out of the gargoyle's throat. Before his comrade's corpse could turn to stone, Jegen pulled the arrow out of his throat to inspect it. The tip of the arrow had been crafted to look like a serrated vampire fang, but that would have been impossible. How could vampire's attack in broad daylight?

Suddenly, an enormous vampire, wrapped in red robes and bandages, leapt onto the remains of his nation's church and stabbed another gargoyle through the chest with his horned broadsword. Jegen and the other gargoyles lunged at the vampire in an attempt to slay their adversary, thinking that surely one vampire could not take on four gargoyles at once. They were proven wrong when the vampire assailant decapitated two of the gargoyles and ripped the wings off of another before stabbing him through the chest. Jegen had attempted one last strike at the vampire, only to have his arm cut off and a mighty kick delivered to his stomach, making it difficult to breath. The huge vampire walked over to his defeated opponent and picked him up by his throat to humiliate him. In an attempt to free himself, Jegen made fire seep out of his pores to loosen the vampire's grip. Much to his dismay, the vampire showed no signs of injury. The vampire assassin unwrapped his head to reveal that he was the vampire lord, Dracula, in order to show his opponents that they were no match for him even when the sun was dampening his powers. Dracula then bit Jegen on the throat and dropped the beaten gargoyle onto the ground.

What happened next scarred Mojhyn's soul for the rest of her life. The properties of gargoyle genetics, mixed with the strong vampire poisons from Dracula's bite made Jegen deteriorate and burn as he liquefied into the dirt he stood on and shattered into pieces. Smiling with evil satisfaction, Dracula turned his attention to Mojhyn, who was drenched in tears. Before he could kill the gargoyle toddler, blades of ice landed at Dracula's feet. Seeing a large group of gargoyles in the distance, Dracula retreated back into the forest he had attacked from. When the gargoyle team arrived at the scene, they found the remains of their six dead friends and a gargoyle girl cradling the stone that was once her father's head. From that point forward, Mojhyn swore that she would rid the world of vampires and other evils that sought to destroy everything good.

Many years of relentless training and hunting vampires had turned Mojhyn into a bloodthirsty killer. Some gargoyles found her ways of fighting beastly and ruthless in the way she would destroy her enemies. One gargoyle even went so far as to describe her fighting style as "concentrated insanity." Mojhyn's teachers had warned her that if she did not check herself, she would become negligent to others around her. Ignoring her teacher's warnings out of stubbornness, Mojhyn continued to fight in her own way.

One night in Italy, around the sixteenth century, Mojhyn, who was now a youthful adult gargoyle, was sent on a hunting session with her peers to complete her tenth level of training. Five senior students, who were training for the status of "master pupil," accompanied her class. Their assignment was to watch Mojhyn and her classmates while they hunted vampires and werewolves and make sure they performed accurately. Once the hunt began, Mojhyn's class separated and began their graduation assignment, while the senior students secretly followed them.

Within moments, Mojhyn had found her first victims. A pack of lycanthropes who were looking for prey of their own. Folding her wings behind her back, Mojhyn pulled out two pairs of twenty-pound nunchaku and began to smash the lycanthrope's heads to pieces. Within a little less than a minute, the werewolves were reduced to steam and fur. Before they could deteriorate completely, Mojhyn took their fangs and placed them into a pouch she was supposed to fill with teeth before an hour had passed. Once the lycanthrope corpses were completely toothless, Mojhyn sped off to her next target.

After forty-five minutes of hunting, Mojhyn's bag was almost completely full of werewolf fangs. Confidence filled the young gargoyle's head as she spotted three shadows reflected on the wall of an alleyway, feasting on what was now a dead streetwalker. As she leapt over to her final targets, Mojhyn froze in her place when she saw that the three shadows belonged to three vampires. The gargoyle's mind overflowed with painful memories as she remembered her father being bitten by Dracula. Images of her father's green blood flashed before her as she saw the blood drip from the jaws of the three urban vampires.

Too frightened to move, the vampires shook when they saw the young gargoyle's bright yellow eyes glare directly at them. Even though gargoyles did not have any notable pupils or irises, something about Mojhyn told the vampire's that any hint of sanity she had was gone.

With a bloodcurdling roar, Mojhyn dove at one of the vampires and repeatedly punched him in the chest. She solidified her fists completely so that her fingers would not break under the pressure of her angry punches. The way Mojhyn's fists rapidly struck the vampire was almost like watching rotating gears in a clock. The vampire screamed out in agony for his friends to help him, but they were too terrified to move after seeing such savagery. Blood and ash flew onto Mojhyn's dark, bronze face as she tore the vampire to shreds. Once one of the other vampires got the nerve to try to run, Mojhyn snarled as she heard his footsteps run out of the alley. She ripped the destroyed vampire's arm out of its socket and threw the limb at the running vampire, knocking him to the ground. Jumping off the pile of ash and landing on the next vampire, Mojhyn grabbed him by the head and rammed her knee into his nose four times before slamming him to the ground, where she stomped on his throat with enough force to decapitate him. With two of the vampires dead, Mojhyn turned to face her last victim of the night. Seeing a trail of urine flow from the vampire's trousers as she slowly walked towards him, Mojhyn scoffed and spit a small ball of fire into the vampire's eyes. As the vampire screamed out in pain, Mojhyn drove her fist into his jaw, sending the punch through his throat and into the wall he stood against.

As her breathing began to relax, other gargoyles had come to her position to see what was wrong. One of Mojhyn's peers stepped towards her to make sure she was alright. Still in a state of mindless violence, Mojhyn tried to throw one of her nunchaku at her classmate. Before the weapon could leave her hands, one of the senior students caught Mojhyn's hand and pinned her to the ground with her arms behind her wings and kept his foot on her tail so that she could not try to break free. This senior gargoyle was in fact Tiogra, who had been watching Mojhyn's hunt with caution. As Mojhyn's breathing and heart rate returned to normal, Tiogra helped her to her feet and escorted her back to the castle.

As they flew back to the castle, Tiogra glanced at Mojhyn's sad expression as she flew. Having witnessed her brutal fighting methods, he saw a woman in need of help, who was lost in her own darkness. He asked Mojhyn what was wrong with her life that she was so obsessed with bloodshed. Mojhyn looked back at her past and told Tiogra the story of how her father and his comrades had fought Dracula and how the vampire lord had butchered them all. She described the fear she felt when she saw the prime vampire bite her father on the throat and watched him deteriorate to the ground. Mojhyn also told Tiogra of how she vowed to personally be the gargoyle to wipe out every vampire from the face of the earth.

After hearing her story, Tiogra explained to Mojhyn that hatred was an emotional disease that could turn anyone into something horrible and how it not only affected whoever was bearing the hatred, but how it made the world into a hell for everyone around them.

Once they arrived back at the castle, Mojhyn was scolded by her teacher for nearly killing her colleague during the hunt and was sentenced to remain in the tenth level of training until she could control her temper. Feeling pity for Mojhyn, Tiogra went to visit the wayward gargoyle in her home in the fourth tunnel on the fifteenth level. Seeing that the lights were still lit, Tiogra knocked on her front door, assuming she was still awake. When Mojhyn answered the door in her gargoyle tailored pajamas, she was shocked to see a senior gargoyle on her porch, who told her that he had an offer for her so that she would not have to remain in her tenth level of training. Starring at him from under her relatively small gargoyle brows in little suspect that he was full of hot air, Mojhyn sighed and invited Tiogra inside her abode to humor her superior.

Looking around at his surroundings, Tiogra admitted to himself that Mojhyn's lifestyle did not surprise him. There was a blanket thrown over one of the living room chairs with a bowl of noodles undisturbed on the seat. One of the other two chairs had been knocked over while the third was buried into the wall behind it. There were holes in the wall with charred edges that were made from a fit Mojhyn had thrown after hearing that she had failed her graduation hunt. Shelves holding pottery had been knocked out of place from the impact of Mojhyn's angry fists. The coffee table was covered with playing cards and an empty smoking pipe, belonging to a habit Mojhyn would eventually break. There was one feature in the mess that caught Tiogra's eye the most. It was a plush gargoyle doll with a note next to it that read, "never forget." Tiogra had remembered that this was the doll Mojhyn had spoken of from her terrible past.

Mojhyn walked over to the chair with the noodles, picked the bowl off of the seat and sat down with her tail wrapped around her leg and the blanket wrapped around her. Tiogra placed the chair that was lying on the floor back onto its legs and sat across from Mojhyn.

As Mojhyn continued eating her noodles, Tiogra explained that there was a way for her to easily overcome her anger if she would be willing to let him help her. Mojhyn eyed Tiogra suspiciously and asked him to continue as she shoveled the noodles into her mouth with her chopsticks. Tiogra then explained that even though the technique was forbidden, through meditation he could take all the overbearing negativity from her soul and place it into himself. The technique was forbidden because gargoyles were required to make their spiritual journeys by themselves without any aid. Since he had many years worth of experience with spiritual influence, it would be easy for him to dispose the negativity he would transfer out of Mojhyn. At first, Mojhyn was hesitant. She asked Tiogra if the transfer process would make her forget what had happened to her father and if she would lose what drove her to be a successful warrior. Tiogra smiled and told her that the transfer process would allow her to keep her memories, but remove what made them painful. Upon hearing this, Mojhyn agreed to let Tiogra help her and sat cross-legged on the floor. Tiogra sat in front of her and asked to hold her hands. She placed her hands palm down on Tiogra's and closed her eyes as she straightened her back.

Almost as if by magic, the lights in Mojhyn's apartment dimmed. Tiogra later told Mojhyn that it was not the room that was getting darker, but that it was the voyage into her subconscious that darkened the room. Through Mojhyn's mind's eye, she could see her entire range of vision burn red with anger as she and Tiogra traveled into the deepest part of her soul. Mojhyn could hear her father's screams of agony and Dracula's howling laughter echo through her head as she reached the core of her spiritual being. Suddenly, the red flames began to flow to the center of Mojhyn's vision as they were sucked from her soul into Tiogra's body, leaving nothing but pure white enlightenment.

When the transfer was complete, Mojhyn woke to see that Tiogra still had his eyes closed. After three minutes, Tiogra woke from his trance and rose off the floor. Mojhyn was overcome with happiness after realizing that her hatred had vanished. It was like ten thousand pounds of burden had disappeared from her soul. She hugged Tiogra and thanked him with tears in her eyes as a memory of her father playing with her in a meadow in England flew through her mind. Tiogra smiled and left her apartment, satisfied that he had successfully helped someone in need. A few weeks following the event, Mojhyn had graduated from her tenth level of training, after showing her teachers that she had control over her emotions. The grandmaster was suspicious though and had asked for a conference with Tiogra. The senior gargoyle admitted to the grandmaster that he had broken the rules to help Mojhyn overcome her personal pain. At first the grandmaster was disappointed, but came to the conclusion to let Tiogra's choice go unpunished since it was an act of kindness and it helped Mojhyn become a better warrior.

For the years following the event, Tiogra and Mojhyn had seen each other throughout the castle and had flirted back and fourth. Mojhyn had admitted that she found Tiogra attractive since the moment he left her apartment the night he helped ease her mind's pain. For Tiogra, it took time for him to realize how attracted he was to Mojhyn. He had said that he liked how Mojhyn's horns curved backward from her forehead and how her ears curved towards her eyebrows from under her horns.

Another feature Tiogra had said he liked were her hooded eyes. These were compliments she considered extremely flattering. Later on, Tiogra had proposed to Mojhyn after he had earned the status of a master gargoyle. She immediately said yes and the two had gotten married, beginning their life together as husband and wife.

Thinking back on their past, Tiogra and Mojhyn sat peacefully in their living room for over an hour. When the recollections were over, they decided to check on Jhonig, who had tucked himself in for the night and was sleeping soundly.

Mojhyn smiled at her son as he slept, thinking about how adorable he was. Tiogra smiled as well, imagining how productive Jhonig would be as a member of the gargoyle nation. Once they finished thinking about their son, the two gargoyle parents left the room to get some sleep themselves.

The next morning, Tiogra woke up to a kiss from Mojhyn. He smiled and followed her into the kitchen, where she had breakfast waiting for him and Jhonig. Even though Mojhyn knew Tiogra was fully capable of making his own breakfast, this was a gesture of kindness from wife to husband, especially since he stayed up late to talk to her and make sure all was right with her world.

A few moments later, Jhonig woke up to greet his parents before school. Mojhyn and Tiogra smiled as their son entered the room.

"Hello, Jhonig." Mojhyn said cheerfully.

"Good morning." Jhonig responded in as much cheerfulness as his mother.

"Did you sleep well last night?" Tiogra asked.

"Like a baby." The gargoyle child replied, smiling.

"Good." Tiogra said, "If I remember, today is the day of your big test."

"Yep," Jhonig replied, "Knock out twenty targets in thirty seconds, without any elements."

As Jhonig sat down and began eating his breakfast, Mojhyn's smile turned into a half smile as she gazed at her son, still troubled about his first kill last night.

"Jhonig…" Mojhyn began, "can I ask you something?"

"Sure." Jhonig replied.

"How do you feel about last night?" she asked, hoping not to trigger any wrong nerves.

"I feel fine." Jhonig said, "Why?"

Mojhyn struggled with her words as her son asked her a question regarding her own curiosity.

"Because…" Tiogra said in an attempt to save his wife from embarrassment, "Most gargoyles learn to kill by the time they are eleven, the fact that you've received a death under your belt is surprising to both of us."

Jhonig then looked down at his cereal almost shamefully. "Every life is sacred, no matter who the life belongs to." The young gargoyle said earnestly, remembering what his teachers had taught in his classes. "But they attacked dad and me, I was only acting in self-defense."

"And that you acted with this knowledge is why we are proud of you…" Mojhyn said reassuringly with a relieved smile, "Since you're developing so quickly."

Jhonig looked back up and smiled. "Then I will continue to make you proud." He said.

The couple smiled at their son as Tiogra sat up and drank the last few gulps of his coffee. "Well," he said, "Time to take you to class young man."

"Ok!" Jhonig said happily.

After his breakfast, the two flew off to Jhonig's class on the fifth level of the mountain. Standing in the doorway, Mojhyn smiled as she watched them leave, thankful for her son's wellbeing.

Resurrection

It was twelve o'clock in the morning when the chief elite vampire team arrived back at the vampire estate. Halton and his comrades were drinking, singing and laughing as they walked down the gigantic halls of the castle after a night of celebration for killing off the rattus a year ago. Even though the event was long over and done with, the vampire elites were too intoxicated at the time to care about current events.

Watching his comrades celebrate gave Halton a diabolical feeling of joy, similar to the feeling he received long ago when he commanded the death of a female gargoyle in Germany and left her comrade for dead in the snow. He was especially impressed by the explosive weapon the vampire scientists were able to produce over the last three years using the magical essence in the bodies of the mummified vampires they had found in Egypt.

As they proceeded to revel in their successful mission, Halton noticed something in the corner of his eye. It was Vlad, starring at him with an unusually deep scowl. This made Halton wonder if he was in some sort of trouble. Vlad beckoned Halton over to the pitch-black hallway he was standing in, and like a good sycophant, Halton obeyed.

As the two vampires walked down the pointed arched hall, Halton noticed the enormous, golden-framed portraits hanging on the walls. At first, the elite warrior thought they were pictures of famous vampires, but he quickly realized that they were various pictures of Vlad in different clothes and postures. Halton wanted to scoff at his master's ego, but dared not make any noise Vlad might not approve of.

At the end of the hallway was Vlad's throne room, which appeared empty. This was unusual, considering by this time of day, it would be full of vampires hanging on the ceiling.

Once they reached the middle of the room, Vlad stopped suddenly. With his hands folded behind his back, he turned around and faced Halton.

"Sir," Halton began, "is something wrong?"

Vlad grinned from ear to ear. Within what seemed to be a flash, the vampire lord bashed Halton over the head with his fist. The blow was hard enough to put a crack in Halton's skull and knock him unconscious, yet not hard enough to kill him. The last thing Halton felt was the burning, sandy taste of ash flowing from his nose and mouth as he hit the floor and passed out.

When Halton awoke, he was startled to find that he was strapped to a medical bed. He tried to speak, but could not due to his mouth being incredibly dry, not to mention there was a giant tube stretching out of his jaws. Lack of blood intake had made his body weak. Tubes with orange liquid flowing inside of them were connected to every part of Halton's head.

Halton tried to sit up, but all he could do was slowly move his head. When he finally managed to look at his body, he was horrified to see that he had been dissected from his chest to his pelvis. Even more tubes were connected to every major organ in Halton's body, pumping orange liquid into his physique. What was even stranger was that there was a glass box filled with ashes resting inside Halton's chest. He muffled what would be screams if he were strong enough to yell. The orange liquid was gently burning him from the inside as it pumped through his body.

The weary elite then heard footsteps coming from the right and tried to break free unsuccessfully. He cursed at himself in his thoughts for being too weak. Even if he could break free, what could he do? He was connected to hundreds of tubes, which would probably interfere with his ability to walk in the first place. What terrified Halton the most, was that the only light in the room was shinning directly on him. He had no idea what the tubes were connected to. For all he knew, the tubes were pumping flammable liquid into his veins.

As the footsteps came closer, Halton saw a figure cloaked in shadow standing over him. As the figure leaned in closer to his face, the elite vampire could see it was his lord, Vlad.

"Hello, Halton." Vlad said, "Comfortable?"

Halton muffled words that Vlad could only make out as curses in his direction.

"Good." Vlad said sarcastically, "I was hoping you'd say that."

As Vlad walked away from Halton, lights began to brighten the room, revealing hundreds of mummified vampires with tubes connected to their chests as well as stakes. Halton's eyes widened as he saw that the tubes from the carcasses were connected to him. He tried to scream, but was once again unsuccessful.

"Don't bother yelling for help, Halton." Vlad said as he typed a password onto the computer that was sitting right in front of his elite vampire assassin. "No one would hear you scream, nor would they even care if they could."

Halton's face was overcome with confusion as his medical bed slowly moved, making it so he was sitting upright.

"You see, Halton," Vlad said. "Everyone in the castle knew about this little project except you. Time and time again you've made the vampire nation proud. Which is why you were the best guinea pig for this little science experiment."

Vlad walked over to one of the bodies and tapped one of the tubes.

"The liquid pumping into your body is called 'Necro-Mag'." Vlad explained, "It's the remaining mystical essence from the bodies you see before you. As you've probably already guessed, Halton, these are the remains of the Cult of Egn."

Halton was shocked. This explained why the orange liquid had such a similar color to the gas from the canisters he and his team had dumped into the rattus' lair. The only question the vampire assassin had was why he was strapped to the medical chair? What kind of sinister plan did Vlad have in store for him?

"Yes," Vlad said, "You can only imagine the agony that came with the hours it took to make the weapons you used on the rattus. I had to make sure there was still enough essence left to make this project possible. You understand don't you, Halton?"

Halton rolled his eyes. He had almost forgotten how much Vlad loved the sound of his own voice.

"Eh, it was stupid of me to ask." Vlad began again, "You're not smart enough to understand it all anyway. I can tell you this though, every detail of this experiment had to be perfect in every way. If any body were missing or too deteriorated, the new body I'm going to create for my father wouldn't be perfect."

Halton looked down at the glass box of ashes lodged in his chest. So that was where the ashes came from, they were the remains of Dracula's body.

"You were the final puzzle piece." Vlad explained, "A vampire of astounding speed, strength, agility and stamina. Not to mention I trained you myself in the ways of shape shifting. Like I said before, Halton, you're the perfect candidate."

Vlad walked over to the wall, opposite from the computer, that had a big red switch on it that was labeled "power." Vlad grabbed the switch with eagerness, yet hesitated. He looked at Halton one final time and smiled.

"Goodbye, Halton." Vlad said, "You will be missed. But think of it this way… you're making a sacrifice for the greater good of the vampire nation."

With his sarcastic goodbye being said, Vlad threw the switch. Sparks of electricity flew out of the tubes as the remaining Necro-Mag flushed out of the mummified vampires and into Halton's anatomy. The sleeping vampires awoke as the stakes flew out of their chests and screamed in pain as their life essence flowed into Halton, reducing them to ashes. Halton screamed as the burning sensation overcame his body. His veins glowed as they seemingly shot out of his flesh. Muscles soon quickly covered the veins as layer upon layer of flesh grew over the vampire assassin's body.

Halton could feel every part of his physique change. His eyes grew bigger and his fangs grew twice their size. He could feel his whole body grow until he was three times the vampire he once was. His memories began to burn away as his sight blackened like he was dying. Smoke rose up out of Halton's pores as the transformation took place.

Soon enough, the area around the medical bed was covered in fumes. Vlad could hear the belts he had used to tie Halton down snap as a large, dark figure emerged out of the vapor. Much to Vlad's satisfaction, a very distinguishable widows peak on a very pale forehead could be seen from within the smoke. It was Halton's body, however this was no longer Halton, it was Dracula, the prime vampire.

Although his face lacked emotion, as Dracula's fiery red eyes scanned the room, this was incredibly surprising to him. It was difficult to fathom being dead for more than a hundred years in torment and suddenly he was one with the living again.

Dracula had not forgotten who was responsible for his untimely death either. As soon as he saw Vlad, his eyes widened with rage.

"Hello, father." Vlad said smiling, fully aware of his father's anger.

Dracula growled and charged at his wayward son, grabbing him by the throat and pinning him to the wall. To his dissatisfaction however, Vlad showed no signs of struggle or pain.

"Well, if it isn't the 'Slaughter Dragon'." Dracula sneered, his voice had the faint accent like the cracking of burning wood. "I guess I have you to thank for my resurrection."

"You could say that." Vlad said smiling back.

"And I suppose I should thank you." Dracula said, "However, you are also responsible for my demise!"

Dracula's grip tightened around his disobedient son's throat. This time Vlad gasped for breath and clutched at his father's wrist. Dracula raised his fist and prepared to punch Vlad's skull into the wall.

"Goodbye, son." Dracula said happily.

As Dracula's fist shot towards his son's face, Vlad instantly turned into mist and freed himself of his father's grip, then reappeared on the other side of the room away from his father. Dracula spun around to see his son materialize from the mist.

"Good," Dracula said smirking, "You remember everything I taught you. You'll excuse me if I rejoice in the fact that I didn't teach you everything, otherwise this would be too difficult."

"Wouldn't expect it any other way, dad." Vlad said, raising his eyebrows in sarcasm.

Dracula turned his right arm into mist and used the vapor to push the medical beds between himself and his son out of the way.

"Such power!" Dracula said in awe at what he had done, "You impress me yet again, boy. Here I thought you had given up your study in sciences."

Vlad shrugged his shoulders. "Everyone has to have a hobby." He replied.

Dracula charged at Vlad again. Within every one of his footsteps, it was as if small quakes erupted when his feet collided with the ground. Vlad jumped out of the way, watching his father collide with the wall and immediately leapt in his direction. The current vampire lord was shocked to see that the body he had made for Dracula was stronger than he expected.

The revived vampire lord's feet then connected with Vlad's face, smashing his head into the ground. Despite the pain, Vlad was surprised it did not kill him in the process. The prime vampire proceeded to pick Vlad up by his head and squeezed hard enough that blood trickled down Vlad's face and turned to ash as it dripped off his chin.

"Perhaps your works are a little too good, my son." Dracula said as he smashed Vlad into the wall to the left.

"Maybe…" Vlad taunted from behind his father.

Dracula turned around in surprise, his son was better than he expected. Usually he would give Vlad a compliment, had this been hundreds of years ago. Yet Dracula figured he had given his murderer enough praise for one day. Mist, from the double that Dracula thought was Vlad, slowly returned back to its source, letting Vlad revert back into his normal weight as the mist poured back into him.

"So tell me father," Vlad said resuming his fighting stance, "How was hell?"

Dracula swung at his son again, only to have his blow avoided and miss his target completely.

"There is no such thing for beings like us." Dracula explained, "As it turns out, when vampires die we go back to our source. The one who created us and our lycanthrope brethren."

"Egn?" Vlad asked, surprised that the god of the damned would want anything to do with the earthly servants who failed him.

"Exactly." Dracula confirmed as he swung at Vlad again.

As Vlad dodged the next swing, a thought popped into his mind.

"So we all become a part of him in the end?" he asked.

"No." Dracula began again, "He recycles our souls for something else, though I never understood what for. However, I did not go back to the source."

Dracula swung at Vlad again, hitting the wall in front of him instead of his son.

"Where did you go?" Vlad asked.

"I was taken by Trog, the original gargoyle, for committing the most sins against his people." Dracula replied, "He was incredibly angry for what I had done when I was alive. I was tortured everyday until I thought I would eventually lose my mind. That is… until you revived me."

As the prime vampire kept trying to hit Vlad, the two of them continued to talk.

"And what did God think of all this?" Vlad asked, assuming the deity the humans prayed to existed.

"As far as I could tell, he didn't exist let alone care." Dracula explained, "I never saw him, unless of course he refused to show his presence to me when I asked for his audience. When I did, Trog would just stare at me and I would be tortured some more. Who can blame him? I am, after all, the master of my kind, it's only natural he should hate me. Even now…"

With sudden, tremendous speed, Dracula then punched Vlad in the chest, knocking him into the giant light above the bed he was resurrected on.

"I am reborn a demon, thanks to you." Dracula chuckled as Vlad coughed up ash, "With this new power, I could take on the gargoyle nation alone and even stand a chance against the grandmaster."

"I've been meaning to talk to you about that…" Vlad said as he staggered to his feet, "I don't know the limits to your power. We're going to need to test you first before you can go out and kill things like in the good old days."

Before Dracula could hit Vlad again, he stopped and stood very still. He then sat down on one of the medical beds and rested his head on his hand.

"Go on…" Dracula said, raising an eyebrow.

Vlad dusted himself off and sat on the medical bed across from his father.

"Well," Vlad began, "Considering the fact that it took the essence of over one hundred mummified vampires to bring you back into the body you have now, there is a great possibility you're a demigod. However, that doesn't mean you can't be killed or beaten in battle. Things have changed since you were last on Earth. For example, you can't just swing at people and expect that you'll hit them. It takes tremendous martial skill to kill someone nowadays, something that the gargoyles have a lot of. Not to mention you might have new abilities, and that is something worth looking into."

Dracula scratched his chin. "What if I think this is a waste of time?" he asked, starring at his son from under his sleek, black brows.

"Trust me, the time we spend on this will be for the better." Vlad said, insulted that his father would suggest such a thing about his work. "You will be happy I did this in the end."

Vlad walked over to the table that had his now destroyed computer scattered on top of it and picked up a briefcase that was resting in the wreckage. He then unlocked the combination and opened the briefcase, which held a vile filled with a violet-red liquid labeled "rattus blood" inside.

"I had my men extract four vials of this from my test subjects before they were killed." Vlad said as he handed the vile to Dracula, "Drink this."

Dracula eyed the vile suspiciously before he drank it in one gulp. At first, he noticed no change in his body until Vlad asked him to run from one end of the room to the other. The prime vampire completed the feat in almost an instant.

"What was in the vile?" Dracula asked.

"The blood of the rattus." Vlad responded, "It's been modified to give you the speed you now possess."

"Interesting." Dracula said, smiling from ear to ear.

"Indeed," Vlad said, smiling in return. "Now come, it's time to be reintroduced to your people."

As the diabolic lords made it up back into the throne room, after Dracula had thrown on some pants and a cloak, the vampires that were resting inside immediately flew down from the ceiling to bow to their returned master. Trang, who had overheard the commotion from the hallway outside, peaked into the throne room to see what was going on. When the vampire princess saw her grandfather standing next to Vlad, she felt as though her head would crack open from disbelief.

"Oh, Lord Dracula, we were so lost without you!" one vampire exclaimed, much to Vlad's displeasure.

"Lord Dracula, it is good to see you alive and well!" declared another.

Dracula raised his hands to calm the crowd, making the room immediately fall silent.

"My people." Dracula said, "My return, as grand as it is, must not be for naught. We must fight this disease that has plagued our people long enough. The plague known as gargoyles!"

The vampires all cheered in agreement.

"Today," Dracula spoke again, "we must train hard for the fight against the gargoyle nation!"

The vampires cheered again.

"Today…" Dracula boomed, "Will be the beginning of a new era of vampires! Today, we will begin to rid the world of our most hated enemy! Starting today, we will slay all gargoyles!"

As the crowd cheered for the final time, Dracula then ordered every vampire to spread the word that he had returned and to begin their training for the upcoming war with the gargoyles.

When the vampires flew out of the room, Trang's face paled with fear. Since Dracula was resurrected, her plan to take the throne could not commence. She ran back down the hall as quietly as she could so she did not alert her father and grandfather of her presence.

Vlad looked up at his father and smiled. "Well," he said, "are you ready to start testing?"

"Wouldn't miss it." Dracula said grinning as he gestured towards the throne room entrance in anticipation.

When Dracula gestured, a ball of fire and bats burst out of his hand and erupted against the wall near the doorway, creating a large crater in the center of it.

Vlad and Dracula eyed the ruined wall in surprise. The display of Dracula's power filled his son with glee.

"I suppose there isn't anytime to waste." He chuckled as he and Dracula laughed, thinking about the destruction and death they would unleash upon the gargoyles.

Jhonig's Dream

It was a wonderful day for Jhonig. Today was his graduation ceremony for completing his third level of training. This also doubled as a birthday celebration, since the young gargoyle was going to be seven years of age in only two more weeks.

Jhonig was as happy as he could be. His friends were happy for him, Tiogra and Mojhyn were proud of him, and his teachers were thrilled with his performances.

The celebration was a sight to behold. Almost every gargoyle that was present in the castle appeared for the graduation. Not just because of Jhonig's birthday, but also due to their own children's accomplishments. The banquet was exquisite as well. There were elegant desserts, meats with a variety of herbs and spices, salads, and beverages of all kinds. It was a truly wondrous celebration. There was even an ice sculpture of a dragon that the gargoyles used to cool their drinks.

The festivities the gargoyles had were excellent for the children. There was dulled dagger-throwing, pin the axe on the demon head, and a paper mache monster that they could swing at with clubs. The false beasts were, of course, filled with candy for the children.

Now that Jhonig had graduated, he could begin the next step in his training. This involved learning to control his elements so that they would not destroy him from the inside, striking with his wings and his choice in which profession he would spend the majority of the time doing within the nation. Due to his grades, he was allowed to choose engineering and medical studies as possible careers. The grandmaster told Jhonig to give it time and to think it over before he came to his final decision. The most important thing to remember in making a professional choice was, "No matter what you decide to do, you are all equally important to the gargoyle nation." These words were what made Jhonig decide to wait until he had a definitive answer on what job he wanted.

Once Jhonig, Tiogra and Mojhyn arrived at their home, Jhonig immediately wished his parents goodnight, went to his room and fell asleep out of exhaustion from the party. Mojhyn and Tiogra sympathized with Jhonig and both agreed that since it was his third graduation, he had every right to be tired. Jhonig then drifted off into a deep sleep once he tucked himself in.

Jhonig awoke in the middle of a field that was pleasant and filled with life. Gargoyle children were playing, dancing and singing, trees were alive with color as flowers bloomed on their branches, dandelions blew in the wind, their seeds floating in the air like spirits of peace. It seemed like it was paradise. Then Jhonig blinked his eyes. The felid turned into a barren wasteland with fire where the grass was. The trees that were once alive were now dead and burned. Wherever there was life, there was now death and decay.

Jhonig then heard marching footsteps in the distance. He looked to his left and saw the vampire nation clad in armor. Even the vampire women were dressed in the strange battle garments. Their armor was colored bright blue, yet kept a frightening image. Their helmets made it seem as if they had two sets of black eyes resting on top of each other. The suits of armor themselves were crafted to resemble demonic bat creatures. The vampires growled and snarled at Jhonig, barring their fangs and roaring into the sky.

Suddenly, a giant vampire on a blood red horse appeared in the middle of the monstrous army. The vampiric titan did not wear a helmet, yet his face was cloaked in shadow. The giant vampire then grabbed one of the smaller vampires and snapped his neck. As the smaller vampire turned to ash, the larger vampire spread the cinders over the army.

Instantaneously, Jhonig heard another army approaching. He spun around and saw the gargoyle nation, standing directly across from the vampire country's army. Though their army was smaller, the gargoyles stood their ground and waited for the command to charge. Each member of the gargoyle nation either held a sword or was unarmed, allowing them to rely on sheer martial skill alone. Strangely enough, the gargoyle nation did not have any armor, they simply wore their traditional uniforms; gray, tattered robes with long sleeves and baggy, loose slacks. Jhonig assumed that this was so they had loose, comfortable clothing to fight in, just like his teachers had instructed him to. He had never seen any gargoyle wear armor, but from what he could tell, the gargoyle nation was in over its head. The gargoyles were outnumbered and possibly equally matched, considering the vampires were wearing armor that seemed thick enough to rival even a gargoyle's hide.

Then the war horns sounded. The two opposing sides ran at each other furiously out of sheer hatred for their enemies and clashed within seconds. Mixes of vampire ash and gargoyle blood flew through the air as swords, bullets and claws tore at flesh and stone. This took Jhonig by surprise, he had never seen a gargoyle bleed let alone die in combat.

The battle was equally balanced. Twenty vampires died with every three gargoyles that fell. Jhonig wished he could help, but for some reason his body was frozen in place. Not even the hardest effort could free him from his paralyzed state. All he could do was watch, witnessing all his friends and loved ones perish under the bullets and blades of the vampire country.

Just then, out of the corner of his eye, Jhonig saw a being made of light run onto the battlefield. The light was dim enough that Jhonig could see that the creature was in fact Tiogra, his own father.

As Tiogra ran through the battlefield, hacking and slashing away at the vampires with a sword, the giant vampire climbed down from his horse and drew his own blade. The sword the giant vampire had was practically four feet of steel, attached to a crude hilt that held the blade together.

Then the brawl between Tiogra and the giant vampire began. The opponents lunged at each other with such ferocity that the earth itself shook under their feet.

Jhonig noticed there was something different about Tiogra. His eyes showed no sign of peace in them. There was nothing calm, cool, or collected, only absolute rage and anger flashed in Tiogra's eyes.

As the two gladiators clashed their swords, Tiogra immediately punched the vampire's head and knocked him back into a nearby tree. The tree proceeded to collapse onto the vampire's torso and nearly crushed him. However, the vampire threw the tree off of himself and continued to fight.

Tiogra lashed out at his opponent with an exchange of blows to the fuller of the vampire's sword. Though he kept his hands hardened for extra strength, Tiogra's fists began to crack apart from the combined force of his punches and the thickness of the enormous blade. Eventually, Tiogra's effort placed a crack in the steel of the vampire's weapon. Both the gargoyles and the vampires stopped their brawl and gathered around the two combatants just to see which champion was better.

After countless hits and blocks, both swords eventually broke and the warriors resorted to using their fists. As they fought, cataclysmic events took place on the battlefield. Rocks exploded up from the ground, vampires turned to ash and gargoyles crumbled into pieces.

In the end, Tiogra punched a hole straight through the armor of the giant vampire and tore his spine out through his chest, then used his power over water to freeze the spine solid. The master gargoyle proceeded to whip the vampire across the face with the spinal structure as the vampire turned to ash. The remaining gargoyles cheered as the surviving vampires collapsed into ash from the loss of their leader.

Jhonig rejoiced to himself and was finally free of the invisible bonds that paralyzed him. He ran towards Tiogra to give him a hug in delight of their victory when suddenly, Tiogra's smile faded. A blade pierced through the master gargoyle's chest and twisted from horizontal to vertical, then cut him straight down the middle of his torso and disappeared.

"No!" Jhonig yelled as he watched his father collapse onto the ground.

As Tiogra fell, the battlefield, the gargoyles, and his corpse, turned to light and faded away, and Jhonig awoke.

Tiogra and Mojhyn had burst into the room after hearing their son scream in his sleep. Mojhyn held Jhonig close as he panted for breath.

"What's wrong, honey?" Mojhyn asked her son.

"Bad dream?" Tiogra asked as well.

"It was a nightmare!" Jhonig started, still shaken by the dream, "It started out really well, but then there were two armies, one was ours and the other belonged to the vampire nation. Both sides had champions, the vampires had a giant and we had dad."

Tiogra smiled at his son's identification of him as a hero.

"But then things got ugly." Jhonig said as he looked up at his parents, "After dad won, someone stuck a blade through his chest and disappeared."

Tiogra and Mojhyn were taken back a bit by Jhonig's strange dream.

"Did you see who…struck me?" Tiogra asked, trying not to upset Jhonig any further.

Jhonig shook his head in disappointment.

Tiogra then told Jhonig to get dressed and to wait for him by the front door.

"Where are you going?" Mojhyn asked, still disturbed by her son's wild dream.

"Babe," Tiogra said holding his wife's marble shoulders, "given all that's been happening with Jhonig… his new powers, his hidden abilities, his first kill. I think there's a pretty good chance he has foresight as well."

"What…he can see into the future?" Mojhyn asked, looking at her husband as if he had grown two extra heads.

Tiogra simply nodded. Mojhyn sighed and, believing that Tiogra was right, simply said, "Be careful."

The couple kissed each other goodbye, but before Tiogra and Jhonig could walk out the door, Mojhyn asked them to wait after she put on her urban gargoyle attire.

"I'm coming with you." She said.

"Are you sure?" Tiogra asked.

"If there's something going on with our son," Mojhyn replied, "I want to make sure we get to the bottom of this together."

Tiogra smiled as the family flew off towards the upper level of the mountain, locking the door behind them.

Once the trio entered the castle doorway from the caverns, the other gargoyles gave Tiogra, Mojhyn, and Jhonig praises and welcomes.

Jhonig had loved exploring the castle section of the mountain, it was always filled with friendly faces and people he knew he could count on. It gave the kind of safe atmosphere that he assumed many human schools produced, giving him a sense of happiness.

After they reached the door to the hallway that led to the castle study, Mojhyn and Tiogra sighed. Despite the fact that Jhonig could have only been dreaming, the fact was that strange events took place in the world all the time. The possibility that he could see into the future was still stressful, given what he saw.

The family of three proceeded down the hallway until they reached the third door on the left. Tiogra knocked on the door until they heard the grandmaster's voice.

"Yes?" the grandmaster's muted voice yelled through the door.

"It's Tiogra, sir!" Tiogra yelled back, "I have urgent news regarding Jhonig!"

"The door is open!" the grandmaster yelled in reply.

Tiogra held the door open for Jhonig and Mojhyn as they walked into the study. The grandmaster was sitting in a large red chair with armrests, reading a book on the Japanese war of Sekigahara in the 1600's, recorded by Tun-Taig.

"Did you know that Oda Nobunaga's son, Oda Nobutada, was a lycanthrope?" the grandmaster asked, "It says here that one of Nobunaga's generals, Akechi Mitsuhide, forced him to commit suicide. It also states that Mitsuhide himself saw Nobutada turn to fur and steam before his very eyes. He then ordered the execution of everyone who witnessed this event."

The grandmaster closed the book and placed it on the desk in front of him.

"I guess he figured what the humans don't know won't hurt them." The grandmaster said, slightly amused at the irony.

The grandmaster then directed his attention at Jhonig, who bowed in respect.

"And what does the young Jhonig have for me tonight?" the grandmaster asked with a friendly smile.

Tiogra walked over to the grandmaster and bowed down to his ear level.

"He's had a strange dream." Tiogra whispered, "We figured that with all his power, he might also have the gift of foresight. We just wanted to make sure he was alright."

The grandmaster looked at Tiogra with concern. Under normal circumstances, if Tiogra reported something strange, the grandmaster would have told him there was nothing to worry about and that it could be handled. Yet, for some reason, the grandmaster felt like this problem needed investigating.

"Tell me what you dreamt about." The grandmaster said calmly to Jhonig.

Jhonig calmly approached the grandmaster and went into great detail about his dream. About the vampire and gargoyle nations going to war, about the vampires having armor that could match the gargoyle's thick hides, about the giant vampire fighting Tiogra and about how Tiogra was stabbed at the end.

The grandmaster slowly stood up and looked at Tiogra with a raised eyebrow.

"Are you sure you're not just a little paranoid?" the grandmaster asked Tiogra, jokingly.

Mojhyn tried not to chuckle at the grandmaster's joke. Regardless of his humor, everyone in the room knew how serious the grandmaster took situations such as this. Tiogra asked the grandmaster to perform a meditative examination on Jhonig to see if there was any other power they might not have known about. The grandmaster agreed and asked Tiogra to close the door.

While Tiogra did as he was instructed, the grandmaster and Jhonig sat cross-legged on the floor, facing each other with their hands on their knees.

As the examination began, the room darkened. Tiogra and Mojhyn felt as if their weight was rising off the floor, reminding Mojhyn of the day when Tiogra had helped her overcome her wild anger. As they watched, they noticed that they both could see the grandmaster's aura flow through the room, which appeared in an unadulterated white color. As it flew through the room, thoughts of happiness and comfort flowed over Mojhyn and Tiogra, as if everything they had ever worried about had faded into nothing for a brief moment.

The examination took several minutes before the grandmaster was finally done. As his aura seeped back into his body and the room brightened, the grandmaster instructed Tiogra to stay in the room and to have Jhonig and Mojhyn wait outside in the hallway. The gargoyle family did as they were instructed without question.

"Well?" Tiogra asked with concern as his wife and son left.

"Well," the grandmaster began, "If there was any doubt that Jhonig was the reincarnation of Trog, this would prove otherwise. In time he'll seem like a demigod, even among our people. And yes, it would appear he now has been blessed with Trog's foresight."

Tiogra looked at the ground with a troubled expression. If Jhonig really had foresight, this could mean that when the final battle between the vampires and gargoyles came, Tiogra would probably die. This was an outcome he was not prepared for.

"I suspect this all has to do with the prophecy." The grandmaster stated, "Trog must have an incredible plan for him. Although I'm not quite sure why the majority of his soul is still in the earth."

Tiogra looked at the grandmaster with confusion.

"From what I do understand," the grandmaster said, "Jhonig is being prepared for the future. In a way, he's being shaped into a vessel that will hold all of Trog's power. But as I said before, I don't have many details about Trog's plan to work off of."

Despite the grandmaster's effort to lighten his student's current mood, Tiogra was still starring at the ground. Even though gargoyles were trained to expect death at any time, Tiogra had lived so long that he had gotten used to being immortal, the fact that he could die in the future was nerve-racking. The grandmaster walked over and placed a firm hand on his student's shoulder.

"Hey, don't worry about it." The grandmaster said. "I can promise you this, when we go to battle with the vampires, I'll make sure no one will get the jump on you."

As Tiogra chuckled at his master's words, the grandmaster gave him a pat on the back for reassurance.

"I wouldn't tell Jhonig this though." The grandmaster warned, "If he found out there was a chance of his father dying, who knows how hurt he'd be?"

"Right." Tiogra said, "Thank you, grandmaster."

"Don't mention it." The grandmaster said, "What are friends for?"

Tiogra smiled back at the grandmaster and walked out of the room into the hallway, where Mojhyn and Jhonig were waiting for him.

"So?" Mojhyn asked.

"Turns out your fine, Jhonig." Tiogra said smiling, "Lets head home."

Walking down the hall, Tiogra's smile faded as he thought to himself of how he was going to break the disturbing news to Mojhyn.

Kin Issues

After the resurrection of her grandfather, Trang was taken back with confusion and anger. This was a major set back in her plans to overthrow her father. She had to come up with a new strategy and fast.

First of all, she had to find out if Vlad had anything else planned for his war. Second, she had to alert the gargoyles of Dracula's revival. Third, if all else failed, Trang had to sabotage her father's plans by herself if necessary, which meant finding a place to create an army of her own in a secluded area, far enough away that her family would not notice. Before anything could happen, Trang had to make sure that her plans with the gargoyle nation could still commence.

While the gargoyles are destroying my father's army, I'll be the one to seize the throne and lead the vampire country to fruition. Once the war is over of course. She thought to herself.

Trang hurried into her father's throne room to find answers. With more stress on her shoulders than usual, she sighed and gazed around at the walls. She was not looking for anything specific, just to quickly reflect on her life and how she had come to this point.

When she looked to her right, much to her surprise, Trang noticed a lever on the wall, which was hidden so that no one would notice it at first glance. However, Trang was not just anyone. She walked over to the lever and pulled it down. An elevator appeared in front of her as the lever retracted back into the wall. Curiously, Trang stepped inside. The elevator then creaked as it descended downward to the basement level.

Trang was not even aware that there was a basement level to the castle let alone an elevator that led to it. Once she arrived at the bottom, Trang's eyes widened in shock. The elevator had taken her to a laboratory filled with experiments and equipment for genetic experimentation. Trang also noticed the racks with dead creatures on them. One was for vampires, another for tortasapiens, another for the rattus (which was now empty), and one for lycanthropes. The only other one that was empty was the rack that said "gargoyle." This was no surprise to Trang, considering the gargoyle's reputation.

As she ventured further into the lab, Trang noticed a giant computer on one of the walls, which had a violet screen that was asking for a password. Trang tried to ponder an answer as she starred at the giant screen.

If my father were to make a password for himself, it'd have to be something I'd never think of. She thought.

After several long minutes of thinking, Trang finally typed "EgnSon59" into the computer. Much to her disbelief, the code worked.

An image of a suit of armor instantly popped up onto the screen. The armor was sleek and bright blue with a helmet that resembled a demonic bat's head with four eyes. Trang looked at the file that said test run and double clicked on it. Inside the file was a video of the armor undergoing all kinds of abuse that confirmed that the armor was as hard and durable as stone. As the video ended with Vlad and other vampire scientists laughing menacingly in the background, Trang knew she had to warn the gargoyles of this sudden calamity. She immediately ran towards the elevator and ascended back into the throne room.

As she ran out of the throne room, down the halls of the castle towards the garage, Trang stopped suddenly. She swore she heard voices coming from behind the walls and pressed her ear up to the wall so she could hear better, yet the voices were still muffled. She could barely make out that it was the sound of Vlad and Dracula, who were probably training.

Just then, an explosion shook the hall and knocked the vampire princess back a foot. Trang guessed Dracula was the cause for it. She remembered that behind the wall was the castle gym, since she had explored every nook and cranny of the castle herself. As of today, there was no secret that was undiscovered by her anymore.

Trang crept down the halls to the fitness center, where the door was slightly open. Peaking inside, she could see her father and Dracula laughing hysterically.

"Ok, do that one." Vlad told his father as he laughed, pointing at a lifeless, stone replica of a gargoyle.

Dracula smiled and concentrated his energy into his right hand. A ball of flame with fiery bats circling around it appeared in his palm. Dracula threw the ball of flame in the statue's direction, where the statue exploded upon contact with the fire. The prime vampire and Vlad then laughed until they were holding their stomachs and slapping their knees.

Those two have gone mad! Trang thought as she witnessed her grandfather's power.

"Ok," Vlad spoke again as he calmly stopped laughing, "so far we've covered your new combat techniques. You can self-levitate, project fire from your hands, and your hypnosis has increased. The powers you had before you died have exceeded that of normal vampires. You're immune to garlic and sunlight no longer weakens you. Now you only have to touch humans to turn them. I'd say you've far exceeded my expectations."

"Excellent!" Dracula said, "Rally the troops. We'll attack the gargoyles in exactly two days."

Trang's eyes widened. A surprise attack on the gargoyles could ruin everything. She had to warn Tiogra right away.

Trang was careful enough not to make any noise or hint that she was spying on her father. She knew she had to leave the castle in order to contact Tiogra to warn him so that there would not be any suspicion that she was rebelling. As she ran down the hall towards the garage, she accidently shoved several vampires out of her way.

Great, Trang thought, *now they're sure to tattle on me for "suspicious behavior."*

Once Trang reached the garage, she grabbed her helmet off the nearby shelf next to the coat hangers and jumped onto a sleek red motorcycle, revved the engine and sped off through the garage door and into the night. Trang knew that she had to get far enough away to escape the reach of any unwanted pursuers. Unfortunately, seconds away from the castle, Trang noticed several vampires chasing after her on motorcycles of their own.

Probably trying to keep me inside, she thought, *have to lose them somehow.*

Thinking fast, Trang pulled her personally crafted, double-edged Russian kindjal out of the saddlebag as well as five shuriken. She then leapt into the air and tossed the shuriken with near perfect accuracy. Luckily, the shuriken hit each of their targets in the head and the pursuing vampires turned to ash while their motorcycles hit some of the assailants behind them. Trang witnessed her successful attacks as she landed back on her bike safely.

As the chase continued, three vampires managed to catch up to Trang, only to have their heads cut from their throats by her Russian-based blade. The next one to catch up was a little more skilled than the last three though. Pulling out a sword of his own, the vampire soldier swung at Trang, only to have his attack blocked.

This vampire was strong and determined. He chased after Trang and swung again. Trang blocked the attack and swung back at him, but her strike was blocked as well. It was as if they were playing a children's game of tag with swords. However, it did not take long before Trang managed to push the vampire down a nearby cliff and into the abyss below.

As soon as Trang thought that she was out of trouble, several more vampires rode up behind her. The vampire princess groaned and continued to ride towards her destination.

It was much to her luck that the sun began to rise, right as soon as she cleared the desert foothills near the castle. The vampires behind her shrieked and turned to ash as Trang continued to ride away, only weakened by the sun's rays through her protective clothing and powerful heritage.

After a few more minutes of covering ground, Trang stopped once she was out of the castle's view. She could not help but notice her cell phone was vibrating. When she pulled her phone out, the screen read

"Vincent." Recognizing her brother, Trang immediately hit talk.

"What's up?" Trang asked, thinking it was urgent.

"Sister…" Vincent said sternly, "Where are you going? If dad finds out…"

"Dad is going to probably kill me for what I'm going to accomplish in this mission, Vincent." Trang said, "I'm sorry brother, but it's something I feel like I must do."

"If you rebel again, I'm not sticking up for you this time." Vincent said harshly, "You can kiss your ass goodbye as far as I'm concerned."

"Dad treats you like dirt and you think I'm the one who's wrong?" Trang asked, "As far as I'm concerned you're dead to me as well, goodbye."

As Trang hung up, she tried as hard as she could not to cry. It would not sound very good to her brother if it sounded as if she had regrets. From what she could tell, she would not want to be back inside the castle walls after the event that just transpired and the conversation she just had. This fact gave Trang an excuse to move into seclusion, but first she had to call Tiogra to warn him about Dracula's plan of attack.

As Trang dialed Tiogra's number onto her cell phone, she thought about all the fun memories she had of playing with Vincent when they were growing up together. This only made her feel worse, so she immediately tried to think of her father's evil plans and focused on the problem at hand.

At the same moment Trang finished her call with her brother, Tiogra was in the kitchen with Jhonig, showing him how to prepare dinner when suddenly, his cell phone rang. It was odd considering Tiogra knew it was his turn to stay home since Mojhyn was supposed to go on patrol that night, and he knew that she usually did not call him when she was working. The only other person that would call Tiogra was Ghin, and he was on guard duty that night as well.

The master gargoyle picked up the cell phone and looked at the screen that read "vampire girl." Tiogra turned off the stove and told Jhonig to hang out in his room for a while. Jhonig, reading his father's concerned expressions, obeyed without a single complaint. Tiogra then hit the "talk" button on his phone and listened closely.

"Trang?" Tiogra asked, "Is this you?"

"Yeah," Trang responded on the other end of the line, "it's me."

"What's up?" Tiogra asked, plainly.

"I'm having problems at the vampire estate." Trang said, still a little shaken by her earlier conversation with her brother, "My father's done something horrible."

"Well," Tiogra said, "spit it out girl."

"He's resurrected Dracula." Trang said, "I don't know how, but it's him."

Tiogra's eyes widened. The vision Jhonig had was true, the vampires did have a champion now. Dracula was more than a match for Tiogra then, if he were truly back from the dead, the events that would take place would truly be catastrophic.

"That's not all." Trang continued, "He has more power now than ever."

Tiogra blinked as his mind went blank for a brief second before he resumed the conversation. "What do you mean?" he asked.

"I mean he has more power." Trang responded, "He can throw fireballs, levitate, and he has increased hypnosis. He wasn't this powerful even when he was the head of the Cult of Egn. There might be more but I don't know if there is."

"Gotcha," Tiogra said as he regained his sturdy mindset, "I'll alert the grandmaster right away."

"There's one more thing," Trang said, "Vlad's been working on some sort of armor. Its density is equal to stone. I think he might be making that for his army. Which, by the way, is going to attack in two days."

Tiogra remained calm. His mind was uneasy, but Trang did not need to know that. "Thank you, Trang." He said.

"Don't mention it." Trang responded, "Good luck, Tiogra."

As Tiogra hung up his phone, he wrapped up the food he was preparing, placed it in the refrigerator, and told Jhonig to follow him to the castle section of the mountain.

"But what about dinner?" Jhonig asked.

"We'll pick something up at the tavern." Tiogra said reassuringly.

"Okay." Jhonig said with a sigh. In his mind, the food from the tavern in the castle was not as good or well prepared as his father's meals were.

Once the two arrived at the castle and reached the tavern, Tiogra and Jhonig flew up to the ceiling where Tiogra showed his son to the booth he had chiseled out for himself and Mojhyn decades ago.

In the castle's taverns, once a gargoyle became a master pupil, it was an optional gift that they could chisel out a booth for themselves in the walls or ceilings that were allowed to have up to three seats. As far as the booths went, there were up to seventeen total, but only eight belonged to the gargoyle masters who were currently alive, in good physical condition and did not throw themselves into solitude.

"Where are you going?" Jhonig asked.

"I need to tell the grandmaster some things about the upcoming war, Jhonig." Tiogra said, "This will only take a second, stay right here."

Tiogra ordered some steak for Jhonig and asked for it to be sent up to the booth before he went to speak to the grandmaster. Once Tiogra left,

Jhonig rested his head on his right hand and drummed his fingers on the table.

As Tiogra walked into the shrine room, he noticed that he had nearly interrupted the grandmaster, who was currently praying in front of the picture of the gargoyle nation's glyph. The picture was used to represent Trog, since there were not any framed pictures of the prime gargoyle to be found anywhere. There was soft, oriental music playing from a small stereo as the grandmaster prayed. It was a sweet and peaceful melody Tiogra recognized as the music some of the gargoyles used to meditate. He also recognized the incense of amethyst the grandmaster was burning as a gesture of respect to Trog.

As he waited for the grandmaster to finish meditating, Tiogra bowed his head and silently stood by the door. Once the grandmaster was done, he turned off the stereo and gestured for Tiogra to enter the room with a relaxed smile as he turned to face his student on his white meditative cushion.

"Tiogra…" the grandmaster said calmly, "What news do you bring today?"

"Grandmaster," Tiogra began, "I have received a report from our agent on the inside of the vampire headquarters."

"The vampire woman?" the grandmaster asked.

"Yes," Tiogra confirmed, "She tells me that Dracula has been resurrected and that he is even more powerful than ever."

The grandmaster's smile faded upon hearing this news. He knew how badly beaten Tiogra was the last time he fought with the prime vampire, the fact that he had been revived and gained even more power was greatly problematic. Nonetheless, the grandmaster's tone remained calm. It was important to keep a cool head under any situation, especially if the head belonged to the leader of a nation.

"I see…" the grandmaster said rubbing his chin, "anything else?"

"Yes sir," Tiogra said, "Trang also told me that the vampires have managed to forge armor that matches the density of stone. Also, Dracula and Vlad are planning an attack on the castle, which will occur in two days."

"Ah." The grandmaster noted with a calm tone.

Tiogra looked at the grandmaster with confusion from his response about the armor. "Sir?" he asked.

"Even after all this time, the vampires still have no clue." The grandmaster said reassuringly, "True, when we harden ourselves for strength, our flesh is that of stone, but our dense anatomy is greater than vampires can comprehend, assuming they based the armor's density off of regular rocks. Furthermore, the stones Trog uses to make gargoyles are from his own body, much like myself, and he has ways of protecting us

96

whether we know it or not. The stones the vampires have compared their armor to are probably no stronger than Alabaster. Nonetheless, there is a chance Jhonig's dream is still accurate on the armor, depending on weather or not Vlad has any tricks up his sleeves. We should still prepare."

Tiogra nodded.

The grandmaster cracked his neck as he stood up and proceeded towards the door, "The nation will be alerted right away. Hopefully this battle will go like it did the last time. In the mean time, Tiogra, you should prepare for war. You are dismissed."

"Thank you, grandmaster." Tiogra said as he bowed, then proceeded to walk out of the room and back into the tavern to retrieve Jhonig.

Once Tiogra entered the tavern, he noticed that several gargoyles were watching the bar with blank faces. Unable to see what they were watching, except for the pile of beer bottles that was growing continuously, Tiogra flew up to his booth to get Jhonig. As soon as he reached the booth, however, Jhonig was nowhere to be found. Tiogra panicked, thinking his son had wandered off in the castle.

Then realization hit Tiogra like a sack of bricks. As the master gargoyle peaked over the side of the booth, he saw what the other gargoyles were watching with shock. There was a young gargoyle drinking and tossing empty bottles of alcohol to his left. It was Jhonig!

Tiogra angrily flew down off the booth and onto the ground. Seeing the master gargoyle so upset made the other gargoyles move aside so that he could reach his son. Tiogra grabbed Jhonig by the shoulder and spun him around to see his face. After the child placed his two hundredth bottle down, Tiogra could see that Jhonig was completely drunk.

"Jhonig?" Tiogra asked.

"Whaht?" the gargoyle youth asked, with ale leaking out of his mouth.

"Are you drunk?" Tiogra asked, pretending he did not already know the answer.

"Nah!" Jhonig responded, "Ah'm juss buzzed."

Tiogra looked around the room and then back at his son.

"Who gave you beer?" Tiogra asked, noticing the bartender who quietly slipped away.

Jhonig tried to point at the bartender, but wound up pointing at himself in the mirror behind the alcohol on the shelves.

Tiogra sighed and grabbed his son by the arm, dragging him off the barstool.

"C'mon, We're going home." Tiogra said as he felt Jhonig pull his wrist out of his father's grip.

"Kiddo, I'm really not in the mo-." A swift, fire charged punch to the face by Jhonig interrupted Tiogra's words.

Tiogra flew backward into a painting of Yemz at the wall on the far left of the room. Along the way he managed to crash into two other gargoyles at a table, who were enjoying drinks of their own. Tiogra looked up with infuriated eyes and rose up out of the damage his son had made from punching him. Jhonig lunged at Tiogra with great force, only to land in the pile of bottles he created. As he stood up, Jhonig took another swing at Tiogra and missed, much to the master gargoyle's disappointment that his son was so heavily intoxicated.

For fifteen minutes, Jhonig continued to lazily throw punches while Tiogra continued to dodge until the young gargoyle showed signs of tiring.

"Jhonig," Tiogra said sternly, "It's time to go home."

"Buht I dun wanna…" Jhonig mumbled as he collapsed on the floor and passed out.

Tiogra picked his unconscious son up off the floor and flung him over his shoulder. As the gargoyle elite carried his son out the door, he punched the bartender, who was hiding by the exit, directly in his exaggerated cobble nose, hard enough to knock him out.

Tiogra took Jhonig to the castle hospital and asked one of the nurses to help his son sober up. The nurse agreed and hooked the young gargoyle up to one of the Intravenous Drips.

"Mojhyn's going to love this." Tiogra sarcastically muttered to himself.

As Tiogra waited outside the medical station Jhonig was in, he thought about how he was going to break the news to his wife that their son had been drunk. Tiogra had received a few calls from Ghin, Mojhyn and Yemz while he waited. He took the call from Ghin, telling him what had happened with Jhonig and saying that he would hope to see his friend soon. The call from Mojhyn, he answered, yet did not tell her what had happened with their son, thinking it would be better to talk to her in person about his mistake. He ignored the calls from Yemz, remembering how obnoxious the master gargoyle was and feeling angry with him for the remark his loose acquaintance made at Mojhyn a few days ago.

You know, it's unfortunate you found her first. Otherwise, she'd be a lot happier with me. Yemz had said.

Naturally, Tiogra did not do anything in response. Not because Yemz was another master gargoyle and not because they were friends despite how terrible the friendship was, but because Tiogra felt that Yemz was just going through a phase and that it would soon pass. Yet regardless of what he told himself, Tiogra had a faint thought in the back of his mind as though he was humoring himself into believing that Yemz was a good person.

For the majority of their association, Tiogra and Yemz fought side by side and even then the bond was unsteady. Only five other instances occurred in life where Yemz was so unpleasant that Tiogra felt like kicking his colleague's stone testicles up through his head. The first was when Yemz made a suggestive comment about Tiogra's mother after she had died in a lycanthrope attack. At the time, Tiogra was young and sensitive. He responded to the insult by punching Yemz in the stomach after he used his power over water to cover his stone fist in ice. The punch was so hard, Yemz coughed up blood and passed out on the floor. When the grandmaster intervened, Yemz said that Tiogra was insane and outrageously suggested that he be killed. However, the grandmaster used meditation to read Yemz's mind and saw the truth. Instead, Yemz was heavily disciplined and Tiogra was scolded for picking fights.

The second time was similar because Yemz made sexual comments towards Mojhyn while she and Tiogra were dating, whipping her posterior with his tail as she was walking with Tiogra one day. Tiogra responded to this by casually breaking both of Yemz's arms when Mojhyn was not around him. The third and fourth time, Yemz repeatedly kept saying that Tiogra was ugly to his face. Tiogra did nothing in response to this. After all, it was common gargoyle belief that true men were meant to be ugly and brutal. However, this did not mean that Yemz's constant immature behavior was not annoying.

The fifth time, Yemz did something totally unexpected. He slapped Tiogra on the rear while they were on a scouting mission near a mansion in Russia that was overrun with vampires. In response, Tiogra grabbed Yemz by the snout and punched him in the face, knocking him out before anyone had noticed them and finished the mission himself.

Suddenly, and much to his surprise, Tiogra saw Yemz walking down the hallway towards his direction. Tiogra heavily sighed and continued to lean against the wall he was next to.

Think about someone enough, they're bound to show up. Tiogra thought to himself.

"Hey, Tiogra!" Yemz exclaimed with a smile.

"Hey, Yemz." Tiogra muttered, as memories of his colleague flowed through his mind like water from a broken dam.

"How're things?" Yemz asked, "What brings you here?"

"Things are ok…" Tiogra said, "and it's nothing important."

Yemz eyed Tiogra with suspicion. "Are you sure?" he asked, "Jhonig's not in there is he?"

Tiogra was getting irritated with Yemz's questions. It really was not any of his business what Tiogra's family was going through. However, Tiogra thought he would tell Yemz what was happening just to get him off his back.

"If the information is that vital to your day… yes, Jhonig is in there." Tiogra said, "Now leave me alone."

"Hey, I'm just asking." Yemz said with a grin, "You aren't still upset about what I said about Mojhyn are you?"

Tiogra refused to look in Yemz's direction. Yemz responded by moving in front of the master gargoyle's face.

"C'mon man," Yemz said as he reached for Tiogra's shoulder, "you need to forgive…"

Before he could finish his sentence, Tiogra grabbed Yemz's hand and threw him against the wall he was leaning against. He then pined Yemz to the wall by ramming his fist into the master gargoyle's shoulder.

"Don't ever insult my family again!" Tiogra bellowed, loud enough that everyone in the hall could hear.

Immediately, everyone's attention was turned towards the two warriors. Yemz was petrified. He could feel the imprint in the wall Tiogra had left when he threw his body against it, along with a now dislocated shoulder joint. He shoved Tiogra off of himself and walked away with an injured ego and a bruised shoulder.

Tiogra glared at Yemz as he walked away, thinking back to what Mojhyn had said years ago.

One of these days, that man is going to be the death of you.

Tiogra tried to ignore the past conversation and continued to wait for Jhonig to recover from his drunken incident. Disappointed at himself for losing his temper, Tiogra tried to think about playing with Jhonig in the French countryside to keep his mind positive. Despite the wonderful memory, Tiogra could not help but think that Mojhyn might have been right about his acquaintance. Regardless of this thought, the master gargoyle reassured himself that in the future, he would try to be more cautious.

Mojhyn's Manhunt

After many hours of stress and patience, a young gargoyle nurse told Tiogra that Jhonig had recovered from his alcoholic state and was currently sleeping. Tiogra went into the medical bed where Jhonig was resting and calmly woke his son, then asked if he remembered anything that happened earlier in the evening. Jhonig responded by shaking his head with incredibly tired eyes. Shortly after, word reached the grandmaster that one of his best junior pupils had been drunk. Upon hearing this news, the grandmaster was outraged. He immediately punished the bartender responsible and scolded Tiogra for allowing his son to be intoxicated. Tiogra humbly asked for forgiveness and told the grandmaster that he would not be so careless in the future. The grandmaster realized that Tiogra was stressed about how Mojhyn would react to his thoughtless mistake, despite his student's calm overtone. The grandmaster forgave Tiogra and told him to tell Mojhyn that he was keeping Jhonig overnight for meditative study regarding the upcoming war. Tiogra thanked the grandmaster profusely, retrieved Jhonig and flew back to their home on the twenty-second level.

After the events that took place that day, the gargoyle nation was placed on high alert and news spread of Dracula's resurrection. Numerous gargoyles were sent out into the world to try to retrieve any information they could on the vampires. With much disappointment, there were hardly any details to be found. The grandmaster reassured the gargoyles to keep their heads cool and to be prepared for anything unexpected. In spite of his collected presence, the grandmaster himself was heavily concerned. If his people could not find anything regarding the vampire nation, Vlad must have had something phenomenal planned.

The next evening, Tiogra was given the day off and was allowed to sleep in. This was an exceptionally good thing, considering he had not slept in several weeks. That evening, Tiogra stayed home and taught Jhonig some lessons on how to make another meal for dinner when Mojhyn went on a scouting mission.

Mojhyn was exceptional when it came to scouting. Despite her love for brawls on the battlefield, she had admitted to Tiogra that the adrenaline she received from urban fights was exhilarating. Now that she and Tiogra were taking turns raising Jhonig, it was only natural that she would have time to herself once in a while. This time was spent the way most gargoyles would spend their free time, scouring the human cities in search for any sign of trouble.

Tonight, Mojhyn's weapon selection was an explosive one, taken straight from her locker in the gargoyle armory. It involved four explosive spiked chakrams, ten explosive stakes, five ten-inch long knives, a pair of bladed knuckles (a personal invention by Boragen), and three pairs of twenty-pound nunchaku. Each weapon was ideal for the combative mindset Mojhyn currently had and tucked away in the single-strap book bag she brought with her.

The gargoyle armory had a vast array of weapons ranging in design from medieval times to the modern day. Few of the weapons in the armory were so far advanced that they made human weapons look like toys. It even had special "reserved" lockers for gargoyles that had their own customized weaponry and preferred weapons.

The racks holding the guns in the armory were only regularly visited by Boragen, but hardly by anyone else. Each member of the gargoyle nation tired to make it a habit only to use guns in their human disguises. Even then, firearms would only be used when hostile situations got completely out of hand. Boragen was an exception, seeing as how the master blacksmith never cared for swords and "old fashioned" ways of combat.

As Mojhyn patrolled around New York City, leaping quietly from building to building so that she would not be noticed without a human disguise, she sighed in boredom. It seemed as if today there would not be any action whatsoever. This was good in the sense that the streets were relatively safe, but it had been too long of a while since Mojhyn had any practice in combat. After a couple of minutes of scaling the buildings around her, the gargoyle woman perched herself on the edge of The Plaza and looked out into the city. As the wind blew through Mojhyn's wild, yellow hair and ruffled through her lime green shirt, she contemplated to herself about how fortunate she was to be a gargoyle and how much of an amazing husband Tiogra turned out to be. She thought of her wonderful son and how he graduated from his first few terms of classes recently. She also thought of the dark pleasure she received from slaying vampires that even she admitted was twisted. Even though Tiogra's meditative practice "cleansed" her in a way, she still could not give up her love for the adrenaline that came from hunting.

After a long time of reflection on the past events, Mojhyn hopped off her perch and sat cross-legged on the roof, where she began to meditate. As Mojhyn began her out-of-body experience, she concentrated on finding prey for the night.

As she scanned the city, Mojhyn could pick up faint traces of talking, but she could not figure out where it was coming from. Then she recognized the speech patterns and accents as those of lycanthropes. Mojhyn could also pick up large traces of movement coming from underneath the city. The lycanthropes were in the sewers and there were a little over a hundred of them roaming around in the sewage. Snapping out of her meditative state and thinking this was an opportunity too good to pass up, Mojhyn retrieved her cell phone out of her bag and dialed the number of her friend, Celan.

"Celan," Mojhyn said, "It's me, Mojhyn, you got a minute?"

"Sure," Celan said on the other end of the line, "What's up?"

"I just picked up a large trace of lycanthrope activity in the sewers near The Plaza." Mojhyn said, "Feel like breaking skulls tonight?"

"Hell yeah!" Celan exclaimed, "I'll be right there."

Mojhyn hung up and waited for the streets to be clear of civilians. She silently flew down to the sidewalk so no one could see her, picked up the nearby manhole cover and dove in, closing the entryway behind her.

As Mojhyn crept down the sewers, she relied fully on her ability to see in the dark to guide her. It was important that she had no source of light at all so she did not alert the lycanthropes.

Suddenly, Mojhyn heard voices coming from the end of the pipeline. It was a group of five urban lycanthropes, two female and three male, who were in their human forms. Each one was wearing an article of clothing that had the lycanthrope symbol on it, two wolf skulls designed to look like angelic wings. The symbol was either on their coats, pants, or shirts.

Mojhyn thought about how it disgusted her that lycanthropes thought they were the only holy forces on the planet, especially since they did things that caused more damage to the world than justice. She watched as the two female lycanthropes turned around, dropped their weapons and proceeded to aggressively grope the males.

Case and point. Mojhyn thought as she pulled out her knives. She had to take the five of them out quietly if she wanted the mission to go smoothly. Within seconds of her thought, Mojhyn took action and threw the knives directly at the heads of the female lycanthropes. The knives hit the heads of the females, pinning one to the wall of the sewer and the other just above the navel of one of the male lycanthropes. Before the werewolf could yell out in pain, another knife was thrown into his throat. The other two lycanthropes retrieved their guns and quickly turned around to face the gargoyle assailant. However, the steam from the bodies of their dead comrades was clouding their vision. Before they could pull the triggers, Mojhyn kicked their guns out of their hands, bending the rifles at ninety-degree angles. She then jabbed her index fingers into their throats, puncturing their Adam's apples so they could not scream.

As the lycanthrope soldiers bled to death, Mojhyn turned to make sure her opponents were completely dead. When the coast was clear, Mojhyn pulled out her cell phone again and called Celan.

"I've already got five down, Cel." Mojhyn said, "How're you doing?"

"I've got ten." Celan said on the other line happily.

Damn, Mojhyn thought as she continued to run. She hung up on

Celan knowing full well that her reaction towards her friend's kill count only made Celan happy.

As she ran along the side of the sewer tunnel so she did not make any splashing noises, Mojhyn could detect the pulse of a tunnel filled with lycanthropes to her right. There were thirty urban werewolves total. Luckily, from what Mojhyn could tell, they had not been alerted to her presence yet. She pulled out two of her explosive spiked chakrams from her bag and made a sharp right turn. As the lycanthropes turned around to see who was behind them, the explosive devices decapitated ten lycanthropes and stuck to two more, followed by a violent explosion. As Mojhyn ran past the lycanthropes, she took out the remaining eighteen with her bladed knuckles and the hooked claws on her wings. A few of the lycanthropes tried to shoot at their assailant, but Mojhyn's skills surpassed their own greatly. She threw the bodies of dying lycanthropes at the direction of the ones that were still alive. With the steam from their dead friends in their eyes, Mojhyn killed all of the remaining werewolves with ease. It was easy considering that centuries of martial training allowed her to feel out the presence of the werewolf soldiers, almost as if they were in broad daylight, despite her lack of recent practice.

As she delivered punches to the heads of the lycanthropes, Mojhyn was curious as to what the pain felt like. Considering the troops had three inches of thick spiked steel going into their skulls and thinking about the pressure points she was hitting, Mojhyn imagined the pain was unbearable.

As the dead lycanthropes dropped to the ground and turned into fur and steam, Mojhyn made a personal body count in her head.

Thirty-five. She thought to herself as she continued to run, disappointed that the werewolves she had killed were only dregs and not from the upper class of soldier.

Further down the pipes, Mojhyn heard a voice coming from even farther down the sewage ways.

"Sir, it's a gargoyle, a female dressed in green and black! She's taken out thirty of our men already!" the voice exclaimed.

"Damn!" the voice of the head lycanthrope responded, "She'll put the whole mission in jeopardy! Find her and stop her!"

"Ahem!" a voice said from above the lycanthrope soldiers. There, Mojhyn and Celan stood in a pipeline, high above the crowd.

"You fleabags in the middle of something?" Celan asked sarcastically, eyeing the place she and Mojhyn had arrived in and noting that there were dozens of lycanthrope soldiers below them.

The lycanthropes immediately raised their firearms at the ceiling of the sewers to shoot down the two gargoyle females. Mojhyn reacted quickly and threw her explosive stakes at nine of the lycanthrope soldiers. When the stakes exploded, the blasts killed twenty troops within range.

The other lycanthropes started firing at Celan, who dropped her stakes on the soldiers below her, killing thirteen of them in the process.

As the battle continued, Mojhyn pulled out her last two spiked chakrams and decapitated twelve lycanthropes as she ran along the walls of the sewers. She then pushed a button on the chakrams and they instantly started beeping. Mojhyn threw the chakrams at the four lycanthropes in front of her and watched as her opponents exploded, taking out ten more lycanthropes with them. She smiled in satisfaction as her prey turned into steam and fur before her eyes.

Then it was Celan's turn. She pulled six chakrams out of her violet, leather messenger bag and flung them in every direction. However, not all the lycanthropes were poorly skilled in the ways of combat. Three lycanthropes managed to dodge the chakrams and rolled out of harms way in time to turn into their werewolf forms. The rest of the lycanthropes followed this example and transformed as well. They lunged at Celan and scratched at her arms, tearing her yellow long-sleeved shirt in the process.

Celan wanted to scream, but remembered her training and remained calm. As she shifted her wounds to stone, Celan pulled out two pairs of her own twenty-pound nunchaku and managed to fend off the lycanthrope horde.

Seeing her friend in trouble, Mojhyn pulled out her two remaining knives and slashed through the crowd of lycanthropes. She hacked and tore through flesh and bone until her knives broke, allowing her to resort to her own nunchaku and continued to make her way through the enemy crowd towards Celan.

The two friends continued to slaughter the lycanthropes until only the leader remained. Celan finished with sixty-four kills while Mojhyn had seventy-one. As the companions looked at each other through meditative vision, Celan could see that Mojhyn had come out the winner of their game, despite her larger supply of weapons. Now the only thing remaining was to interrogate the group leader.

As he crawled out of one of the piles of fur, the leader of the lycanthrope troupe moaned in pain, still in his beast form. He was abruptly turned over onto his back after Mojhyn kicked him in the chest.

"Why are you here?" Celan asked after she and Mojhyn punctured his arms with their claws, making it so the lycanthrope leader would be unable to fight back.

"We came looking for the rattus city." The lycanthrope groaned in pain, "We were informed there might be some survivors."

"What do you care about surviving rattus?" Mojhyn asked sternly.

"I wanted to capture some of them for my master's experiments." The bleeding lycanthrope explained.

Mojhyn and Celan looked at each other with raised eyebrows. Celan punched the lycanthrope in the chest, hard enough that he coughed up blood.

"There are no survivors of the rattus." Celan growled, "The vampires killed them off a year ago."

The lycanthrope turned his head away in disgust. How could he have been so foolish? This explained the explosion in New York that he had heard about so long ago. Mojhyn raised her fist, ready to punch a hole through the werewolf's head.

"Wait, wait!" the lycanthrope shouted, eager to save his life. "We also heard that the vampires are planning an attack against the gargoyles!"

Mojhyn lowered her fist in slight confusion. "So? What do you care?" she asked.

"We figured you might want our help." He said shaking, "We hate the vampires just as much as you do after all. We just want some credit incase you fight back."

Mojhyn and Celan glared in disgust at their prey. "You are as useless as the humans you prey upon." Mojhyn said, "The gargoyles need no allies. Take that to the grave with you."

The lycanthrope shrieked as Mojhyn and Celan both obliterated his head with their strikes. Mojhyn later thanked Celan for her aid and the two went their separate ways once they left the sewers.

On the way home through the window, Mojhyn thought she would tell her husband about the events that happened that night and then rest. Perhaps she would play a game with her son before he went to bed. Maybe she would watch the news or something funny on the television before she began work again tomorrow. The thoughts she was having as she climbed out of the portal to France were pleasant, but for now, all Mojhyn wanted to do was sleep for the first time in weeks.

Once Mojhyn arrived home, she hung her book bag by the door and slumped in the big leather chair. She could smell the beef stroganoff Tiogra was making with Jhonig from inside the living room. Jhonig ran from the kitchen and hugged his mother before she sat in the chair, despite the smell of rotten sewage she was emitting. Mojhyn smiled and returned her son's hug. As much as she loved the thrill of action, it was always good to be home.

"You're just in time for dinner, mom!" Jhonig said happily.

"Really?" Mojhyn asked with a smile.

Tiogra then walked into the room and smiled to see his wife tired after a long night of work.

"Jhonig was a very big help for me today." Tiogra said.

"Is that so?" Mojhyn asked.

"Yep!" Jhonig exclaimed happily.

As Mojhyn eyed the food on the kitchen table, she smiled and kissed Jhonig on the head.

After dinner, Mojhyn, Tiogra and Jhonig played a game of Go Fish and then sent Jhonig off to bed. Tiogra closed the door to his son's room and turned to face his beautiful wife. "Wonderful kid isn't he?" the master gargoyle asked.

Mojhyn just stood in the hallway, holding her right arm and looking at a picture on the wall that was taken when she and Tiogra took Jhonig to an amusement park for the first time when he was three years old. Despite having to disguise themselves in clay, it was a wonderful experience for everyone, especially when Jhonig laughed himself into exhaustion from all the fun he had.

Tiogra held Mojhyn by the shoulders and kissed her cheek. "Is everything ok?" he asked.

"Can Trang be trusted?" Mojhyn asked.

"Well, I know she's a vampire," Tiogra said, "but I've been given no reason not to trust her so far."

Mojhyn looked at Tiogra with a worried expression in her eyes.

"However," Tiogra explained further, "that doesn't mean I haven't been on my toes."

Mojhyn smiled, grabbed Tiogra by the hand and led him to the couch where they sat down. Mojhyn rested her head on Tiogra's shoulder as he held her hand and they intertwined their tails together. As she ran her fingers along one of the horns that curved towards the back of Tiogra's head, Mojhyn tried her best to retain a happy face and hide the stress she felt from what the lycanthrope team leader had told her.

"Why do you ask?" Tiogra wondered.

"One of the lycanthropes I fought told Celan and I that he knew about the vampire's plan of attack." Mojhyn explained, "I was just wondering if it had anything to do with Trang."

Tiogra looked up and starred at the reflection of himself and Mojhyn in the television. If Trang was seriously telling the lycanthropes everything she had told him, it could mean a three-way war.

"That's pretty bad news." Tiogra said calmly, despite what he just heard.

"Are you going to tell the grandmaster?" Mojhyn asked.

"No," Tiogra said, "I'll handle this myself."

Tiogra calmly rose off the seat and proceeded to head for the door when Mojhyn stopped him.

"Are you ok?" Mojhyn asked.

"I'm ok." Tiogra said, reassuring his wife, "I just need to make sure everything will be ok for the rest of the nation. I'll be back in a little bit, alright?"

Mojhyn nodded in response. Tiogra could tell his wife was worried at his response from the news and kissed her goodbye before he left.

"Don't worry." Tiogra said as he gazed into Mojhyn's eyes, "I'm sure everything will be fine."

"Ok." Mojhyn said softly.

Regardless of the uneasy tension, Tiogra flew off towards the castle's landing pad for the window makers. He had to confront Trang and make sure that she was not planning a double-cross on the gargoyle nation. Otherwise, there would be no telling what kind of damage would be done from a battle involving vampires, gargoyles and werewolves.

Sabotage

It was four o'clock in the afternoon at the vampire estate. Vlad had completely ignored the fact that his daughter had disobeyed him and ran away from the castle. Instead, he was focused more on his reanimated father and the newfound power the prime vampire now possessed.

As he walked down the halls of the vampire estate, Vlad could hear his father's words ring through his head from the day before.

That daughter of yours desperately needs to learn some manners soon. Dracula had said, *her attitude is going to get her killed one day.*

Vlad proceeded into the castle's study to see if he could find any inspiration for destruction to help in the upcoming battle. To his surprise, inside the study, sitting at the ivory desk and reading a book on swords, was Dracula, who was dressed in his favorite, golden oriental robes.

"What is it you want, son?" Dracula asked, still focused on his book and playing with one of the black, skull shaped toggles on his robes.

"I was going to ask you about the upcoming battle with the gargoyles, father." Vlad stated, "I don't think we have enough men."

Dracula closed the book and starred up at Vlad from under his sleek, black eyebrows. He then slowly stood up and placed the book back on the shelf where he had taken it from.

"How many vampires are there?" Dracula asked.

"A little over five thousand, currently." Vlad replied.

Dracula smiled. "Well, we're going to need a lot more soldiers if we are to survive this conflict you've started." He stated, "Do you know of any people who'd be willing to donate a few?"

Vlad thought to himself. "What about Austria?" he finally asked.

"Too big." Dracula said, "We'll need something a little less conspicuous."

Vlad thought to himself again. "Vatican city?" he asked.

"Too small." Dracula replied as he walked over to a world map hanging on one of the walls. He then pointed to a spot located on the southern end of the Lberian Peninsula at the entrance of the Mediterranean.

"Gibraltar?" Vlad asked, starring at the spot his father had pointed to.

"Give me one night." Dracula said, "I'll have the vampire population increased by a few more thousand."

Vlad smiled broadly enough that it stretched from ear to ear. The thought of his father causing destruction and chaos filled him with glee. It was the perfect opportunity to spread terrorism and gain from it as well.

"Very well." Vlad said, "However, I think we'll need something more."

Dracula eyed his son in suspicion. "What did you have in mind?" he asked.

Vlad looked at the bookshelves directly at a preserved claw that was sitting in-between two rows of books. The claw belonged to the lycanthrope leader, Ulric. An old and currently inactive enemy of the vampire nation.

"I was thinking that maybe our troops wouldn't be enough, even with the reinforcements." Vlad said, picking up the claw and moving it between his fingers. "Maybe our canine brethren would be willing to help us wipe out this threat."

Dracula paused for a minute and chuckled at the foolish idea.

"You must be joking." The vampire lord said, "There's no way in heaven, hell or earth those mutts would help us. Especially since we've been at war with each other for so long."

"But think about it father..." Vlad began, "we share the same god and the same hatred for gargoyles. Surely, they might be willing to aid us."

Vlad saw that Dracula was about to dismiss the idea without a second thought to it.

"Besides," Vlad began again in an attempt to save his plan, "Once we're done killing off the gargoyles, we can kill off the lycanthropes when they least expect it! It'll be killing two birds with one stone... figuratively speaking."

After hearing his son's reasoning, Dracula stroked the hair covering his chin in thought. Vlad had made a good point. In one swift move, they could execute both problems in a matter of hours, then the only problems left would be the tortasapiens and the human populace.

"Alright." Dracula said, "Do what you can to negotiate with the lycanthropes. In the meantime, I will be increasing our populace."

As Vlad nodded in agreement, Dracula turned into mist and flowed out the window.

Once he reached his destination, Dracula eyed his surroundings with pleasure as soon as he rematerialized, thinking about the havoc that was about to commence. A homeless man, who was sleeping underneath a newspaper the vampire lord materialized on, stumbled to his feet to confront the stranger who interrupted his nap.

As the homeless man looked up, he saw two bright, violet, flashing lights, which were emitting out of Dracula's eyes, shining directly into his face. Dracula commanded the man to walk towards him, and the man obeyed. The vampire lord then proceeded to brush some trash off the man's coat, making the homeless man's eyes turn blood red and his teeth grow twice their normal length. The homeless man hissed into the night as he completely transformed into a vampire. All it took was a touch from the vampire lord and the man simply turned. Dracula smiled and commanded the man to wreak chaos upon the city. The newest addition to the vampire race obeyed and leapt into the window of a nearby house, where he bit and turned a young couple living inside.

Watching his newest servant perform a dance of chaos, Dracula turned into mist and flowed into five separate households, then materialized back to where he was originally standing within seconds. Several new vampires leapt out of the windows and doors of the houses Dracula had passed through and began to prowl the streets looking for victims. Along the way, the new vampires found and attacked a few gargoyles who were out on patrol in the area. The gargoyles managed to kill as many vampires as they could before they realized they were outmatched, but the vampire infestation was spreading faster than any other attack ever had before, proving too much for these gargoyles to handle. The turning process continued until the entire population of Gibraltar was bled dry. By the time Dracula was finished, over fourteen thousand members increased the vampire population.

Meanwhile in Hong Kong, Tiogra had called Trang from his cell phone and asked her to meet him at the last place they saw each other, two years ago. Trang, who had no idea of what was going on, agreed and followed his request.

After Tiogra placed the call, he flew across the city, unnoticed, to the rooftop where he had first met Trang and waited for her to arrive. It was two hours into the afternoon before Tiogra saw Trang appear on a nearby rooftop. Quickly and quietly, he ducked behind a wall to catch the vampire princess off guard. Luckily enough, Trang walked right into his trap. Tiogra lunged out from behind the wall and punched the space directly in front of the vampire princess. Startled, Trang fell backwards and landed on her back. Before she could get up, Tiogra grabbed her by the shirt and slammed her against the wall he had punched.

"How do the lycanthropes know about the battle?" Tiogra yelled.

"What are you talking about?" Trang asked, trying not to shake in fear.

Tiogra punched the wall again to show his frustration.

"Lie to me again and get a mouthful of garlic." Tiogra said through gritted stone teeth. "Now tell me why you told the lycanthropes about the battle!"

"I needed a backup plan incase your people didn't agree to help me!" Trang explained, "I only told a few of them, enough that I might have a chance against my father."

"Sure you weren't trying to kill off my people?" Tiogra asked, looking at her pulsing blood flow through his meditative vision.

"Yes!" Trang yelled in pain as the gargoyle's grip tightened.

Noting that Trang's pulse had not changed as she spoke, Tiogra could see that she was not lying and released his grip. Trang grabbed her neck and regained her breath as she dropped back onto the roof. "How did you know that the lycanthropes knew about the battle?" she asked.

"My wife told me." Tiogra said, "She went on a hunt and interrogated one of them."

Trang made an expression of understanding and rose up to her feet. She could see that Tiogra was only concerned about the protection of his people, hearing that she had spoken to the lycanthropes would certainly be unnerving. "I'm sorry you thought I had betrayed you." She said.

"I'm sorry I assumed you did." Tiogra said, looking down at the ground in shame for his impudence.

Trang held her left arm in slight pain. "Eh, it's ok." She pardoned.

Tiogra looked back up and smiled, but the truth was he would probably never forgive himself for assuming the worst. He had known plenty of idiots in his lifetime who had done the same thing and who paid for their ignorance dearly, which he assumed was all because of their poor behavior. He knew he was concerned for the wellbeing of his nation and was stressed from preparing about his possible death and seeing Jhonig intoxicated, but this was still no excuse for acting without full knowledge of what was going on. Beliefs aside, Tiogra had a job to do and had to focus on the task at hand. With Trang actually being innocent, this meant that he had sent himself on a personal quest for no reason other then to threaten an ally of the gargoyle nation. The worst part was Trang did not even deserve the threat.

"Well," Trang began, "assumptions aside, I'm glad you're here."

Tiogra raised an eyebrow in the vampire princess's direction. "Why?" he asked, "What's up?"

"My grandfather has made a personal trip to Gibraltar," Trang explained, "He planned on turning the human population into vampires. By my calculations, there are fourteen thousand more vampires by now at the most."

Tiogra retained a calm expression. There was no need to get anxious or excited in any way in front of Trang. It occurred to the master gargoyle to contact the gargoyle castle to make sure they were not under attack. If Dracula was seriously adding new members to the vampire nation, this could either be catastrophic or just another battle to be fought. Either way, more vampires meant more killing.

Tiogra immediately pulled his cell phone out of his pocket and dialed in the number for the gargoyle castle. It took a few rings, but eventually Bok received Tiogra's call.

"Bok, are you there?" Tiogra asked.

"Yeah," Bok grunted and confirmed, "I'm here."

"Listen," Tiogra said, "I think the vampires are planning an attack on the castle."

"Really?" Bok asked sarcastically, "that might explain the thousands of suck heads at our front door."

Tiogra's eyes widened in shock, he was too late. The attack had already started. This explained the sounds of gunfire on the other end of the line.

"Crap!" Tiogra exclaimed, "I'll be right there!"

"You'd better hurry," Bok said, "they've already breached the gate."

Shoving his cell phone back into his pocket, Tiogra quickly unfolded his wings and flew off towards the window maker as fast as he could. Trang stayed behind, thinking that the vampires had already started their attack by the urgency of Tiogra's leave. Once her gargoyle ally was gone, she leapt off the building, landed on her motorcycle and sped off into the night.

Once Tiogra arrived at the castle, he immediately had to duck three shots that were fired at his head. Rolling forward with his wings tucked behind his shoulders, Tiogra grabbed two vampires with his feet and punctured their skulls with his retractable thumbs while snapping the neck of a vampire that was in front of him with his tail. His eyes widened in shock as he regained his footing, the castle had been thrown into chaos. There were shots being fired and explosions going off around the castle as gargoyles were fighting as hard as they could to keep the vampires from going any further into the mountain. Tiogra used his meditative vision to scan the mountain and saw that there were over seven thousand vampires swarming the castle like termites on a log. Without hesitation, Tiogra flew into the air and dove down through one of the windows of the castle as he headed towards the armory. As Tiogra was flying through the halls, ash fell on his face from the vampires dying around him. Almost every gargoyle over the age of thirty was helping to fight and defend the castle while the others remained in the caverns to keep their people and cities safe. From what Tiogra could see as he flew through the castle, the gargoyles were winning.

The strange part about this battle was that the vampires were not wearing the armor that Jhonig had seen in his dream, which made Tiogra wonder if the dream his son had was a false vision. Bullets whizzed by Tiogra as he flew further down the halls. Gargoyles were being tackled and vampires were flying left and right out of being hit, burned, cut open or torn apart. Once Tiogra arrived at the armory near the entrance to the caverns, he saw that a large group of vampires was blocking his way to the door.

"Tiogra!" a voice called from Tiogra's right, trying to grab his attention.

Tiogra noticed a single-edged gargoyle sword being thrown at him in time to catch it. The sword was shaped like a jagged, Chinese broad sword, yet thicker and heavier with a straighter blade. The form fitted, leather grip of the sword was curved downwards towards the edge of the blade for a more fluid wield.

After Tiogra caught the blade, he sliced through five vampires behind him and then turned to face the voice that yelled his name. The voice belonged to Ghin, who was slicing through ten vampires with a weapon of his own. A huge, double-bladed battle axe with horned edges.

"Where the hell have you been?" Ghin asked, as the two friends sliced through the crowd of vampires to get to the armory.

"I had to interrogate someone." Tiogra explained, "I thought we had been betrayed."

"You mean the vampire girl?" Ghin asked, "I've never trusted that bitch."

"You've never met 'that bitch'." Tiogra stated.

"Still," Ghin replied, "no vampire can be trusted, no matter who they are."

Tiogra felt an uneasy pain in his stomach as Ghin spoke poorly of Trang. The pain was not out of physical contact, but out of emotion. As much as history had shown the gargoyles that vampires were evil natured, somehow Tiogra felt that Trang was honorable and could be trusted. This also mixed with the feeling of guilt he had from being hostile towards the vampire princess earlier. Though the dishonor of speaking about an ally as if they were nothing was enough to make Tiogra feel rattled, he did not let the ache interfere with his fight.

The two master gargoyles continued to slice their way to the armory with only one objective on their minds; open the armory to allow the other gargoyles to get their weapons. As Tiogra and Ghin fought their way through the crowd of vampires, Tiogra noticed the blind gargoyles from the main library fighting off the vampire hordes. The way they fought was in perfect synchronization. After one of the blind gargoyles performed an attack, another one struck within seconds.

It was almost too difficult for Tiogra and Ghin to make their way to the armory door. It took nearly fifteen minutes until they finally got halfway to the entrance. Unfortunately, other vampires had noticed the struggle the gargoyles had to get to the door and had stopped what they were doing to help their comrades attack Tiogra and Ghin.

As they continued to fight, the gargoyle duo suddenly heard a loud boom behind the armory door. The boom was so loud that it practically shook the halls of the castle. As the booming continued, the vampires turned around to see what was making the noise.

After the fifth boom, the door blew off its hinges and crushed twelve vampires from its impact with the floor. Smoke emitted from the entryway as the vampires crowded around the door to see what caused the explosion. Ghin and Tiogra smiled in satisfaction, knowing what awaited the vampire scum.

Out of the smoke, a large gargoyle, armed to the teeth with guns, gigantic knives, and any other gadgets he could find, trekked out of the smoke. This gargoyle was what people from the medieval ages would define as a beast from hell. His pointed nose gave him a goblin like tone, yet the thick horns on his cheeks and chin made him look more demonic, along with his gray skin and dim yellow eyes. A thick coat of black fur covered his back, completing his beastly presence. The twelve foot tall gargoyle was Boragen, the chief blacksmith of the gargoyles.

Boragen let out a bellow of happiness as he saw the vampires step away in fear. Immediately, he fired his custom-made battle rifles at the vampire mass, reducing them to nothing but ash within seconds. Tiogra and Ghin ran inside the armory and grabbed whatever weapons they could find as their friend tore away at the vampires.

"What took you so long?" Ghin asked Boragen.

"I had to get the armory ready," Boragen replied in his deep European accent, "You know? Make sure everyone's weapons were in shape and alright to use."

"Took you long enough." Tiogra said sarcastically.

"Just shut up and fight." Boragen laughed in response.

The three warriors spread the word to the other gargoyles that the armory was now fully functional. In return, the rest of the gargoyles ran to get their weapons. In no more than a couple of hours, the vampire attack had been subdued, leaving only piles of ash and minor damage to the castle.

The gargoyles cheered in their victory and later on mourned the several casualties that occurred during the attack. One pair of gargoyles that had died was a couple named Grynin and Adah, who were much like Tiogra and Mojhyn.

Grynin and Adah were an ordinary gargoyle couple. They were proud of their success, honored and respected by their friends, and happy for the fact that they were in each other's lives. They were also some of the first gargoyles to greet Jhonig as an infant after he was adopted. Although Grynin and Tiogra were not the closest of friends, they had helped each other in combat many times and it was sad to accept the fact that he and his wife had departed from the world of the living.

Many friends gently wept for the loss of their relatives and comrades. Nonetheless, they had to move on and stay strong to honor their loved ones and live lives worthy of their memory. A token funeral was held for the deceased gargoyle warriors. Later on, the gargoyles would take a yacht out to sea and place the bodies into the water, like the grandmaster had done to the bodies of his brothers, centuries ago.

Repairs had to be done to the castle after the vampire attack. Luckily, the damage was not so great that any of the castle towers collapsed. The gargoyle nation immediately worked around the castle after the funeral, helping one another to fix their home.

Gargoyles were running about the castle placing tables right side up after they had been knocked over, boarding up the doors where they had been crushed, and fixing windows where they had been smashed. While everyone else was making repairs, Tiogra went to see the grandmaster.

As he ran down the hall, Tiogra thought about why the grandmaster had not been seen during the attack. It was not like the grandmaster to hide. Perhaps he had his hands full, fighting off some vampiric assailants of his own. Either way, Tiogra could sense that the grandmaster was in the transmissions tower.

Once Tiogra reached the tower, he walked through the door to see large piles of ash on the floor as well as an ember covered grandmaster, along with three other gargoyles, who were placing the equipment back together and setting it upright. The grandmaster was sitting cross-legged in the middle of the room, meditating while his students worked. When the grandmaster came to, he immediately saw Tiogra but did not smile. He walked over to his master pupil, jumped up and slapped him on the head. Tiogra winced and held his head in pain while the other three gargoyles looked over in his direction to see what the grandmaster would do.

"Where were you?" the grandmaster sternly asked.

"Forgive me, grandmaster," Tiogra said bowing, "I was in China, trying to get information."

"You were with the vampire girl?" the grandmaster questioned.

"Yes, sir." Tiogra said with his head still facing the floor, "I had received news that the lycanthropes knew about the war and thought we had been betrayed."

"I see." The grandmaster said, "Very well, you are pardoned, but only this once."

"Thank you, grandmaster." Tiogra said as he bowed again.

"Don't get me wrong, Tiogra," the grandmaster said calmly, "there is no doubt of your loyalty and sense of honor..."

The grandmaster then leaned in towards Tiogra, so they met face to face.

"...However," the grandmaster murmured as his tone changed from calm to stern, "if you are out and about when your nation needs you and you don't have a good excuse, a slap to the head will seem like a walk in the park, ok?"

"Yes, grandmaster." Tiogra humbly responded. He knew that he had brought the news that the vampires had planned to attack last night himself, but was so caught up in emotional disorder that he had forgotten to station himself for the attack.

The other gargoyles were stunned. No one had ever personally seen Tiogra receive a reprimanding before. Despite this, they immediately continued repairing the transmissions room.

Shortly after he was reprimanded, Tiogra suddenly remembered what he was going to tell the grandmaster in the first place.

"Grandmaster," Tiogra began, "I noticed the vampires weren't wearing any armor when they attacked the castle."

The grandmaster's expression remained dull. "The vampires were not supposed to wear armor in this fight." He told Tiogra with sadness, knowing his student had hoped for different news.

"Oh." Tiogra said with slight disappointment.

"This attack was an invitation to the final battle with the vampires. They have the armor, they just plan on using it at their palace on their own territory." The grandmaster explained.

Tiogra nodded his head in understanding. It made perfect sense. Dracula of all beings would be the only one to try something as egotistical as sending an army to attack his enemies as a way to "invite" them to try to destroy him. The fact that the gargoyles were still alive only meant that they survived the invitation and would accept the challenge.

"What should we do sir?" one of the other gargoyles asked the grandmaster.

"We do what Dracula wants," the grandmaster said as he turned away from the destroyed equipment to face Tiogra, "we take the fight to him. You, Ghin and Boragen will accompany nine thousand gargoyles to Transylvania and finish this battle with the vampires permanently. The rest of our nation will guard the mountain with my nephews and niece."

"Yes sir." Tiogra said as he bowed in respect at the grandmaster's strategy. As the grandmaster looked at his master pupil, he could see that Tiogra was still troubled by Jhonig's vision. The grandmaster walked over to Tiogra and placed a bumpy, callused hand on top of his student's head.

"I know how you must feel." The grandmaster calmly told Tiogra, reassuringly, "You and the rest of our people have been taught that death can come to someone unexpectedly and to live everyday like it is your last. The knowledge that you might die in this battle changes your perspective. You are like my own child to me, Tiogra, as are the rest of the gargoyle nation's members. If I could, I would have you stay here to guard the castle for your safety, but you are one of the gargoyles who knows how to combat vampires better than anyone else I've ever seen and we will personally need you to help destroy them once and for all. I can't promise you that I will single everyone else out for your safety, but right now I need you to keep a cool head and focus on the mission at hand. Trust me, everything is going to be ok."

Tiogra nodded and smiled at the grandmaster's words. He and the other gargoyles then followed the grandmaster out of the room and down the stairs into the grand hall of the castle. The three other gargoyles flew in separate directions after they descended the stairs to spread the plan of attack on the vampire estate. Within hours, nine thousand gargoyles were preparing for the final battle with the vampires along with Ghin and Boragen. Tiogra had spent the hours mentally preparing himself for a possible death in this final fight with his nation's lifelong enemies. During this time, he spent a few hours with Mojhyn and Jhonig playing board games and sharing laughs with his family. Afterwards, Trang had sent Tiogra a text message, telling him that she was sending the coordinates to the location of the vampire estate to his phone as well as how many soldiers her father had left. Tiogra thanked Trang and gave the message to the grandmaster, who invited Tiogra to accompany him in one of the castle taverns for what might be Tiogra's final drink. There, the grandmaster and Tiogra were sharing laughs and memories of good times as the time for battle drew near.

"We're going to be in for one hell of a fight, sir," Tiogra said as he finished the last drop of his whiskey, "if the rumors of Dracula are true."

"They're true." The grandmaster said as he finished his own drink, "But his being more powerful doesn't make this a suicide mission. It just means he'll fall harder."

The grandmaster's confident words gave Tiogra a sense of encouragement as the two friends rose from their seats and headed for the tavern exit. If there was any hope to be had for Tiogra that day, it was that if he were to die, he could die with good memories.

Moments later, Tiogra joined Boragen and Ghin in the armory as they prepared their weapons for battle.

Soon after he had entered the room, the armory door unexpectedly slammed behind Tiogra. The three warriors turned to see that surprisingly enough, it was Yemz who slammed the door. What disturbed them most was that Yemz had a sickeningly broad smile across his reptilian face.

"I thought you'd be out on duty somewhere." Ghin said to Yemz with a false smile.

"You think I'd miss out on the final battle with the vampires?" Yemz responded.

Boragen and Ghin looked back at their weapons, trying to ignore Yemz. They knew how much he pretended hate the other races out of his "concern" for other gargoyles, and quite frankly it bothered them. The only one that smiled was Tiogra, which surprised Boragen and Ghin since they remembered how much Yemz had gotten on Tiogra's nerves recently.

After a few moments of preparation, Boragen had finished polishing his blades and cleaning his guns.

"Well," he said, "better go get ready. The grandmaster's giving a speech before we go and I don't want to miss it."

"Wait for me!" Ghin exclaimed as he sheathed his sword.

Boragen and Ghin jogged towards the door and turned back to see if Tiogra and Yemz were ready.

"You guys go ahead," Tiogra said smiling, "we'll catch up."

Boragen and Ghin nodded and closed the door behind them.

"I don't know about you, Boragen, but Yemz kind of gives me the creeps." Ghin said as the two master gargoyles walked down the halls.

Boragen nodded in return and continued walking.

Meanwhile, back in the armory, Tiogra and Yemz were nearly finished preparing their weapons.

"I don't get this." Yemz suddenly said.

Tiogra looked up in confusion. "Get what?" he asked in a monotone voice, still remembering the insults his acquaintance threw his way not too long ago.

"Why we bother protecting the humans." Yemz explained, "At the rate these killings and turnings are going, we're bound to just wipe them out anyway."

Whatever Tiogra had of a small smile quickly faded. He knew sometimes Yemz could be full of himself, however, his cocky attitude was getting unbearably annoying.

"I thought you once said you envied humans." Tiogra reminded Yemz, "Doesn't that mean you can relate to them on a certain level?"

"What do you mean?" Yemz asked. "I'm more powerful than them. How could I ever relate to weaklings?"

Tiogra slammed his sword down on the bench they were sitting on, grabbing Yemz's attention.

"God, Yemz!" Tiogra yelled as he leapt up from his seat in frustration, "What the hell is your problem?"

"What-?" Yemz began.

"You damn well know what!" Tiogra continued, "First you act all sorry for yourself because you're 'mistreated' by everyone else. Then you get all high and mighty because all of a sudden you discover that you're stronger?"

"Maybe I know where I stand on the food chain." Yemz said as he stood up from the bench.

"Food chain?" Tiogra yelled, "Are you nuts? We're supposed to protect humans, not bully them!"

"I know that!" Yemz yelled back, "I just don't see the point! These are weaker beings! They don't deserve what they have! As far as I'm concerned, they don't even deserve to exist!"

"What would Chem think of this?" Tiogra asked.

Yemz walked furiously back over to Tiogra and punched a dent into a nearby locker, mainly to try to scare his uneasy friend back for when he had slammed him into a wall.

"Don't you dare bring her into this!" Yemz yelled, "You hear me?"

Seeing Yemz try to mimic Tiogra's anger regarding his honor was so sickening and pathetic, Tiogra nearly felt like vomiting.

"Don't even pretend like you've got a conscience now, you ungrateful waste of rock!" Tiogra yelled back.

Yemz's eyes widened in shock from Tiogra's insult. The master gargoyle did his best to ignore Yemz's expression, thinking that there was no logical reason for Yemz to act surprised. The terrible truth was that the fact that since Yemz had been so oblivious and disgustingly shameful to their friendship, current events had not even phased him.

Tiogra walked back over to bench, grabbed his weapons, and walked towards the door, feeling ashamed for arguing with someone who he considered immature.

"Now look," Tiogra began, "we've got a war to finish, so I pray that you don't do anything stupid on the battlefield. But so help me Trog, if you do I will hit you so hard and fast you'll blink out of existence."

As Tiogra walked out of the room, Yemz glared at the door and sharpened his sword in anger.

Lycanthropes

It was a dark and rainy evening in Cologne, Germany. A man dressed in formal German attire, who looked to be in his early forties, was walking down the street of Gotenring towards a boarded up house. Before he entered, he looked around to make sure no one was watching him and then pulled a key out of his coat pocket, unlocked the door and quickly went inside the abandoned building before anyone could notice him.

The building was dusty and empty without a single hint of life. As the man ventured further into the house, he watched his feet for a loose wooden plank in the floor. Once he found it, he knelt down and pulled the plank upward. Just then, a section of the floor to the man's right moved apart, revealing a hidden stairway. The man proceeded down the stairs as the floor closed behind him.

Once the man reached what seemed to be the bottom of the stairs, he pulled out a flashlight and flashed it three times. Immediately, the sound of cranking gears was heard, followed by light flowing through a crack in an enormous gateway at least twenty feet in front of him.

As the doors opened, the man saw what his people, the lycanthrope kingdom, knew as home. It was an enormous cavern filled with a rusting city, composed of dirt and steel, that was large enough to house thousands of lycanthropes. Along with the lycanthropes' homes were shops, armories, and a church dedicated to Egn, for those who still worshiped him. Faith in the evil god was dwindling nowadays, due to the gargoyles winning most of the battles that currently took place.

Lycanthropes were incredibly secretive and only went out into the world whenever necessary. There was hardly any time when they would use their powers like the vampires did. Mostly, they would hunt woodland creatures for food and rarely would they bring humans down into the city to feast upon. Their numbers were moderately reduced as well, due to the fourth battle they had with the gargoyles. Once that battle was over and their leader, Aldalfrid, was slain, the lycanthropes decided it was in their best interest never to even touch the surface world for a long time. Ulric, the current leader of the werewolf kingdom, completely agreed with his people's decision. So the lycanthropes hid underground, waiting patiently until the day they could rise again. Sadly, as far as they could tell, that day was not coming anytime soon.

As the man from the street walked down the boulevards of the city, he was greeted by many of his comrades.

"Good evening, Medwin." A lycanthrope woman said to the man as she dusted her child off from playing in the streets.

"Evening." Medwin responded with a smile, "I see young Gustav

---

121

has been playing with his friends again."

"Yes," the wolf woman confirmed with a smile, "ran into a shelf outside of Heinrich's shop."

The young, blonde haired lycanthrope looked up at Medwin with a smile, showing that he was not in extreme trouble, which made Medwin happy in return. From what he remembered, Gustav was a good child and never meant any harm. Medwin only wished that the boy could have been born under different circumstances.

As he ventured down the thoroughfare, he passed by Heinrich's shop and saw that there was not any serious damage done, just a small shelf of dusty books that had been knocked over. The shelf itself was not broken and the books seemed to be in good condition, despite being knocked to the ground.

When Medwin walked past the shop, he helped Heinrich pick up the books that were knocked to the ground and replaced them in the proper order they were in.

"Ah Medwin, it's good to see you again." Heinrich said, smiling at his friend's kindness "How are things on the surface world?"

"They are good, my friend." Medwin said as he smiled back, "Besides it being over populated by snack food."

Heinrich laughed at Medwin's joke.

"Thank you for the book you let me purchase the other day." Medwin added.

"Not a problem." Heinrich said, remembering the occasion. The book Medwin had purchased was called *The Celtic Twilight* by a human author named W.B. Yeats. Heinrich never understood what fascinated Medwin with that specific author, mainly because the author was human. To Heinrich, only books by lycanthrope authors were ever worth reading.

"Well, I must be off." Medwin said, "Ulric is expecting me. I suspect it's for something important."

"Alright then, Medwin." Heinrich said, "Take care of yourself!"

"Thanks!" Medwin said smiling as he walked towards the cavern keep.

The keep was built at the farthest end of the cavern to protect a passageway that led to the surface world and also housed the leader of the lycanthrope nation. The passageway was made as an escape route if the underground civilization of the lycanthropes were ever discovered and attacked.

As Medwin ventured down the streets, he looked at a window of one of the keep's towers, seeing electricity and sparks flashing from inside the room. Medwin assumed that this meant Ulric was at work on another invention.

Once he arrived at the keep's giant steel door, Medwin knocked twice to alert his king of his presence. A lycanthrope servant answered the door, first peaking through the slot to see who it was and then opening the door with a greeting.

"Hello again, Medwin." The servant said.

"Hello, Armon," Medwin replied, "Is Ulric busy?"

"Yes," Armon responded, "But he is expecting you."

"Alright," Medwin said, "well I hope you have a pleasant evening, Armon."

"Thank you, sir." Armon replied as Medwin walked down the hall to the stairs that ascended to Ulric's lab.

As Medwin climbed the stairs, he could not help but think of the current battle that would take place with the gargoyles and the vampires. This battle had sprouted a general question that was on every lycanthrope's mind: Who would come out the winning party in this conflict? One thing was for sure, Ulric was not going to like the news Medwin had for him. Medwin had seen other werewolves give Ulric bad news before, the aftermath of which was not pretty.

Once Medwin arrived at the door to Ulric's lab, he reached for the knob, but before he could open the door, an explosion emitted from the room and broke the door off its top and bottom hinges. Medwin could hear Ulric swearing and cursing through the broken door and tried not to laugh at his master's expense. He had always secretly found it funny whenever Ulric was upset, due to the facial expressions the lycanthrope king made. Whenever Ulric was really mad though, people tended not to bother him until his mental storm had calmed.

As Medwin walked through the broken door, Ulric was throwing around beakers and lab equipment in anger. The lycanthrope monarch's lab coat was charred and burnt from the experiments he was conducting earlier in the day in an attempt to develop stronger lycanthropes. Medwin, being the loyal servant that he was, was concerned for his king.

"Is everything alright, my lord?" Medwin asked.

"No, Medwin..." Ulric said, stroking his gray hair and trying not to pull it out in frustration, "Everything is not alright."

Ulric proceeded to drop his lab coat onto the floor and walked around the mess he had made towards his throne in the lab.

"Our race is nearing the brink of extinction." Ulric said as he walked, "My sciences are failing to come up with a way to evolve our race, Egn has forsaken us, and on top of it all, I am failing my duties as king."

As Ulric slumped onto his throne, he pulled out a bronze pocket watch from his vest and starred at the craftsmanship of the trinket, pondering a solution to his problems. Medwin walked over to the bar on the far left of the throne and poured a drink for his leader and himself.

"Come now, your majesty." Medwin calmly said, trying to reassure his friend as he handed him the beverage, "Things will get better for the wolf race. Your sciences will prevail. You're doing a wonderful job as king of the lycanthropes. The people love you and your father would be extremely proud. As far as Egn is concerned, eventually he will see the error of his ways and take us back into his burning arms as the people he has always loved."

"Ah," Ulric said as he accepted the cold glass of scotch, "my friend, to speak such things of Egn is blasphemous. It would be wise of you to watch yourself. Still, hopefully you are right."

As the two werewolves drank, Medwin remembered the news he had for his king.

"I hate to be the bearer of bad news, my lord..." Medwin began, "but did you send a squad of nearly two hundred urban lycanthropes into the sewers to patrol the remains of the rattus city?"

Ulric eyed his friend in suspicion. "No," he said confused, "I ordered no such move. Why?"

Medwin paused for a minute, afraid of what the bad news would bring to him.

"Well," Medwin began, "Sven took a squad out to search the remains of the rattus city for any survivors, I figured you ordered this movement."

Ulric slowly buried his head in his hand in angst. Medwin could see the robotic index finger, which replaced Ulric's missing digit, stroking his skull in agony.

"How many men did we lose?" Ulric asked, afraid of the answer.

"All of the ones that left with Sven, sir." Medwin regrettably stated.

Ulric sighed and rubbed his eyes, allowing the cold steel of his finger to cool his overheated head for a brief second. "How many men do we have left?" he asked heavily.

"A little under ten thousand, sir." Medwin responded.

Ulric looked up from his hand at Medwin, who was expecting a fit from his lord. Instead, Ulric simply stood up and looked out the window at the underground city.

"Well..." Ulric said, "at least Sven is out of our fur."

Medwin nodded in agreement. Sven, though a good fighter, was often disobedient and would have rather done things his own way. These were traits in a commanding officer the lycanthrope nation could have done without.

Just then, a transmission came through on Ulric's holographic messaging system. Ulric and Medwin looked at each other in confusion. Unless something was urgent, the messaging system was hardly ever used. Ulric flipped the "on" switch and within minutes, a face appeared below the hologram projector.

"Vlad." Ulric muttered with disgust as he glared at the vampire leader.

"Hello, Ulric." Vlad responded with a smile, "I see you're still up to your sciences."

Ulric ignored his enemy's jest at his work. "What do you want?" he asked, trying to fathom why his enemy would ever want to call him.

"Well, if we must get right down to business." Vlad said, "I have sent over seven thousand vampires to the gargoyle's base in France. I have not expected them to return, but I do hope that they have done some damage along the way. The gargoyles have probably already started planning a counter attack on my castle, and my father alone will probably not stand up to as many soldiers as I estimated they are sending."

"Your father?" Ulric asked in surprise. The latest news he had heard regarding Dracula was that the prime vampire was dead.

"Yes, my father." Vlad said with a twisted smile, "Unlike you, I actually care about my family. Enough to resurrect them, at least."

"Get to the point, suck head." Ulric snarled.

Vlad eyed Ulric with contempt. "My point is..." Vlad continued, "that if we do not join forces, my nation will fall and yours will follow shortly after."

This took Ulric by surprise. He would have never suspected that in all his decades alive, a vampire would ask for his help. The werewolf king then glanced at the floor and pondered. If the vampires truly needed help in this battle, it would be wise to help them so that they would be rid of the gargoyles once and for all. However, if this was a trap, then Vlad planned on killing off the lycanthropes once they were done with the gargoyles anyway. Knowing Vlad, the second option was probably the most likely.

"I think not." Ulric finally said.

Vlad's eyes widened in shock, as well as Medwin's from hearing his king's response.

"Now listen, I...!" Vlad began.

"No, you listen." Ulric interrupted, "The vampires have been nothing but cruel and unjust to my people. We may share the same god, but that doesn't mean I have to like you. As far as I am concerned, you're all better off dead anyway."

Vlad's face froze from hearing Ulric's response.

"Besides," Ulric continued, "I have a better idea. Why don't you try whatever demonic steroids you used to bring your father back on your soldiers? Maybe then you'll stand a chance."

"That was different." Vlad responded, "It was a resurrection process, I can't just..."

"This conversation is over!" Ulric interrupted again, "I'd sooner spit on my father's grave before I ever help you!"

Vlad chuckled before Ulric angrily flipped the switch off, making the hologram vanish. Vlad's chuckle rang through Ulric's head as he returned to his throne, where he rubbed his bearded chin with his robotic finger in thought.

"Your highness, may I speak?" Medwin asked.

"You may." Ulric permitted in a gruff tone.

"This may have been our chance to rid ourselves of the gargoyles once and for all!" Medwin exclaimed, "Surely Vlad was serious about the partnership!"

"You don't know Vlad like I do!" Ulric yelled back, "When you fight someone for a few hundred years, who mocks your work, your ambitions, and unjustly steals your god's love for you away, then come and talk to me! Besides, with Dracula resurrected, there's no telling what he was planning. Not to mention this gives me twice the reason not to trust him."

Medwin was unsettled by his lord's madness. It must have been hard for Ulric to accept defeat at Vlad's hand so many times before. Due to the past events, it was understandable why Ulric would reject a plea for help from the vampire lord. If there was one-thing lycanthropes were full of, it was pride. To have their dignity wounded over again and again was demeaning to their very souls.

As Ulric pondered, his mind went from one thought to the next. What would happen if he did go to Vlad's aid? Had the vampire lord truly gone mad? What would happen if he were to find a way to fight off the gargoyles without help?

The last thought was the one that hovered in Ulric's mind the longest.

I would need something even stronger then the gargoyles themselves if I wanted to wipe them out. He thought.

Then an idea popped into Ulric's head. He remembered a story he had read from long ago about a scientist who created a monstrosity from different parts of dead men. The monster was so strong it could crush anything with it's thumb and index finger and was seemingly indestructible.

"I've got it!" Ulric exclaimed.

Medwin looked at his king with confusion. "Got what, sir?"

"Its so obvious!" Ulric declared as he jumped up from his throne and hurried over to the door that led to the stairs. He was so excited that he practically forgot his street coat by the broken door.

"Sir?" Medwin asked, a tad shaken by his king's excitement.

"Medwin!" Ulric exclaimed happily, "Round up a small squad…we're going grave digging!"

The End of Traditional Enemies

The mood of the castle courtyard was silent. Nine thousand gargoyles, who were armed with swords, maces, axes and hammers, chattered amongst themselves in preparation for the final battle with the vampire country. For some, nervousness was common, considering it was their first battle. For others, they were as calm as bowls of water with confidence that they would win. All together, everyone was eager to meet the new Dracula in battle. There was not a single gargoyle that would shirk from this fight.

The grandmaster stood before his army and smiled. Each gargoyle who stood before him had seen him as a father figure and had shown him loyalty and honor their entire lives. They were the most infamous, lionhearted warriors the supernatural world had ever known. This was an army he had trained himself, each combatant with enough discipline and might that would make Trog proud to call them gargoyles.

Behind the grandmaster stood four of his master pupils, Boragen, Ghin, Yemz, and Tiogra. The four warriors stood with their hands folded behind their backs and under their wings, waiting for orders from their master. The grandmaster scanned the room and raised his right hand above his head to direct his students' attention towards himself. The gargoyle army immediately stopped talking and paid direct attention to their nation's leader.

"Warriors!" the grandmaster shouted, "In moments, we will walk into the window that leads to Transylvania. There will be over twelve thousand vampires waiting for us on the other side. They have made armor for themselves to try to match our strength. However, we have all fought vampires before. For every one of us that has fallen, twenty of them have died. This battle will be no different. For we are gargoyles, the guardians of the earth! For too long, they have threatened peace and harmony for their own selfish needs, but that ends here today! Today, balance will be restored!"

The gargoyles cheered as they flew behind the grandmaster, out of the courtyard and onto the landing pad, where the window to Transylvania was open and waiting for them.

As the gargoyle army stepped through the window that led to a cliff in Transylvania, they followed the coordinates that Trang had provided and flew west towards the vampire estate. Moments later, the gargoyles noticed the sun rising from the east as they reached the location they were sent to. Once they arrived, the vampire's cloaking field had vanished and revealed the castle that resided within it. The castle was bigger than any of the gargoyles had thought it would be and twice as demonic as they had imagined it was. As the gargoyles looked down below, they noticed a huge crowd of thousands of vampires that were clad in blue armor, standing directly in front of the castle entrance and positioned along the black, spiked, steel walls that fortified the stronghold. A few miles away from the castle, Boragen signaled for the gargoyle army to land. Without delay, the gargoyles dropped down to the ground across from the castle and stood patiently as they waited for the order to attack. The vampires hissed in anger as they recognized their lifelong enemies and barred their swords, guns and claws for the fight that would decide the fate of their race.

As the opposing armies stood across from each other, they glared each other down in spite. The vampires spat and gnashed their teeth while the gargoyles maintained their calm, disciplined breathing.

The grandmaster held his fist in the air, ready to give the order to strike. Using his godly meditative sight, the grandmaster looked directly across the battlefield and saw Dracula and Vlad on the highest tower of the castle, clad in the fiery, exotic red, black, gold and silver battle garments they had worn centuries ago. A smug grin stretched across Dracula's face as he saw his old enemy for the first time since his death. Suddenly, a flare shot up out of Dracula's hand and burst across the sky. The vampires then aimed their custom rifles at the gargoyles, ready to slay their enemies where they stood. Seeing this, the grandmaster used his elemental power to form ice over his knuckles, signaling to his master pupils what to do.

"Barrier!" Tiogra shouted.

Immediately, Tiogra, Boragen and the other gargoyles with power over water, projected a thick barrier of ice in front of their comrades, which stopped the bullets from hitting their targets. The vampires continued to fire upon the gargoyles, thinking that the barrier would have to give in soon. Luckily, the wall of ice held, thanks to the water gifted gargoyles adding more ice to help keep it steady.

The grandmaster listened closely for the chance when the gargoyles could counter attack. When the bullets stopped, he could hear the vampires unload the magazines from their guns, ready to load the next round.

"Now!" the grandmaster yelled as he saw the chance to attack.

The gargoyles roared as the ice wall shattered apart. The water gargoyles immediately took to the skies while the fire gargoyles violently sprinted towards the castle as fast as they could.

Hearing their enemies' battle cries, the vampires quickly reloaded their guns and fired upon the gargoyles again. As they saw the vampire's bullets fly towards them, Ghin, Yemz and the other fire talented gargoyles folded their wings in front of them as they ran and used their power over fire to set their wings ablaze, while hardening their flesh to withstand the bullets. The flames the gargoyles were producing were enough to make it difficult for the vampires to aim correctly. Unfortunately, not every gargoyle was safe from the wall of bullets, despite their hardened flesh. A fraction of the well-aimed bullets managed to pierce the stone flesh of the gargoyle's hardened wings and hit their targets in the head, killing some of them instantly.

Watching his comrades die as they charged and with the memory of Rejan's death sitting in his mind, Ghin intensified the flames on his wings, increasing the heat until the impact from the bullets felt like nothing more but annoying pricks against his body. The other fire talented gargoyles followed Ghin's example and increased the heat of their own flames as much as they could. Meanwhile, the gargoyles with the gift of water flew over the vampire army and began to shower large shards of ice on top of their enemies, crushing some of the vampire soldiers where they stood. While the vampires were distracted by the gargoyles flying overhead, the fire gargoyles took the advantage and launched the flames from their wings at their opponents, knocking some of the vampires back while burning others to ash.

Though the armor the vampires wore was impervious to the flames, some of the gargoyles with greater experience and martial discipline made the fires seep into the armor and burned the vampires within. However, some of the bullets the vampires shot at their last moments of living managed to kill some of the gargoyles as they made contact with the vampire army.

As the gargoyles landed on the battlefield and along the walls of the castle, weapons and claws clashed as the gargoyles collided with the vampires. Blood and ash flew left and right as blade, element and stone tore through armor, flesh and bone. While the two nations fought each other, the master gargoyles used their own methods of combat to pave their own way through the field of soldiers. Boragen used his enormous, personal war hammer to crush the vampires and used his battle rifles to blast them to pieces. Ghin used his brute strength and flames to furiously tear the vampires apart and ripped the helmets off of others to expose them to the sun. Yemz and Tiogra were hacking away with their swords as the vampire legion threw themselves upon them, blasting some with fire and crushing others with water. The grandmaster was the most magnificent fighter of the gargoyles. Using his martial arts and combined power over fire and water while still in his diminished form, he managed to eliminate the majority of vampires he came across. His aggressiveness was derived from the oath that he personally had to make sure his students were kept safe.

From their position on the castle, Dracula and Vlad could see that despite their numbers, chances of the vampire army winning were looking slim.

"Things aren't looking good father." Vlad said from behind the prime vampire with a worried expression.

"Don't worry." Dracula said, "I've learned some new tricks in my spare time."

Dracula raised his hand above his head and gestured towards the sun. Immediately, rain clouds covered the sky and blocked out the solar rays while thunder rolled across the battlefield.

"Now, we will win." Dracula said with a smile as he proceeded to throw fireballs at the gargoyles.

The gargoyles, however, were not as easily destroyed as their vampire counterparts. Thankfully, Dracula was aiming blindly as he threw his fireballs at the sea of warriors below, destroying some of the vampires in the process. Keeping their focus on the soldiers in front of them, the gargoyles did their best to avoid being struck by Dracula's attacks. Those who were directly hit shattered into chunks of stone or managed to block the impact with their wings and were severely burned.

As the battle raged on, the vampire numbers were still becoming thinner and thinner. Tiogra fought valiantly, decapitating and eviscerating as many vampires as he could. As he fought, the gargoyles around him were deeply motivated and tried to match his intensity.

While Dracula continued to cast his fireballs, Vlad pushed a button on a remote he pulled out of his armor that opened the castle's main door. Some gargoyles saw this as a chance to charge the castle and immediately ran towards the darkness within the entrance.

Tiogra, Ghin and Boragen continued to fight as they watched the gargoyles enter the castle suspiciously. After a few minutes, without any sign of struggle, Tiogra and the other master gargoyles became increasingly skeptical, since it made no sense for Vlad to invite the gargoyles into his home without any traps waiting for them inside. Suddenly, a loud booming was heard from within the castle and four gargoyle soldiers were thrown back into the battlefield. Tiogra leapt into the air and caught one of the gargoyles before he hit the ground. The strange thing was that these gargoyles were dead and sickly gray, but had not crumbled into pieces.

As he inspected the corpse and noted the imprint of a giant fist on the dead gargoyle's chest, Tiogra looked up to see what monstrosity Vlad had created that was able to fend off so many gargoyles. As the monster stomped out of the shadows, Tiogra and Ghin's eyes widened with disbelief. They recognized the face from the archives in the castle's main library. It was Vincent, Vlad's oldest child and only son. The gargoyles knew that Vlad was scum, but what amazed them was the fact that the vampire lord would steep so low as to turn his own child into a living vampiric nightmare.

As Ghin and Tiogra starred at Vincent in incredulity, they clenched their stomachs, as did every other gargoyle within twenty feet of the deformed vampire prince. A very unfamiliar feeling of weakness washed over the gargoyles bodies as they knelt down in pain. Looking around at the other gargoyles, Tiogra could see that his comrades were unable to use their elemental abilities in defense against the overwhelming sensation. Apparently, along with his new enhanced strength, Vincent had become a gargoyle nullifier. As he looked over the vampire prince's new form, Tiogra assumed the glowing blue veins within Vincent's chest displayed where the nullifying power came from.

The terrible experiments Vlad had subjected Vincent to had rendered his face horribly deformed in an attempt to alter his son's appearance to look more like his own. The vampire prince now stood thirteen feet tall and was covered in unnatural muscle. The weight of the muscle mass made Vincent's back completely hunch over like a beast. Small pieces of machinery that were used to amplify Vincent's strength covered his back like abnormal quills, further increasing his frightening image.

Regardless of his intimidating presence, the gargoyles charged at Vincent with as much vigor as they had, only to have him beat them back with enough force that he killed some of them. One gargoyle managed to jump onto Vincent's head and whipped his face with her wings. However, her attempt to kill the abomination was in vain as the giant vampire plucked the gargoyle off his head and squeezed the life out of her with his enlarged fingers.

Seeing this, Tiogra charged directly at Vincent in rage. The monstrous vampire glared directly at Tiogra and tried to stomp the master gargoyle into the ground. Luckily, Tiogra was nimble enough to dodge the monster's attack and parry the other blows that followed. It seemed as if Tiogra would kill this vampire like he did every other that crossed his path. However, Vincent's combative instincts proved differently. He blocked Tiogra's sword with his forearm and broke the blade by twisting it within his limb. He then threw the master gargoyle to the ground and stepped on his chest to pin him under his heel.

Tiogra looked up at the giant vampire with wide eyes, thinking this was his last moment on earth. As Vincent's enormous fist seemed to come down at Tiogra in slow motion, the master gargoyle thought about how he would never see his wife or son ever again. He thought about the events he experienced with the people of his race, about the laughs he had shared and the comfort he gave to relatives of lost friends. The thoughts were pleasant, but it was all over now. Regardless of his previous stress, the experience almost felt peaceful. It was time for Tiogra to die.

Just then, a hammer was thrown at Vincent's hand, hard enough to break his arm. Vincent howled in pain as half of his forearm dangled by a strip of skin. This action was followed by a fiery kick to Vincent's skull by

Ghin, knocking the vampire off of Tiogra and sending him crashing into Boragen's fist, which sent the altered vampire prince flying towards the castle.

"Get inside the castle and find Vlad!" Boragen yelled to Tiogra as Ghin repeatedly slashed at the vampire prince's face with fire in his claws, "We'll take it from here."

Tiogra nodded and ran inside the castle, followed by three other gargoyles.

As Boragen and Ghin made sure their friend made it inside the castle safely, their attention quickly turned back toward Vincent, who slowly stood back up from their combined assault and glared at the two warriors in a rage that was not his own.

"C'mon!" Boragen yelled as his knuckles cracked within his clenched fists.

Vincent chuckled and picked up a nearby vampire, then swallowed him much like a snake would swallow a mouse. Steam hissed outward and flesh and bone grew out of the stump where Vincent's arm had been. In an instant, the monstrosity's arm was healed.

"Well that's disgusting." Ghin said as he witnessed the repulsive event.

Vincent charged at Boragen and Ghin with enough force to match a steam engine. Ghin ran off to the right of the deviant as Boragen stood his ground. When Vincent collided with the gargoyle blacksmith, a shockwave emitted from the force of the two behemoths colliding, creating a crater where they stood.

Boragen tried to hit Vincent, only to have his punch blocked and countered with another punch, which managed to knock Boragen to the ground. It was the first time a vampire ever blocked a strike from Boragen, let alone managed to knock him off his feet. This shocked the gargoyle blacksmith greatly, yet he retained his warrior's attitude.

Ok... Boragen thought as he got up for another strike, *...a little less arrogance this time.*

Regaining his focus, Boragen stood upright and starred his opponent directly in his deformed eyes. Vincent tried to strike Boragen again, only this time, it was his strike that was blocked and it was he who was punched in the jaw, knocking him to the ground.

After the counter strike, Vlad's devilish smile stretched across Vincent's altered face as he regained his footing, spitting out blood as well as one of his fangs.

Meanwhile, Ghin was keeping the other vampires from interfering with Boragen and Vincent's battle. Shooting bursts of flames out of his hands like blasts from cannons along with his incredible martial skill, Ghin managed to keep a thirty-foot radius around his friend and the thirteen-foot monstrosity clear of interfering vampires. Eventually, other gargoyles joined in, helping Ghin to keep the enemy soldiers out by forming a circle around Boragen and Vincent, pushing the vampires back as much as they could. It was incredibly difficult considering every time a vampire was slain, three more appeared where the other had been.

Simultaneously, Boragen and Vincent continued their fight. With every punch thrown, there was a counter blow. It seemed that along with his mutations, Vlad had altered Vincent's fighting methods to become a match for even a master gargoyle. Boragen and Vincent were progressively covered in welts and bruises through each second of the fight. Eventually, the enormous gladiators grappled and locked themselves in place, trying to throw the other to the ground.

The combined force of the mammoth warrior's struggle created a tremor upon the earth they stood on. The ground vibrated until Boragen finally threw an uppercut to Vincent's jaw, sending him flying backwards into one of the castle's walls, which crumbled on top of the vampire prince. Even though Vincent was completely covered in rubble, Boragen knew the fight was far from over and the exchange of blows he had with Vincent was merely a warm up. Sure enough, the rubble shook, and a very bloody abomination burst from the pile of concrete and steel.

"Great," Boragen said to himself, "I was hoping you'd be better than your previous friends."

As the blood fell from Vincent's body, it turned to ash and mixed with the rain pouring out of the sky. The rain began to fall heavily from the summoned clouds as the gladiators glared at each other from across their fighting zone. With a satisfied smile, Boragen cracked his neck, which harmonized with the thunder in the sky.

Vincent grinned in return as blood fell off his face. He leapt over the pile of rocks and charged at Boragen, who countered this move by leaping into the air himself, catching Vincent's head and slamming him into the ground.

Before Boragen could continue his attack, Vincent rolled backward and kicked the gargoyle blacksmith in the back of his head. Boragen fell forward, but caught himself before his face collided with the ground. As soon as he began to rise back up, Vincent jumped on Boragen's back and pinned him to the ground. The vampire experiment proceeded to punch and scratch at the back of his opponent's head in an attempt to rip his brain out of his stone skull. Before a fourth blow could be dealt, Boragen grabbed a nearby stone, cut Vincent with the serrated claws on his wings and rolled over, grabbing Vincent by his jaw and then striking his foe in the side of the head with the rock. Seeing an opening for an attack, savagery overcame Boragen's mind as he repeatedly bashed the rock into Vincent's head while holding onto his lower jaw. Once the rock was reduced to pebbles, Boragen resorted to tearing chunks of Vincent's face off of his skull and placing dents in his reinforced head.

At this point, Vincent's right eye had been swollen shut while the other had been torn off along with his right ear and left cheek. Hanging from his jaw, Vincent tried to grab Boragen with whatever strength he had left. With no mercy to be shown, Boragen grabbed Vincent's arm with his thumb and index finger and snapped the wrist off of its joint. Vincent moaned in pain as the gargoyle blacksmith tossed him into the air and delivered a sidekick to the vampire's chest, breaking the elemental neutralizer within his body and sending him flying into another wall of the castle. Before Vincent could even think to react, Boragen was punching him in the stomach with jagged, ice hard fists. Realizing his elemental control was slowly returning, the gargoyle blacksmith continued to punch Vincent until he broke all of the monster's ribs.

Even after the beating, Boragen did not stop there. Since the battle began, he knew that whatever remained of the vampire prince was already dead and that this creature was now a deformed clone of Vlad. With the vampire lord in mind, he grabbed Vincent by the back of the head and used his elemental power to drown the vampire by having water forced out of his hand and into Vincent's mouth.

As the water rushed from his hand, Boragen became lost in thought about the gargoyles he had known that brutally died at the hands of vampires. He thought about all the gargoyle children that suffered from the news that their parents and siblings had perished from the vampire country's selfishness. The one thought that hovered in Boragen's mind the most was the memory of his newborn son, being taken away by vampire soldiers centuries ago, never to be heard of again. The life his son would never get to live, along with the deaths of his friends, was enough for Boragen to want more than just the deaths of vampires, but to have them feel as weak and helpless as he had felt when his son was abducted.

Choking on water as it leaked out of the holes in his face, Vincent tried to claw out of Boragen's grip with his one good arm. Seeing this, Boragen stomped down on the vampire's calf, reducing the bones to powder and severely crippling the vampire prince. He then flipped Vincent over onto his back and began to slowly pull the vampire's chest apart. Moaning wearily in pain, Vincent could only roll his head from side to side as his opponent carelessly yanked his heart from his chest. The heart still had a fraction of the gargoyle nullifying energy within it, which sharply stung at Boragen's hand as he crushed it within his grip. Vincent gasped for breath as he slowly died at Boragen's feet, turning to ash within minutes. The only remains from the vampire were a mechanical leg and numerous metallic pieces from his body that amplified his strength.

As Boragen slowly regained a calm mindset, he saw that Ghin and five other gargoyles had finished fending off the vampire attackers and were watching the beating with widened eyes.

"Sorry," Boragen said to Ghin as he spat out some green blood, "I forgot to share. Did you want some?"

Ghin smiled at his friend's dark humor and his reference to Rejan. "I protect my nation with the best I can offer." He said, "That's all she'd want from me."

Boragen smiled as he walked out of the giant hole in the wall he had made with Vincent's mutated body. Looking out over the battlefield, Boragen and Ghin saw that there were still gargoyles and vampires who were locked in combat and that Dracula and Vlad had retreated back into the castle. The grandmaster was busy fighting a crowd of elite vampires in the distance, Yemz was roaming the battlefield slaying vampires wherever he could, and nothing had been heard from Tiogra since he entered the castle.

As he looked back towards the castle, Boragen could see that the other gargoyles were still dumbfounded by the blacksmith's brutality.

"If you think that's savage..." Boragen said chuckling, "Wait until you see what Tiogra does to Vlad."

Ghin nodded in agreement. Every gargoyle had been scarred in one way or another, whether it was the loss of a loved one or witnessing the cruelty of vampires and lycanthropes firsthand. What mattered was how that pain was dealt with. Since Boragen never meditated, it was understandable to Ghin how he could be so brutal towards his enemies. As far as Tiogra was concerned, Ghin knew that stress was being stacked upon his friend like never before with the visions Jhonig had received and the way current events were playing out. However, as he and Boragen flew back onto the battlefield, Ghin reassured himself that after this battle, things would go back to a relatively peaceful state.

Meanwhile inside the castle, Tiogra and the three other gargoyles were running through the halls, trying to find Vlad and Dracula and slaughtering every vampire that got in their way without hesitation. When they finally reached the throne room, Tiogra walked to the center of the room and quietly stood his guard, waiting for the vampire lords to appear. Even though the lack of light was not a problem, Tiogra was bothered that he and the other gargoyles could not see the vampire lords, yet could feel their strengthening auras fill the space around them without being able to pinpoint exactly where they were. They had also noticed that the booming noises from Dracula's fireballs had stopped, which meant that the prime vampire must have definitely retreated into the castle and was most likely preparing for another diabolical attack.

"Quickly," Tiogra said, "we need to find Dracula before he..."

Tiogra was interrupted by the sight of mist flowing into the room through the door. As quickly as it came, the mist flowed over to the gargoyle warriors and drained their life from them, making their bodies crumble to pieces.

"No!" Tiogra yelled as he witnessed his comrades die before him.

The mist then materialized right in front of Tiogra, revealing that it was Dracula and Vlad, standing proudly with grins that stretched from ear to ear. Tiogra glared at his opponents, thinking about how many gargoyles and innocent lives they had destroyed in their existence.

"I must admit, I am quite happy to see you, Tiogra." Dracula taunted with a grin.

Tiogra scowled back at Dracula, keeping his eyes directly on his opponents, watching for any tricks they might pull.

"You seem... different, Tiogra." Dracula said, "Stronger, in someway."

"I've been working out." Tiogra responded, "Using your minions as practice."

Vlad growled as Dracula simply continued to smile.

"I was going to say," Dracula said, "You look like you've been doing a lot of killing lately. Becoming a little bit more evil everyday."

Tiogra chuckled at the vampire lord's words, "Come on, Drac..." he said, "you know better than to use super villain propaganda on me."

Dracula snickered at Tiogra's jest. "No propaganda needed." He said confidently, "If you think about it, you're just like me. A being of power. A beast of destruction. A creature of death."

Tiogra scowled at Dracula, wondering why he had not been able to blast the vampire lords with water. Then it occurred to him that Vlad had a nullifying ability of his own. Another strategy quickly formed in Tiogra's mind. He knew he could still kill Vlad, if not both of them.

"Whatever you say." Tiogra said calmly as he recovered his combative mindset, "Are we doing this?"

"As you wish." Dracula said, cracking his gigantic knuckles, "To the death!"

I'd want nothing else. Tiogra thought to himself as he growled.

Dracula and Tiogra assumed their fighting stances, and the final duel began.

The Sorrow of a Nation

Tiogra lunged at Dracula while Vlad stood against a wall with an arrogant smile. As Tiogra was about to strike Dracula, he noticed that the vampire lord did not move. Then, a seemingly impossible thing happened, Tiogra's punch was ineffective. It was like an infant hitting it's father. Tiogra's eyes widened in shock. Never before had anyone taken a direct hit from any gargoyle and was left standing, let alone still breathing.

"You're a fool if you think I'll be so easily beaten this time, boy." Dracula taunted, grinning as he struck Tiogra in the chest, sending the master gargoyle flying backwards into the throne.

The throne crumbled underneath Tiogra as he collided with it. After the impact, the master gargoyle clenched his thorax as he lay in the pile of gold debris.

"Come to think of it," Dracula said as he walked over toward his adversary, "you didn't technically beat me last time. As I recall, your master had to come dig you out of the pit you put yourself in."

Tiogra leapt up and delivered a flying roundhouse kick to the prime vampire's throat. Dracula, however, caught the kick and sent Tiogra flying into the mirrored wall to the right.

"Yes..." Dracula hissed, "but this will be radically different."

As Dracula approached his opponent again, Tiogra tried to punch the vampire lord in the nose, only to have his fist caught and crushed. Dracula then sent the back of his fist crashing into the side of Tiogra's head, hurling him into the entrance of the throne room, completely demolishing the doors.

"This time..." Dracula sneered as he materialized out of his mist near Tiogra, "I doubt your master will be able to save you."

Dracula picked Tiogra up by the neck and clenched his grip, making the master gargoyle gasp for air as the vampire lord's hold tightened around his throat. The prime vampire proceeded to repeatedly strike the master gargoyle in the stomach until he coughed up blood, then delivered a heavier punch, sending Tiogra flying across the room again and leaving a crater in another mirrored wall. As Tiogra collapsed on the floor of broken glass and stone, he noticed Dracula's eyes glowing violet.

"Stand down!" the prime vampire commanded.

Tiogra slowly stood up with pain coursing through his body. Once he regained his footing, he weakly tossed a rock he had picked up from the rubble at Dracula's head.

"Interesting." Dracula noted as he caught the stone and crushed it, "It figures you gargoyles would be immune to hypnosis."

Dracula's hands suddenly burst into flame as he spoke. Tiogra eyed the fiery bats floating around the vampire lord's arms as the flame blazed around his fists.

"Let's see if there are any other powers you're immune to." The prime vampire chuckled.

The vampire lord heaved a fireball at Tiogra, only to have his flame blocked by a spout of water that shot up out of the ground. Vlad, still leaning against the wall, eyed the spout with confusion.

"I see you still have your elemental abilities to help you." Dracula teased, "Unfortunately, they will do you no good."

Truthfully, the amount of strength it took for Tiogra to use his elemental power near Vlad's nullifier was exhausting, but there was no reason for either of the vampire lords to know the truth. Dracula then used his enhanced speed to grab Tiogra by the throat again. This time, the prime vampire used his supernatural abilities to ignite the gargoyle's face in fire.

"Though I can never traditionally steal your people's strength for my own," Dracula sneered, "I can still find rapture in killing you all. One by one."

Reacting as fast as he could, Tiogra put a barrier of water around his head to protect himself from the flames. Despite his attempt, he was struggling to keep Dracula's power from scorching his head. Soon enough, the flames proved too strong for the master gargoyle and fire engulfed his face. Tiogra roared in pain as the flames seeped inside his ears and nose.

Suddenly, a ball of water splashed onto Dracula's hand, snuffing out the flames. As Dracula turned to see who had suppressed his power, a small stone foot had flown into his face and kicked him across the room. Regardless of the surprise, the prime vampire smiled as he flew through the air. He knew there was only one being who could have kicked him hard enough to send him flying, even with all his current power. Sure enough, as Dracula looked up, the grandmaster was standing in the throne room, starring him down with ash-covered claws. Though his face was calm, Dracula could feel the rage the grandmaster held specifically for him.

"Your fight is with me." The grandmaster said to Dracula, motioning for Tiogra to stand back up.

The weakened master gargoyle rose to his feet, hardening his near-broken arm to stone and straightening his back. As the cracks from Tiogra's spine echoed in the room, Vlad threw off his red cloak and revealed his golden suit of skeletal armor underneath.

Looking over Vlad's armor, Tiogra could see that the golden knuckles and shins of the suit had three, inch long, black spikes that were no doubt used for enhancing the vampire lord's kicks and punches. This made Tiogra chuckle at the fact that Vlad needed handicaps to help him fight.

"So…" Dracula said as he walked back into the room, "The grandmaster has finally come to face me, again. It's come down to this. The master against the father and the student against the son. Got to admit, I didn't see it ending exactly like this."

"You prattle too much." The grandmaster stated, focusing on his opponent.

"Only because I can afford to." Dracula said snickering.

The prime vampire's moment of transcendence was short lived as the grandmaster quickly kicked him in the jaw, knocking him back through the walls into the castle's gymnasium. As this happened, Vlad was frozen with shock to see his father knocked back with such force. Before Vlad could react, Tiogra ran up and smashed the vampire lord with an ice hard fist, beginning his final fight with the once proud "Son of the Impaler."

As Dracula was knocked backward, he flipped in the air and landed on his feet, sliding back into the wall of the gym. He then flew across the room to clash with the grandmaster, who was flying straight at him.

As Dracula's fists flew towards the grandmaster, the elderly gargoyle grabbed the vampire lord by the wrists and slammed him into the ground. On instinct, the grandmaster struck at Dracula's head, only to hit the floor as the prime vampire turned into mist and materialized at the other end of the gym.

"Prime form!" Dracula suddenly yelled.

"Huh?" the grandmaster asked, frozen where he stood with confusion.

"I want you to fight me with everything you've got." The vampire lord clarified, "This will be our last battle, and I want to kill you when you're at your best."

The grandmaster scoffed. Even after death, Dracula was still as arrogant as ever. Still, the grandmaster did not sense any tricks the vampire lord would be hiding and regardless of the request, the elderly gargoyle secretly yearned to use his full power against his lifelong enemy. With that in mind, the grandmaster obliged his nemesis and transformed.

As the grandmaster altered his appearance, his entire body felt incredibly stiff, as if it were a muscle he had never used before. The first feature to extract was the grandmaster's giant moss covered wings, which smacked against the ground, creating terrible quakes that the entire province felt. The grandmaster's joints furiously cracked as his arms and legs expanded and his muscles grew immensely. Ivory talons and organic spikes popped out of the grandmaster's gray, moss covered legs and forearms as the horns that ran along his neck and head emerged out of their ligaments. His serrated tail furiously slammed into the ground as it regained its original size. The grandmaster's face morphed into an even beastlier creature as his silver hair weaved its way into his dark crimson fur. Though not entirely humanoid anymore, the grandmaster's true, aged form had an uncanny resemblance to Trog, only the grandmaster stood on his hind legs instead of all fours.

Dracula watched the transformation in horror and astonishment. It had been so long since he had seen the grandmaster's true form that he had nearly forgotten the overwhelming appearance of his adversary. Only when the grandmaster stopped growing did Dracula regain his combative mindset. The memory of seeing this creature who, although daunting, still only stood up to Trog's ankle brought back so many adrenaline pulsing emotions for the prime vampire, who was more than delighted to feel the sensation once more.

After he had finished transforming, the grandmaster tightened his own gargoyle slacks and dove at Dracula, dragging the vampire down into the castle's lab, where the two titans tossed each other around the room until the entire castle came crashing down on their heads.

Meanwhile, Tiogra and Vlad were busy with their own fight until they suddenly felt the ground shake. Realizing what was transpiring within the fortress, Tiogra quickly broke down one of the walls and climbed to the top of the castle, while Vlad made his way through the hallways to avoid getting crushed. Before either one was out of harms way, the castle began to crumble and collapse upon itself as vampires and gargoyles ran from the falling debris. Once he was outside, Tiogra flew into the sky and observed the falling castle, searching for any sign that Vlad was still alive. Just then, a giant creature burst up from the collapsing structure with Dracula clutched in it's foot. Realizing the creature was the grandmaster in his original form, Tiogra and the rest of the battlefield's occupants watched in awe as the gargoyle leader flew into the summoned rainclouds with the vampire lord in tow. The gargoyles cheered as the vampires gazed up in horror at the sight of the grandmaster's true form before they continued their battle.

Once they were inside the storm, the grandmaster tossed Dracula into the air and punched him further into the clouds with hope that the vampire lord would be smart enough to catch himself before he fell. As he predicted, giant black bat wings sprouted out of Dracula's back. The vampire lord laughed as he and the grandmaster hovered in the depressing clouds.

"I applaud you, gargoyle." Dracula said, "This was better than I expected."

The grandmaster glared at the vampire lord through his reptilian yellow eyes and snarled.

"However," Dracula began, "You will find that in death, I have become even more powerful. So powerful, that I have been granted the abilities of the god I worship."

With that being said, Dracula raised his hands up just below his shoulders with his arms outstretched and his palms facing towards the sky. The lightning and thunder intensified as the prime vampire began to channel his energy through the storm.

Curious as to what Dracula was doing, the grandmaster used his meditative vision to find the source of the vampire lord's sudden power. For the second time in his life, dismay ran across the grandmaster's face. He could see the vampire's immoral power source was Egn himself! The unholy god's face was more horrific than the grandmaster had remembered. It was a constantly burning, ineffable face with flesh melting off the many bones it was composed of. The face hung over Dracula as the vampire lord roared in pain and ecstasy.

The grandmaster could see black veins grow out of Egn's mouth and reach into the vampire lord as he began to make his own beastly transformation. Dracula's skin became fiery and scaled as the evil god's energy pulsed into him. The muscles on the vampire lord's body did not become bigger so much as they became longer and leaner. Another strange trait was that every one of Dracula's muscles doubled. The sight of numerous, red demonic abs folding over themselves along Dracula's torso as his armor fell off of his body was not what made the grandmaster take a look of disgust, so much as the tiny, out worldly maggots crawling in and out of the prime vampire's pores. Even stranger features were the teeth that took the place of Dracula's eyelashes. Then the grandmaster began to realize that Egn was turning Dracula into a diminished version of himself, especially when smoke rose off of the vampire's skin as the majority of his clothes were burnt away and his eyes turned completely white from the heat. With enormous horns growing out of the prime vampire's head completing the image, Dracula had become a true monstrosity.

Laughing menacingly, Egn's face disappeared as Dracula starred down at his opponent.

"Now..." the prime vampire said smiling, "we finish this."

Concurrently in the remains of the castle, a wounded Vlad emerged from the rubble with an incandescent anger from his home being demolished. Feeling the cold rain on his face and snapping his shoulder back into place, Vlad rubbed his arm and began to search what were the remains of his lab for the stone catcher sword.

As soon as he began searching, the vampire lord gleefully noticed the hilt of the blade sticking up out of the ground. Before he could reach the blade, Tiogra plummeted out of the sky and tackled Vlad into the rubble. As he lay on his back, Vlad groaned in pain as Tiogra snapped his forearm back into place from the impact. Hearing the master gargoyle's footsteps heading in his direction, Vlad struggled to his feet, but lost his balance on the slippery rocks he lay on. Still exhausted from his fight with Dracula, yet not wasting any time, Tiogra leapt into the air and tried to drive his feet into Vlad's chest, only to see that the vampire lord avoided his attack and instead destroyed the rock Vlad was situated on. Vlad quickly hobbled over to the blade as Tiogra wearily followed, both determined to kill the other as quickly as possible. When the vampire lord was within reach, Tiogra weakly lunged at Vlad and tackled him to the ground where he pinned Vlad onto his back again and wearily, yet forcefully, punched at his face. Vlad tried to strike back at the master gargoyle, only to have his blow blocked and countered. The vampire lord then kicked Tiogra off of himself and tried to crawl away, only to have the master gargoyle tear his shin guards off of his legs. Feeling this, Vlad's eyes widened as he saw Tiogra notice the glowing blue nullifier located in the sole of his armored boot. Smiling with satisfaction, Tiogra crushed the boot and snickered as the dampening energy stung his arm. A powerful blast of water then shot out of Tiogra's arm and launched the vampire lord forward, past the sword. Given Vlad's distance from the sword and the current physical state the vampire lord was in, Tiogra used his elemental power to revitalize himself for the next attack.

Watching the master gargoyle revive himself, Vlad quickly searched the area for another weapon he could use. Suddenly, he heard the sound of something shattering. Looking back, Vlad saw that Tiogra had successfully healed himself, covered the sword in ice and had smashed it to pieces. Panicking, the vampire lord frantically searched the remains of his lab for anything he could use. All the experiments and test subjects were completely destroyed. All the test tubes and microscopes had been smashed. All seemed hopeless for Vlad until he noticed a vile that read "rattus blood." Laughing hysterically, the vampire lord grabbed the vile and drank the blood in a single swig. Before Tiogra could reach Vlad, the vampire lord grinned at his foe and instantly vanished.

Shocked, Tiogra starred at the spot where Vlad was, thinking that there was no way the vampire lord could have just disappeared. Then an incredibly fast punch unexpectedly hit Tiogra across the face as he tried to ponder how his enemy had managed to regain his strength so quickly. As he hit the ground, Tiogra could make out Vlad's menacing laugher through the heavy raindrops. Before he could rise back onto his feet, Vlad delivered a superfast kick to Tiogra's back, smashing the master gargoyle back into the ground. Hearing the vampire lord's annoying laughter again, Tiogra groaned as he stood back up. Luckily, Vlad was known to toy with his opponents before he killed them. This gave Tiogra some time to think of a plan, he only hopped he thought of something fast before the vampire lord would decide to kill him.

At the same time, Dracula and the grandmaster had continued their battle in the sky. The prime vampire was franticly throwing his enhanced fireballs, while the grandmaster caught them and snuffed them out within his grasp. Irritated at having his power diminished so easily, Dracula began to evaporate into mist. Reacting with his opponent, the grandmaster spit a fireball of his own at the prime vampire, burning the mist before the vampire lord could completely vaporize. Howling in pain, Dracula quickly healed himself and clenched his fists tightly in anger until he drew blood from his palms. Completely igniting his arms, the vampire lord charged at the grandmaster in rage. The grandmaster reacted by projecting jets of water from his hands, completely soaking the prime vampire. Once Dracula regained his position in the air, the grandmaster struck him in the face, multiple times before delivering a crushing blow with his tail, tearing one of the vampire lord's wings.

Enraged, Dracula gestured towards his opponent and conjured a lightning bolt from the surrounding clouds that struck the grandmaster in the chest. Severely injured, the grandmaster fell towards the earth, but quickly caught himself before he fell too far and proceeded to fly directly at Dracula while spitting fire in the vampire lord's direction.

As he dodged the fire from his adversary's mouth, Dracula gestured again, this time having the lightning strike the grandmaster in the back. The grandmaster roared in pain, yet kept his focus on the battle. Hardening his flesh for further attacks from the vampire lord, the grandmaster continued to fly in Dracula's direction.

As Dracula gestured for the third time, lightning began to roll across the clouds. Noticing where the lightning was coming from, the grandmaster quickly grabbed the prime vampire and held him in front of the bolts. Since the lightning was made from Dracula's own power, he only felt a numbing sensation when the massive bolt struck him. It was only when the grandmaster combined the mystical energies of the summoned lightning with his own elemental fire that Dracula felt overwhelming pain. Once the blast was finished, the grandmaster used his power over water to freeze the prime vampire in a thick layer of ice. The elderly gargoyle then drove the frozen vampire lord directly into the ground, where their nations fought below.

When the colossal warriors collided with the burnt soil, there was a loud crash, and a cloud of dust swept over the battlefield. Once the dust settled, a charred and severely burned Dracula rose up out of the crater the grandmaster had made with his body and slowly started to crawl back toward the castle's remains. Before the prime vampire even came inches away from the crater, the grandmaster landed directly in front of him to halt his progress. Dracula starred up at the massive gargoyle in pain, knowing that this was his time to die yet again. He could only hope his adversary would be merciful, but given the circumstances, Dracula knew the grandmaster would not be kind in his execution.

The grandmaster began the execution by slowly tearing off Dracula's wings, then stomped on the lower half of the vampire lord's torso and pulled his legs off of his pelvis. After which, he tore off Dracula's arms while channeling his flames through the vampire lord's ligaments before stepping on his head and slowly crushing him.

"This cannot be!" Dracula screamed in agony, "I was destined for greatness!"

"You were destined for demise!" the grandmaster exclaimed in retaliation as Dracula's head was squashed under his foot.

As the prime vampire's storm clouds dissipated from the sky, the gargoyles cheered as their traditional enemy died under the heel of their master and subsequently slaughtered the last remaining vampires on the battlefield who were not immediately destroyed by the sunlight.

As Vlad perched himself on a nearby rock after striking Tiogra multiple times, he noticed the gargoyles chasing down his minions and slaughtering them effortlessly. The sound of his nation's victory roar caught the attention of Tiogra, who smiled at his master's success in killing Dracula.

"It's over Vlad!" Tiogra yelled from the center of the debris.

Vlad glared at Tiogra and gritted his fangs until they broke in anger as he realized that the battle was lost. If anything, he could have a small victory by collecting the master gargoyle's head. Using his amplified speed, Vlad charged at Tiogra with his claws barred, ready to slash Tiogra's throat away. Once he was inches away from the master gargoyle, a wave of water pulsed out of Tiogra's body and sent Vlad flying backward. Before the vampire lord had time to react, Tiogra tore the upper half of Vlad's head away with his claws. As Vlad's body slowly dropped to the dirt, his mouth moved up and down with chunks of his teeth falling into the dirt as he gasped for air.

"I can see it," Vlad said with what little energy his body had left, "I can see hell... I'll be waiting for you Tiogra..."

Hearing this and remembering the promise he made to Sadik, before the rattus prince had died, Tiogra crushed the lower half of Vlad's skull, turning the rest of his body to ash. Taking a deep sigh of relief, Tiogra strolled towards the remains of a nearby wall and tiredly leaned against it. The grandmaster was at the top of the rubble in his true form, starring at Tiogra and smiling at his master pupil's success. Tiogra looked up at his master's glorious form and smiled back with satisfaction. The war with the vampires was finally over, the gargoyles had won.

Just then, a slicing sound rang through Tiogra's ears and a cold sensation flowed through his throat. Tiogra looked directly in front of himself and saw a blade punctured five inches through his throat, which then slowly turned horizontally and decapitated the master gargoyle. As his head flew through the air, the last sound Tiogra heard was the grandmaster yelling in rage at the site of one of his master pupils dying before his eyes. As Tiogra's head landed on the ground and his body slowly crumbled to pieces, his last view was of Yemz standing over his body, cleaning his blade and smiling with sinister satisfaction.

The grandmaster leapt down from the ledge he was standing on to confront Yemz, who saw the elderly gargoyle leaping down and reacted as quickly as he could, pulling out a second sword and flying directly above the castle ruins to address the gargoyle army. The grandmaster chased after Yemz in a fit of rage, but halfway through leaping off the ground, the elderly gargoyle was distracted by a sudden awareness of intense heat. Looking back towards the battlefield, he saw over a thousand gargoyles throwing fireballs in his direction.

"Brothers!" Yemz yelled as the grandmaster was pummeled by the flames, "The time is now!"

On command, three thousand gargoyles cheered as their eyes changed from yellow to violet. This horrific sight froze the other remaining gargoyles in disbelief as they realized that their comrades and Yemz had somehow aligned themselves with Egn. The gargoyle rebels roared into the sky and started to attack their former comrades, who were completely taken by surprise as the gargoyles they once called friends attacked them mercilessly. Some gargoyles were unable to defend themselves out of shock and disbelief. Boragen and Ghin were some of the only gargoyles that retained a combative mindset as they miserably destroyed their former friends. The grandmaster burst out of the rubble with seven wayward gargoyles in his clutches, killing them as quickly and tolerantly as he could.

"Retreat!" Boragen yelled to the gargoyles that remained loyal to the grandmaster.

The loyal gargoyles obeyed and flew off towards the window maker that led home. As Boragen and Ghin took off, they flew back and helped the grandmaster fly towards the portal, knowing that their leader would not be able to successfully slaughter his own people despite his power. Directly behind the grandmaster, chasing him with barred claws and teeth, were the gargoyles that had betrayed him. It was sickening to Ghin how these creatures, who had served their nation loyally for decades, could suddenly turn against everything they had believed in and fought for.

Using almost all of the energy he could spare, the grandmaster gathered up enough fire to throw at the traitors in order to buy the loyal gargoyles enough time to escape. As the enormous burst of fire shot out of the grandmaster's hands, few of the traitors flew in opposite directions, far enough that they would be unaffected by the blast. Despite their lives of constant training, the sudden bloodlust made some of the traitors lose their tactical awareness and discipline. As soon as the fire made contact, the gargoyle rebels that were hit were immediately killed and fell apart. Those that were not struck either had a stone limb fly into their face or were blinded by the fumes emitting from the blast, making them fly around aimlessly until they could see again.

The grandmaster, exhausted from using up the rest of his energy on his wayward students, fainted and started to plummet to the ground. Boragen, Ghin and a few other gargoyles noticed their master was in trouble and immediately flew to his aid. Luckily, the gargoyles managed to catch the grandmaster before he fell too far.

As the group of gargoyles flew off towards the window with their master in their grasp, a sudden wave of bullets flew past their heads. Ghin looked behind them to see that the traitors had secretly managed to bring guns with them and had hid them among a pile of rocks near the portal. Each rebel was desperately trying to shoot the grandmaster down, but missed horribly.

"Get the grandmaster through the window!" Ghin yelled at the other gargoyles, "Fast!"

The loyal gargoyles flew down to the portal and managed to get the grandmaster inside, before the rebels got too close. Ghin had stayed behind and used his fire to hold the rebels off a little longer for his friends to get through.

"Get in!" Boragen yelled to Ghin as bullets whizzed by his head, "Hurry!"

Having bought his friends a little extra time, Ghin dove inside the portal as it closed behind him. Noticing the window closing before they could reach their target, some of the traitors flew past the opening mechanism and right into the rock formations behind it. Luckily, the grandmaster had prepared for a situation such as this centuries ago, only he had expected that it would be vampires or lycanthropes trying to kill his people, not other gargoyles. Before the window could be reactivated, a small ticking sound was heard and the window maker detonated, killing the rebels around it.

Once the loyal gargoyles reached the other side, they saw their friends and relatives waiting for them on the landing pad as well as other gargoyles who joined them in battle. Everyone was shocked to see the grandmaster being carried by his students, exhausted from the fight. Most of them were taken back by surprise since they had never seen the grandmaster's true form before. Despite this, they feared that the grandmaster would not be able to recover from his wounds, due to his old age. Boragen and Ghin helped their comrades bring the grandmaster to a medical station within the castle, where an entire room had to be cleared for the gargoyles to be able to fit the grandmaster within the walls for medical treatment.

The grandmaster's niece and nephews arrived at the medical station immediately after hearing the news and began to help their uncle heal. The gargoyles that had survived the battle broke the horrible news to the rest of the nation that some of the gargoyles had defected to Egn and were being led by Yemz. Husbands, wives and children shed tears from the news that their loved ones had died and were angered by the report of Yemz's betrayal and his foolish mission for power.

There was one gargoyle in particular who was incredibly nervous about his father's wellbeing. Standing next to his mother, Jhonig waited anxiously for the window to reopen and for Tiogra to come flying out of the portal, waiting for the hug from his son and the kiss from his wife. He strongly wished that the dream he had would not come true, but there was nothing in this moment that would prove otherwise.

Jhonig searched the castle until he found Ghin, who stood in the center of a crowded tavern with Boragen, shaking his head as they told another gargoyle about the unfortunate death of her sister at Vincent's deformed hands.

"Ghin!" Jhonig yelled, grabbing his friend's attention, "Where's dad?"

Ghin and Boragen looked at Jhonig in surprise. With all that had happened, it had never occurred to them that Tiogra was even gone. As quickly as they could, Ghin, Boragen, Mojhyn and Jhonig flew to the medical station to ask the grandmaster where their friend was. Once they arrived, the grandmaster's heart filled with sorrow as he noticed his students, knowing full well what they were going to ask.

"Grandmaster!" Jhonig exclaimed, "Where is dad?"

Noticing the grandmaster's expression, an overpowering feeling of sadness washed over the gargoyle child.

"I'm afraid Tiogra is lost to us." The grandmaster said sadly as he saw Jhonig's eyes fill with tears, "Yemz betrayed us."

Hearing this, Jhonig collapsed on the floor, trying his best to keep his emotions from overpowering him. Boragen and Ghin were taken back with grief and guilt for not realizing that Tiogra was not with them. Mojhyn sobbed from hearing that her husband was killed, proving that her paranoia about Yemz was right. Ghin tried to comfort Mojhyn while Jhonig was still in a state of shock. Before Boragen could put his giant hand on the child's shoulder to comfort him, he noticed that Jhonig had clenched his fists, hard enough to make his gray hands turn white. Feeling an incredible mix of rage, sorrow, confusion, and guilt, Jhonig's wings shot out of his back and he flew directly out of the castle, deep into the surrounding forest. Some gargoyles noticed this and miserably watched as

147

the prophesized gargoyle child sped into the forest, tearing down trees as he flew.

When he was far enough away from the castle, Jhonig finally stopped and roared as loud as he could into the sky. Flames and water rushed out of the young gargoyle's body, crushing and burning the surrounding trees. A giant pillar of lightning shot out of Jhonig's wings and pulled the fire and water into itself as it discharged into the sky. The gargoyle child continued to howl and emit his elements out of anger until it felt that his body would burst apart. His roar echoed through the forest to the castle, where other gargoyles could see the pillar of elements in the distance being launched into the sky. An hour after he had calmed from his episode, Jhonig flew back to the gargoyle castle, where his friends Beihdah and Lokk were waiting for him.

Sadness and pain were in their eyes as they saw Jhonig return from his fit of anger. He walked past his friends, still feeling anger and sorrow from hearing about his father's death, over to the edge of the landing pad and starred into the sea on the horizon. Beihdah looked at Lokk as if to say that she wanted to talk to Jhonig alone. Knowing that Beihdah strongly cared for their friend, Lokk nodded his head and headed back into the castle.

As Beihdah approached Jhonig, she resisted the urge to place her hand on his shoulder, thinking he did not want to be touched at the moment and seeing the pain in his eyes as he starred off into the distance.

"Are you ok?" Beihdah asked.

"No, Beihdah." Jhonig calmly said as he began to walk back inside the castle door, "Not even a little."

"What are you going to do?" Beihdah quietly asked.

Jhonig paused for a moment and turned back around to face his friend. He was careful not to glare in her direction so that she would not think she did anything wrong.

"Nothing." Jhonig grimly said, "Right now, we need peace, not anger. To be honest, I don't know if I'll do anything at all."

As the mature words left the youth's mouth, Beihdah reassured herself that Jhonig was going through a moment of incredible grief but that everything would be all right.

The Worst Kind of Evil

It was a dark night like never before in Dublin, Ireland. A priest was at St. Patrick's cathedral, preparing the alter for mass the next day. After the priest finished cleaning, he grabbed his coat and was about to leave when suddenly, the lights went out. As soon as the priest pulled a flashlight out of his coat pocket and turned the light on, his was overcome with fear. The light from the flashlight revealed that the cathedral was crawling with some of the rebel gargoyles, who were starring directly at the priest, grinning and licking their lips in excitement. Before the priest could react, a large hand gripped his face and squeezed his head until it popped like a balloon full of blood and bone.

As the priest's lifeless body dropped to the floor, the gargoyle traitors turned their attention to the back of the cathedral, where Yemz stood before them on top of the alter.

"Brothers!" Yemz exclaimed, "Phase one of the plan is now complete. We have destroyed our old comrades, releasing us from our moral bonds. Now we must confirm Egn's acceptance."

The rebels cackled from the thought of the goal Yemz had heavily influenced upon them, a new world order where gargoyles ruled with iron fists.

"Egn has heard our cries for help." Yemz said, "Now, we must wait for him to speak."

After his short speech, Yemz turned around and faced the wall behind him. The entire room fell silent as a fiery red light shown in front of Yemz, with faint images of tortured souls being tossed around it.

"Lord Egn!" Yemz began, "We have done as you've commanded! What is your wish now?"

No words were spoken from the red light. Instead, an uneasy feeling of chills rolled down the spines of the rebel gargoyles as if a giant creature with a raspy, hissing voice were speaking to each of them individually, yet simultaneously. Yemz knew that unlike Trog, who spoke to his followers through the earth, Egn spoke through emotions. It had been said that this was because emotions were tools that could bend the wills of lesser creatures. The evil god praised the rebel gargoyles for their betrayal and gave them instructions to slaughter the humans that resided in the city around them, showing him that they had abandoned the labors Trog had placed on their shoulders.

The rebel gargoyles gladly obeyed and flew out of the cathedral, where the other rebels were waiting for them, and began to tear the city apart. Throats were slit and bodies were burned and drowned as the rebel gargoyles terrorized the residents of Dublin. Pieces of men, women and children were thrown about in a barbaric frenzy. Some gargoyles even drank the blood coming out of the humans they were slaughtering, just from the sheer sickening joy they received from the experience.

Yemz smiled as his followers continued to slaughter the humans. Later, he joined in on the killing and even the consumption of blood.

"Kill them!" Yemz yelled, laughing with a mouthful of flesh, "Every last one of them!"

The gargoyle rebels cheered as they set the human buildings ablaze and tore down their homes as the butchering continued.

"Make sure no one escapes!" Yemz yelled as his followers continued attacking the mortals they once protected.

After two hours of slaughter, the gargoyle traitors reveled in their brutality. Most human bodies were stacked on top of each other or scattered around in pieces from being torn to shreds. However, some humans were kept alive so that the rebels could torture them later. There had not been carnage this brutal since the time Dracula had celebrated the day Vlad had "grown a spine" after he killed his brother, Radu.

Yemz looked around the crumbling city in satisfaction. The sight of his followers destroying a human city and massacring its people brought a feeling of self-righteousness to the gargoyle turncoat. Yemz realized that this feeling was Egn praising his work. As his followers continued to tear the city apart, Yemz walked away from the crowd to secretly speak with Egn.

"What is your next command, sire?" Yemz asked, once he had placed himself in seclusion.

A prickly, itching sensation washed over Yemz as Egn instructed him to walk back towards his accomplices and raise his left hand to them. Irritated at his new master from the sensation he was given, Yemz did as he was instructed and stood before his army with his arm outstretched. Suddenly, Yemz's arm glowed red as power surged from his hand and flowed over his followers. The first beings who were affected by the power were the humans who were left alive. The energy was too great for them to handle and they disintegrated. Seeing this, the other gargoyles panicked, having no knowledge of what would happen to them as they were touched by the red light. Their bodies twitched and folded into themselves as the light of chaos began to deform them into slaves of evil.

The transformation made the rebel gargoyles wail in pain. Whatever color and fur they had on their bodies was burned away and replaced by slimy, dark green flesh. Some of their muscles were magically torn away from their bodies and replaced by sharp bones, making regular mobility difficult. Their wings twisted and bent until they looked like the wings of creatures fabricated from mayhem. The faces of the rebels became entirely warped as well, completely sagging in certain areas and gaining more edges and angles in others. It was even stranger when some of the rebels grew extra limbs, horns and claws or developed elongated limbs.

Yemz looked over at his army as the transformation began to change him as well. His muscle mass greatly increased as brutal features took the place of his elegant characteristics. Instead of having smooth, leathery skin, Yemz now had rough, studded flesh. Bones grew over his left arm, covering the sinister energies that Egn was channeling through his limb. Yemz's arms grew in width and length until his hands almost dragged on the ground. The new feature Yemz admired the most were his new, powerful jaws and teeth that overlapped each other. Starring at his reflection in a nearby puddle, Yemz was overcome with joy as he took on an appearance he found wonderfully intimidating.

Once the transformation was complete, Yemz looked back over his deformed army and noted that they were starring back at him with mindless, violet eyes. With a thought, Yemz commanded his army to line up in front of him. Hearing his mental command, the chaotic creatures obeyed their master without any sign of faltering.

Yemz smiled at the power that had been bestowed upon him by his new master. Before he could get too comfortable with his new ability, Egn told Yemz that his next task was to take his brainwashed minions to New York, where the next stage in his plan could commence.

Yemz foolishly asked why he would bother attacking New York and not the gargoyle castle first. A feeling of overbearing weight and pain came over the new servant of evil as Egn explained that the presence of gargoyles would have to be made known to the rest of the world sooner or later. According to Egn, New York was a very important symbol for a country that was currently considered to be the most powerful human nation on the planet, attacking it would make the gargoyle nation respond and try to defend the humans that lived there. With the new power that was given to him, Yemz would be killing two birds with one stone.

Yemz nodded, smiling in satisfaction and then ordered his army to head for New York. Watching the deformed gargoyles take flight made Yemz wince as some of them had trouble rising off of the ground due to their new features, making the turncoat leader almost regret his decision to rebel. Still, every choice in life Yemz had made led to this moment. Soon the world would fall under his control, and with the help of Egn, no one would be able to stand in his way and humans would be put right where Yemz felt they belonged; under his boney, deformed heels.

The gargoyle traitor had sacrificed everything to make his goal a reality. He had betrayed his nation, he had abandoned the beliefs he was raised on and he had killed gargoyles, very few of which considered themselves his friend. In the back of his mind, Yemz had thought, much to his own dismay, that others would have gladly been his friend if jealousy, vanity and fear did not strangle all reason and goodness out of him.

However, none of that mattered now and it as too late for Yemz to undo the past, even if he wanted to.

As he flew in front of his minions, Yemz thought about how the definitive moment of his actions was drawing near and now that he had gotten this far, what his first order of business would be once he eliminated the grandmaster and his pupils. Perhaps he would take the fight to the tortasapiens and destroy the race he viewed as the most useless. Maybe he would head straight for the lycanthropes and flaunt that Egn held a gargoyle in higher regards than a race who had failed him so many times. Afterwards, he would enslave the humans completely and make a name for himself as ruler of the world.

The thoughts of destruction made Yemz completely giddy as he flew. In a matter of moments, he could see the city located directly in front of him. His personal fantasy would have to wait, now was the moment when the proud traitor would finally make the world aware of his greatness and pave a stronger path to victory.

Irreverence

Many members of the gargoyle nation mourned the passing of their loved ones on a huge ship out in the North Atlantic Ocean. The fog that had fell over the water seemed fitting for this moment of grieving. Over four thousand gargoyles were slain by the vampire nation and three thousand gargoyles had betrayed their people under Yemz's order. It was difficult for some gargoyles to stay strong and not become taken over by stress, especially since the loss was so great.

There were not any ceremonial instruments to be played that day and no remains to be buried. Instead, large rocks with the names of the fallen gargoyles inscribed on each one were dropped into the ocean as symbolism for their deaths. After the funeral, the gargoyles wandered around the ship aimlessly and sad. Regardless of the misery at the loss of their loved ones, they were distraught over the news of the traitors, many of which were family and friends to the gargoyles who were still loyal to the grandmaster. It did not make any sense for them to betray their nation and yet they had helped kill so many members of their own race. To add insult to injury, three gargoyles had reported to the grandmaster that the remains of Yemz's wife, Chem, had been found in her home along with a knife that was stuck in the stone that was once her throat. Using his meditative techniques, the grandmaster could see that it was Yemz who had killed his wife, just before the battle with the vampires and had help from Egn to keep the murder a secret until the traitor and his followers were in Transylvania. The disbelief that a member of the gargoyle nation would do such a thing made the dishonor almost too much to bare for the others.

Jhonig was leaning on one of the ship's banisters with Beihdah and Lokk, looking out onto the water with uneasy sadness. Lokk was using his ability over fire to move a trail of flame from one wrist to the other by passing it down his arms and across his shoulders. Beihdah admired her friend's attempt to try to keep a positive mindset, but eventually, Lokk lost the flame and dolefully leaned back against the banister.

From behind the gargoyle children was the grandmaster, who was still healing in his full form and discussing current affairs with Ghin and Boragen.

"It was completely predictable that he would betray us!" Boragen exclaimed, almost choking as he mentioned Yemz, "We should have done something."

"Even if we did, what would have happened?" Ghin responded calmly, "He had over three thousand gargoyles who sided with him. Let's just be thankful they weren't smart enough to stay here and kill us all in our sleep."

"They did not side with him entirely by their own free will." The grandmaster stated.

Boragen and Ghin looked up at the grandmaster completely puzzled, as did every other gargoyle on the main deck of the ship.

"What do you mean, grandmaster?" Ghin asked.

"It was as clear as the violet in their eyes," the grandmaster began to explain as he loomed over the crowd of his students. "Yemz had been secretly dissolving their inner voices of reason for years. Poisoning them. Turning them into slaves for his rebellion. Egn was helping him by blocking Trog's senses and my ability to take notice. If I had known this already, none of this would have ever have happened."

"So we can change them back, right?" Boragen interrupted.

The grandmaster slowly looked at the gargoyle blacksmith with sad, solemn eyes. "They are completely under Yemz's control now." He explained, "Whatever power Egn gave Yemz to help in his crusade is permanent. We cannot save them."

This news did not upset the gargoyles any further. They had already accepted the fact that their friends who had betrayed their nation were already dead to them. Hearing that they were under a diabolical influence made it somewhat easier to accept.

Suddenly, Bok came running up the stairs that lead up from the lower deck and interrupted the conversation. "Grandmaster," he said, grabbing everyone's attention, "there's something on the news I think you should see."

Two other gargoyles brought one of the televisions up to the main deck for the grandmaster to see. When it was ready to use, Bok unmuted the television and increased the volume for everyone to hear. A female reporter was seen broadcasting on the channel they had turned to, just outside of Manhattan.

"Bill, this is nothing like I've ever seen before." The reporter said, "There appear to be over thousands of giant flying, bat-like creatures, circling around Times Square in a cyclone formation. We are unaware of who or what these creatures are. They look like nothing that I've ever seen. The N.Y.P.D were slaughtered as soon as their units arrived and a military strike was ordered a while ago, but their divisions have yet to appear."

As the gargoyles on the ship watched the broadcast, the grandmaster shook his head in disappointment. It was against the law of the gargoyles that humans should be known about their presence. Everyone on the main deck recognized the bat-like creatures to be former comrades who had been warped by Egn's power. As the broadcast continued, the gargoyles noticed the cyclone formation of the mutated rebels began to shift like a swarm of disturbed bees.

"Ok, there appears to be motion from the creatures." The reporter said, "It appears the monsters are breaking up formation and…oh my… they're attacking the citizens!"

The gargoyles watched in dismay as the rebels attacked the people of New York. Some rebels picked up humans and threw them in the air, just to watch them hit the ground in a bloody mess. Other rebels simply tore the humans apart. As the mutated gargoyles buzzed around Times Square, Yemz was seen walking in the middle of the chaotic horde, laughing hysterically as blasts of the red power burst from his hand and tore apart the concrete and steel within the city. One gargoyle rebel attacked the reporter and stuck his tongue out at the camera before it lost its feed.

The grandmaster maintained a calm expression. Regardless of this stressful predicament, there was no reason to overreact. The thought of Yemz's ego as he put on a diabolical show for the world was comforting, seeing that he still was still arrogant enough to defeat. Even through witnessing it on the television, the treacherous gargoyle's arm reeked of Egn's power. However, this was something the grandmaster knew could be avoided as well. When the broadcast was over, other gargoyles eagerly waited for the grandmaster to speak, with hope that he had a plan as he looked at his students with heavy eyes.

"My pupils," the grandmaster said as he addressed the crowd, "as you saw, Yemz and his followers have attacked New York, making our presence known to the rest of the world. He hopes that he will draw us out as a response to this attack against the human populace. Unfortunately, we must do what I had hoped would never come to pass. We must fight our own kind."

The gargoyles slowly bowed their heads as they heard the grandmaster's words.

"You need not worry…" a voice that was familiar to the grandmaster said from above the fog.

The gargoyles looked up to see who spoke. Hovering down from the fog, Aro, Xong-Zox, Tun-Taig and Durin landed on the boat and bowed before their uncle.

"… we will go and fight for our nation." Tun-Taig said as he bowed.

The grandmaster was taken back with shock. "You cannot go!" he exclaimed as he grabbed his tallest nephew by the shoulders, "I promised your fathers I would look after you. I would rather go myse-…"

"You are in no condition to fight, uncle." Xong-Zox interrupted, "And besides, we haven't been able to hold up to our reputations as members of this nation we helped create."

"Aye," Aro continued, "T'would be nice to stretch our legs again."

The grandmaster smiled at his nephew's statement, but remained skeptical. Suddenly, his face calmed, but the expressions that followed were as if he were having a conversation with voices in his head. Finally, the grandmaster closed his eyes and tilted his head towards the ground as if he had come to a conclusion in the silent discussion.

"Alright." The grandmaster sighed.

The gargoyle cousins eyed their uncle in astonishment. "Really?" Aro asked.

"Yes." The grandmaster calmly said.

"What made you change your mind?" Tun-Taig asked.

"You already know your grandfather isn't the only one I talk to from time to time. They say hello, by the way." The grandmaster muttered.

Enormous smiles grew across the master gargoyle's faces after hearing their uncle's words. "We won't disappoint you, uncle." Xong-Zox said as she bowed with her brother and cousins.

"Just hurry up before I go against my brothers' judgment... and please, be careful." The grandmaster said.

"No need to worry." Xong-Zox reassured.

Seeing an opportunity to fight his friend's murderer, Ghin abruptly walked up to the grandmaster.

"I'll go as well." He said.

"Are you sure?" the grandmaster asked as he calmly looked down at his student.

"Yes," Ghin began, "Tiogra was my friend and I was unable to keep him safe. If it means anything, I would like to help defend the world from this new threat."

The grandmaster smiled at Ghin's sense of honor and then looked over at Boragen, thinking that the master blacksmith would want to help in the fight as well.

"I will stay here." Boragen said, "Should Yemz have anymore tricks, I will be here to help defend our home."

"Very well." The grandmaster confirmed as he turned back towards the rest of his master pupils, "Good luck to you all."

Ghin and Boragen respectfully nodded at each other before they went their separate ways. After their nation bowed and bid them good luck in their battle, the master gargoyles took to the skies and headed for New York. From a distance, Jhonig had overheard the entire conversation and snuck down to the lower deck to a porthole. There, he watched the masters fly away and waited until they were far enough that they could not sense him nearby. Once the coast was clear, Jhonig opened the porthole and began to climb through when suddenly, he felt a soft hand pull on his arm. When he turned around, he was taken back to see that it was Beihdah who had tugged on his arm.

"What do you think you're doing?" she asked through gritted

stone teeth.

"I'm going to follow the masters to New York and fight Yemz." Jhonig said as he looked into his friend's eyes.

"You can't be serious..." Beihdah said, "Once Yemz sees you, you'll be dead!"

"I don't care." Jhonig stated.

"There's no way you'll survive!" Beihdah exclaimed as tears began to form in her bright yellow eyes, "He's a master gargoyle and you're only almost eight years old! You can't even master your elements yet! I'm not going to let you do this just because you want vengeance!"

"I'm not doing this just for me." Jhonig sternly explained, "I'm doing it for my dad and for my nation."

Beihdah took a long look into her friend's eyes as if she were starring into his soul and sighed. Not only did she see that Jhonig fully understood that Yemz had greatly dishonored the gargoyle nation through his betrayal, she realized that Jhonig would never forgive himself if he could not address his father's killer, let alone fulfill his destiny as the prophesized gargoyle. The last fact was what made Beihdah decide to let Jhonig go. Before she let go of his arm, she bounced up and kissed Jhonig on one of his knobby cheeks. "Be safe, Jhonig." She quietly said.

Slightly taken back by the random peck on the cheek, Jhonig nodded and dove into the ocean. Using his power over water, he was able to swim without surfacing for air and could see where the masters were heading as he sensed the spiritual trail their auras left behind.

Meanwhile, back in New York, Yemz was overcome with delight as his minions destroyed the humans around them. The storm clouds in the sky gave him a personal feeling of theatrical satisfaction. Police officers and civilians ran frantically as they were chased by the mutated gargoyles, who shot acidic blasts and concentrated bursts of toxic gas instead of water and flames.

"Look at them." Yemz said to himself, "The weakest race in the world and yet they dominate the planet. They bury themselves in materialistic lifestyles and disgusting libidinal vibes, covering them with smiles and false sympathy for one another. They all know how disgusting they can be, and yet they sweep their problems under rugs and humor themselves like the oblivious sycophants they are. If only they knew what awaited them in ten years, right my lord?"

A faint image of an out worldly, maggot-covered skull made itself visible to the right of Yemz, grinning at every word it's new lackey spoke. Though it's happiness was not out of agreement from the rebel leader's hatred, but out of the fact that a practitioner of it's rival's lifestyle had been turned against him.

A smile cracked across Yemz's deformed face as he leapt down from the building he was perched on, killing seven policemen when he landed. S.W.A.T. teams, that were waiting for him below, opened fire upon the supernatural terrorist as the dust cleared from his landing. As he slowly rose out of the crater he left in the ground, Yemz allowed the frail, human bullets to make contact with his altered flesh, showing his imminent victims that he was a threat they had never dealt with before. Using the gas that replaced his control over fire, along with the power in his arm, Yemz covered the area around him with a giant cloud of toxic vapor and unholy energy. The humans around him disintegrated and melted, while the nearby vehicles exploded and collapsed into ash.

Yemz laughed hysterically as the carnage persisted when suddenly, a feeling of overwhelming power coming from the east fell over the rebel leader. Looking towards the North Atlantic Ocean, Yemz cracked another ungodly smile as he saw the five master gargoyles approach the city.

"About time." Yemz cackled as his minions flew next to their master, perching themselves along the unsteady buildings and devastated streets, waiting for the order to attack.

Once the master gargoyles reached the city, they stopped on a nearby building to see where Yemz was. Ghin and Aro's eyes were the only ones that widened in shock as they, along with their comrades, scanned the city that was being consumed by chaos. A few burning buildings crumbled to the ground and distant screams could be heard from where the masters were perched.

"Well this is peachy." Aro said sarcastically, "The humans are going to looove us for this."

"Focus on the mission at hand, Aro." Xong-Zox reminded, "We can't afford to lose our concentration."

"Right." Aro muttered.

Just then, Ghin caught sight of the gargoyle rebels heading in their direction. Each one salivated at the mouth in a mindless rage as they landed across from their former superiors.

"There!" Ghin exclaimed as he pointed towards the rebels.

The other masters looked in the direction Ghin was pointing and immediately leapt off their perch, towards their opponents.

Jhonig had just arrived on land as he saw the masters flying off toward the rebel army. Being as cautious as he could, the gargoyle child leapt to the side of a tilted, demolished building and followed the masters without being noticed.

Landing across from the rebel army, the gargoyle masters glared their opponents down, waiting for Yemz to show himself. Sure enough, the middle of the mutated swarm parted as Yemz walked towards the front, his disgusting smile still imprinted on his altered face.

The master gargoyles prepared themselves as they waited for the battle to begin. The bones in Durin's arms hummed as they vibrated from his elemental power. Tun-Taig slowly rubbed his fingers together as electric currents flowed between his fingertips. The gills on Xong-Zox's forehead buzzed as she used her power over wood to sprout three wooden staves in the palms of her hands with thick vines linking the sticks together, forming a triple section staff. Aro clenched his fists as liquid metal flowed around his hands, ready to solidify into weapons when needed. Ghin was the only master who had not readied his element as he waited for the right opportunity to strike.

From a secluded position on the rooftop of a nearby building, Jhonig watched the standoff that took place before the two forces clashed. Yemz raised his hand above his head for the master gargoyles to see, for the sake of dramatic effect. The seconds that passed after his hand was raised were filled with anxiety, yet the master gargoyles stood perfectly still. Then, with a flinch of his fingers, Yemz's army dashed past him and charged at the masters.

Ghin's hands burst into flame as the mutated gargoyles shot blasts of their toxic gases at their enemies. Durin used his power over air to push the gas back towards the rebels as Ghin shot his fire at the poisonous clouds, watching them ignite and burn some of the rebels to ash. Tun-Taig, Aro and Xong-Zox sped off in separate directions to attack the horde form multiple sides. Seeing this, the rebels divided into three more groups and attacked the masters from different sections of the battle zone.

Aro stopped near the entrance to a subway terminal and began to slice away at his opponents like butter. As some of the mutated traitors launched their acid upon him, Aro used thick layers of metal to catch the liquids and then threw the dissolving plates back at his opponents. His disciplined skill over his element also came in handy against the rebels that produced gas. Concentrating on his power, Aro was able to create a filer around his face to keep himself from inhaling any of the vapors and armor to keep the gas from eating away at his flesh.

Xong-Zox had flown up to the top of a building and struck down her opponents as they flew up to her. Her choice in weaponry proved masterful as she used the staff to break the rebels' bones with every strike. Though her power over wood was not very useful as a defense against the acid and gas, Xong-Zox's gills hummed violently as she channeled her power through her feet and made massive vegetation burst from the building she was positioned on, making the gigantic barbed vines constrict her opponents and squeezed the life out of them.

Tun-Taig had positioned himself in the center of an alleyway, luring the rebels into the space between the walls until there was barely any room left to move. Before the mutated gargoyles had a chance to use their altered powers, an explosion of electricity emitted from the passageway and fried the rebels to crisps. Casually stepping out of the back lane, Tun-Taig brushed a burnt piece of mutated flesh off of his black robes and began to electrocute more rebels along his walk through the demolished city.

Ghin and Durin were still situated at the spot where the battle had begun. The combined teamwork of their elemental powers and martial skill was incredibly effective against the mutated rebels. Durin repetitively used his powerful winds to fatally cut the rebels while Ghin mortally burned them into charred corpses. It was disturbing to the masters how the mutated gargoyles did not crumble to pieces when they died, but simply deteriorated into decayed shells. During the havoc, the two masters were becoming separated as the rebels pushed on. As he became increasingly irritated with the constant attacks, Ghin finally channeled most of his energy into a wave of fire that burst from him and burned the rebels around him. Durin, seeing Ghin's attack heading in his direction along with the gas the rebels were blasting at him, flexed his wings and slammed them into the ground, sending an intense gust of wind outwards and redirected the attacks away from himself. Looking around to see the damage he had done and finding nothing too devastating, Durin charged at the remaining rebels and continued to fight.

As the battle continued, Jhonig waited for the right moment when he could leap in and aid the masters. Suddenly, the young gargoyle noticed Yemz approaching Ghin from across the battle zone with another sickening grin on his horrible face. Jhonig noticed the rebel leader slowly raise his arm as it began to brightly glow red with diabolical energy. Realizing that Yemz was about to kill Ghin, the young gargoyle jumped off the ledge he clung to and dropped as fast as he could to the ground level.

Yemz's grin disappeared as he noticed an unexpected gray blur dive down from a nearby building. Before he could tell who it was, Jhonig drove his feet into the rebel leader's chest, sending him flying back into another building across the battle zone. The booming sound of the impact rang throughout New York, grabbing the attention of both the rebels and the masters.

"Jhonig!" Ghin yelled as he fought, recognizing his deceased friend's son, "What are you doing here?"

Jhonig did not answer as he angrily charged at Yemz again. Before Ghin could try to protect Jhonig, a flash of blue electricity exploded from within the building, sending the structure crashing down to the ground. Just then, Yemz and a very angry gargoyle youth burst out of the collapsing structure and flew back towards Ghin.

After they grappled in the air, Yemz broke away from Jhonig's grasp as they landed across from one another in a pile of rubble. Seeing

Tiogra's adopted son made Yemz giddy with thoughts of crushing the youth between his claws.

"So..." Yemz began, "this is fitting, huh? The prophesized child, come to fight the wayward slave for the honor of his dead father."

Jhonig said nothing in response to Yemz's taunt and glared his father's killer down as rain began to lightly fall from the light, gray storm clouds overhead. Seeing Jhonig's scowl made Yemz's smile stretch even wider than before.

"I suppose it's only fitting that one of us die here. That one of us being you, brat." Yemz continued.

Jhonig remained silent and assumed his fighting stance as a gesture for Yemz to stop his chatter and fight him.

The young gargoyle's resilience only made Yemz chuckle as he assumed his fighting stance as well. "Get ready for hell, kid!" the rebel leader threatened.

"You first." Jhonig responded. Though it was a whisper, somehow Yemz could hear Jhonig's words clearly, as if the young gargoyle were right in front of him. Before he could begin to fathom what just happened, Jhonig sprang forward, and began the fight that would define his role in the world.

To Be a Gargoyle

Jhonig flew at Yemz in a furious rage. Before he could hit Yemz, the rebel leader leapt upward with his arms folded across his chest, completely avoiding the young gargoyle's attack. Seeing this, Jhonig stomped on the ground and stopped himself from colliding with the wall in front of him. As he hovered in the air, Yemz saw the devastating hole in the ground from the young gargoyle's imprint as fire emitted from his foot, shoving nearby debris out of the way. Jhonig leapt into the air and tried to tackle Yemz, only to have this attack dodged as well as the turncoat dropped to the ground.

A bolt of lightning was shot from Jhonig's hands as he tried to hit the rebel leader where he stood. Yemz dodged this attack by rolling to his right with his arms still folded and continued to stare at Jhonig, goading the young gargoyle to attack him further. Aggravated, Jhonig swooped down and tried to blast Yemz with water, but Yemz avoided this attack as well and drove his knee into the back of Jhonig's head, sending the child flying into another building.

From within the hole in the wall that was made from his body, Jhonig rose out of the rubble and saw that Yemz was starring directly back at him, chuckling at how the battle was progressing. Even though he was older and more experienced, Yemz still found pleasure in toying with Jhonig until he was ready to kill the child. Infuriated at his failed attempts to fight, Jhonig burst out of the building and charged at Yemz again. As he was inches away from the rebel leader, Yemz drove his knee into Jhonig's chin and then struck the young gargoyle with one of his deformed wings.

Stunned, Jhonig stumbled around the wreckage, trying to regain his focus. Before his sight stopped spinning, Yemz delivered a punch to Jhonig's face, breaking off one of the young gargoyle's horns in the process. Another three blows accompanied this, followed by a roundhouse kick to Jhonig's stomach. As the young gargoyle knelt down in pain, Yemz grabbed him by the throat with his tail and began to strangle the vengeful minor until he felt the tendons in the child's throat begin to collapse from the pressure.

Tossing Jhonig to the side, Yemz leapt into the air and pinned the young gargoyle to the ground with his chaos-enhanced wings. Then, holding his left hand over the child's head, welts, bruises and cuts began to form on Jhonig's flesh as the red energy flowed over his body. Jhonig's bones and horns were broken as he lay under Yemz's pin, unable to move. Every wound that was placed on the young gargoyle's body felt like invisible knives, fists and bullets were injuring him from within the red energy.

Finally breaking free from the crowd of the mutated rebel slaves, Ghin leapt to his feet and ran for Yemz, but was immediately tackled by more mutated gargoyles. Tears rolled down Ghin's angry face as he helplessly watched his best friend's only son being elementally beaten by his killer.

Too exhausted to yell, Jhonig groaned in pain as the sinister element flowed over his body. Once he was satisfied, Yemz retracted the red light back into his arm and grinned once more. As saliva dripped from Yemz's mutated jaws, Jhonig looked up at the rebel leader, disgusted with himself at his failure to avenge his father.

"Sorry kiddo," Yemz said as his arm began to charge itself with the red energy, "looks like that whole 'prophecy' didn't work out after all."

Yemz held his fist in the air, ready to send it crashing into Jhonig's face. Jhonig shamefully closed his eyes. He had failed to live up to his nation's prediction, he had failed his friends, his family and Tiogra. There was nothing he could do now. He had been beaten to the point where he could not move. Now he would die with guilt rustling inside his head.

It was at this point, when all hope seemed lost, that the world around Jhonig froze. Confused, the young gargoyle rose off the ground as if he did not have any injuries and glanced back at Yemz. As he starred back at the rebel leader, Jhonig realized that this was a spiritual experience when he saw his physical body still pinned under Yemz's hold. At first, the youth wondered if he were dead. Before he could further comprehend what was happening, a blinding blue light shown from behind a forest of buildings to Jhonig's right, covering the world with its color. Jhonig turned to see what was producing the light and jolted back in awe as a creature the size of a mountain climbed over the buildings towards him. As it turned out, the creature was the light source, seeing as it was completely composed of the radiance. Though he could not discern any definitive features, Jhonig could see that the beast was glorious and had an energy about it that made him feel secure in it's presence. When the creature stopped in front of Jhonig, it looked down at the young gargoyle as he looked up in return.

"Be calm." The beast's radiant, earthly voice suddenly boomed, "This might sting a bit."

Without warning, Jhonig awoke back in his own body as time resumed. Yemz was thrown back as a bolt of energy shot out of Jhonig's chest, creating a large crater in the wreckage where he lay. The masters and rebels watched in disbelief as the bolt stretched towards the sky. The appearance of the bolt was like a tree of light in the center of a pit of demolished concrete. Jhonig hovered inside the bolt and roared as the current flowed through his body, healing his flesh and mending his bones and horns.

From within the bolt, Jhonig was overcome with knowledge and events that had led up to this point in his life. He saw the grandmaster training with Jung and Dorgran while he happily watched from a distance. He witnessed Trog's transfer into the earth from within the prime gargoyle's eyes, while the grandmaster and his family fought the undeveloped vampires. Jhonig saw the grandmaster bury his brothers with his niece and nephews and the beginning of the gargoyle nation. He saw the vampires and lycanthropes build their countries and destroy countless innocent lives while he was unable to directly interfere. Jhonig witnessed the laughter and happiness of his people as well as every tragic event that fell upon their shoulders. The next vision showed the day when Jhonig was born and how happy Tiogra and Mojhyn were to have him in their lives. Happy memories of growing up under the care of his foster parents flashed before Jhonig's eyes before he received the vision of Tiogra's death as if it were firsthand. After the history of the earth was completely processed in Jhonig's mind, he regained his sight and immediately noticed Yemz standing across from him.

Once he had healed completely, a now spiritually attuned Jhonig dropped down to the ground with electricity and steam emitting off of his body. Yemz's eyes widened in fear as he saw the gargoyle youth stand upright and stare back at him with incandescent, unadulterated emerald eyes. The way Jhonig starred at Yemz was serene, but deep within the rebel leader's soul, he knew that those eyes held nothing but disappointment and pity for him.

Frightened at the gargoyle child's newfound strength, Yemz mentally ordered a few of his minions to attack his young opponent. As the rebels flew to their master's defense, one of them attacked Jhonig with an overhead strike to the head. The strengthened youth countered this by jabbing his fiery fist straight into the rebel's mouth. With his fist firmly planted into the rebel's head, Jhonig flexed his forearm and made the brainwashed rebel explode from the ribcage up. Two more minions attacked Jhonig with roundhouse kicks to his torso. Before their legs could make contact with Jhonig's body, two powerful gusts of wind erupted from the ground and cut the rebels to pieces. The last five servants Yemz had summoned lunged at Jhonig as fast as they could. However, their attack was for naught as Jhonig kicked the heads off of his opponents and eviscerated them with his wings and tail.

Watching the revitalized gargoyle child slaughter his servants with ease made Yemz become motionless from fear. The fact that Jhonig maintained the same calm expression through the entire fight made the experience even more terrifying, as if killing the deformed rebels meant nothing to him. In a desperate attempt to destroy Jhonig, Yemz ordered the rest of his minions to attack the child.

Hearing their master's mental cry, the rebels leapt away from the master gargoyles towards Jhonig. Xong-Zox, Aro and Durin were irritated by their opponents' sudden choice to leave them in the middle of a fight and obliterated some of them before they were completely out of reach. Only Tun-Taig stayed his hand as the deformed gargoyles leapt away from him.

"Oy, cousin!" Aro yelled as he noticed Tun-Taig leaning against a wall with a relaxed smile, "What makes ya so calm?"

Tun-Taig pointed to where the rebels were heading to explain his relaxed state. When Aro saw why Yemz's deformed minions ran from him, he too smiled in satisfaction. Soon, Xong-Zox, Durin and even Ghin noticed as well. As he witnessed Jhonig tear and cut away at the gargoyle traitors, Ghin was taken back with disbelief. Watching the young gargoyle transform from an angry child into a seasoned warrior in a matter of seconds made Ghin smile, thinking about how proud Tiogra would be of his son.

Lightning, fire, water, wind, wood, metal and stone rapidly flew in numerous directions while Jhonig butchered the rebels as they threw themselves at him. The way the young gargoyle used the elements in multiple inventive ways was a stunning sight within itself. First, Jhonig stomped on the ground, making various rocks shoot upwards and buried them into the chests of the rebels. Then the rocks burst into flames, burning the rebels from within until they were reduced to ash. Next, Jhonig splashed water on top of the deformed gargoyles, freezing them in place. What was new about this traditional gargoyle attack was that Jhonig snapped his fingers, which made tiny particles of electricity within the ice explode and electrocuted the rebels inside. Following this, Jhonig gestured his hands together in a pulling motion and unfolded his wings. Instantly, thin and sharp wooden and steel shards were launched out of the gargoyle child's wings, lacerating the rebels into bloody chunks of deformed meat and bone. Jhonig then conjured mighty blasts of wind from his arms, which developed into small cyclones that picked up the steel and wooden projectiles and moved over the rebels, ripping them apart.

Jhonig's martial prowess was not to be taken lightly either. After he was revitalized, the young gargoyle's strength had quadrupled along with his speed. Heads shattered apart and entire sections of skeletons were reduced to powder from Jhonig's kicks and punches. The young gargoyle's wings and tail were able to cut through the rebels as if they were made out of foam. Despite the massive amounts of blood and gore, Jhonig still maintained a calm expression.

In the middle of the bloodshed, Jhonig noticed Yemz trying to retreat from the battle. With an incredible roar, a wave of fire, wind and lightning pulsed from the young gargoyle and blew over the remaining rebels, destroying them completely. Deformed gargoyle limbs landed in front of Yemz before he could escape Jhonig's range of vision, startling the rebel leader and making him jump back into the remains of the demolished portion of the city. Terrified, Yemz turned back around and saw the gargoyle child slowly trek towards him with the same calm eyes he had from when he was healed.

Using the evil energy within his arm, Yemz made four duplicates of himself and had them attack Jhonig. Seeing this, Jhonig assumed what was known in martial arts as a "horse-riding stance" and began to shake the ground with his power. Three rocks that were Jhonig's size rose up from the ground and broke apart, revealing clones of his own underneath. As the copies of Jhonig and Yemz clashed, Jhonig's clones tackled Yemz's replicas and pinned them to the ground. Suddenly, Jhonig's clones began to spark and then exploded into clouds of fire and lightning, destroying Yemz's copies along with themselves.

"This is impossible," Yemz said to himself as he trembled, "How can he destroy his own kind so easily?"

Without warning, Jhonig appeared behind Yemz and clutched the rebel's left arm, squeezing the limb until chunks of the deformed bones broke off and the limb was severely crushed.

"They aren't gargoyles anymore." Jhonig said with a radiant voice that mimicked the sound of crumbling boulders, "And neither are you."

Swatting the rebel leader's arm out of his hand, Jhonig lightly flicked Yemz in the chest and sent the deformed gargoyle flying backwards into a large chunk of debris. Holding his bleeding chest, Yemz looked up at Jhonig, infuriated that his plans had led him to this point in his life.

"Perhaps you're a rattus." Jhonig said, "Small, gentle and timid, but fearful because your fragile mindset cannot allow you to look at your own reflection, and deep down you know others will see you the same way."

Yemz dove at Jhonig and tried to kick the young gargoyle in the face, only to have his leg caught and his ankle yanked out of its mutated socket. The gargoyle turncoat yelled in pain as he collapsed on the ground and tried to crawl away from his young opponent.

"Or maybe you're a tortasapien." Jhonig began again, "Peaceful, strong and wise. You try to teach the world about your methods of peace but you're shot down at every opportunity you give."

Leaping onto his good foot and using his tail for balance, Yemz dove at Jhonig again and tried to smash his fists into the gargoyle youth's shoulders. The relaxed child caught Yemz's wrists and snapped his forearms into pieces before the rebel's fists were inches away from his shoulders.

"Maybe you're a vampire," Jhonig said, "You are your god's oldest and favorite creation. Spoiled rotten and having no idea how to rule your own people or how to prepare for the future, because you're too distracted by your own personal glory."

As he squirmed on the ground, Yemz tried to strike Jhonig with his tail as a final attempt to kill the youth. Much to his dismay, Jhonig caught this as well and ripped the traitor's tail off of his backside.

"It could be that you're a lycanthrope." Jhonig continued, "You have far more potential than the race who shares your god and all you want to do is win over your creator's love and favor. But over time, your anger and jealousy turns into transcendence, and you foolishly seek out ways to take the authority your creator has by gradually increasing your own strength."

Yemz tried to crawl away on his elbows and knees as Jhonig continued to speak. Before he could even cover the first few inches away, Jhonig stepped on Yemz's broken ankle and quickly tore the rebel's mutated wings off his back.

"You definitely aren't a gargoyle." Jhonig stated, "You don't even know what a gargoyle is."

Jhonig kicked Yemz onto his back and picked him up by his deformed throat. The gargoyle child flew fifty feet into the sky with Yemz in his grip and dangled the rebel in the air as the traitor gasped for oxygen from the young gargoyle's choke.

"But let me explain our purpose to you in words you can understand." Jhonig whispered.

Spinning his arm backward, Jhonig delivered a downward strike onto Yemz's nose, sending the rebel leader plummeting to the ground. The devastating effect from Jhonig's blow and the impact from being smacked into the ground was enough to cripple Yemz even further. Jhonig hovered down to the deformed traitor and grabbed him by the throat again, pressing his thumb into the turncoat's trachea.

"Gargoyles are guardians." Jhonig said as he threw Yemz up into the air and delivered a sidekick to the rebel's stomach, sending him halfway across the wreckage area.

"We guard the world from evil." Jhonig continued as he walked toward Yemz, "And we guard to honor Trog. Not just because he is our creator, but because along with our amazing abilities, he chose to give us freewill. The ability to develop as a people and become more than mindless sentinels."

As he approached Yemz, Jhonig stomped onto the ground, throwing himself and the rebel leader up into the air, then front flipped and dropkicked the traitor into the ground. Yemz groaned in agony as he felt a faint imprint of the child's heel where his wings used to be.

"We fulfill his request to protect, and that requires a lot of violence on our part." Jhonig said as he stood on Yemz's waist, pinning him to the ground. "Along with humans trying to kill each other without any other race's help and raising families of our own, the stress never ends, regardless of the meditation we do to balance ourselves."

Bolts of electric fire discharged from Jhonig's feet and scorched the rebel leader as he lay under his young opponent's clawed heels. The pain continued until Jhonig was sure that Yemz could not revive himself at all. The young gargoyle also noted that the red light in Yemz's arm was flickering on and off from the abuse it was receiving from the improvised punishment.

"But we learn to cope with our burdens and push through the struggle…" Jhonig said as he picked Yemz up by his diminished, diabolically charged arm, "all for the honor of our responsibility. To our forefather and ourselves."

Jhonig then tore Yemz's diminished arm out of its socket and burned the severed limb to ash. The rebel leader yelled out in pain as his mutated gargoyle blood gushed from the wound. Clutching the wound with whatever feeling he had left in his other hand, the turncoat tiredly squirmed on the ground in pain. Jhonig grabbed Yemz by the shoulder by knocking the rebel's hand away and dug his claws into his opponent's wound. As he held Yemz off of the ground, Jhonig slowly broke off each one of the rebel's horns from his head.

Master, Yemz thought as he slowly bled to death in Jhonig's grip, *why have you forsaken me?*

A sharp pain began to form in Yemz's stomach as Egn spoke to the gargoyle traitor. *What made you think I'd actually help a gargoyle, let alone have him directly involved in my plans?*

Tears began to roll down Yemz's deformed face as he heard the evil deity howl with laughter. He began to regret every selfish decision in his life that had led up to this point. Yemz thought about how he should have treated his fellow gargoyles with more respect and about how he should have placed more energy into his marriage with his insecure wife instead of neglecting her. He thought about how he had lashed out at the gargoyles who cared about him in anger and mental pain that he now realized he had essentially brought upon himself from his own fear. As Yemz looked deeper into his soul, he realized that the fear he felt was from the personal phobia that he would never be able to live up to his unrealistic expectations and narcissistic goal of being the perfect gargoyle. He also saw that the unnecessary jealousy he felt towards his peers, for the individual talents they had, only fanned the fumes of his anxiety. All his life, he had wanted to be the best at everything, to be the one that everyone would idolize, worship and envy. Now, through a struggle that he had placed on himself, Yemz knew he was going to die.

As the thoughts of self pity ran through Yemz's head, he slowly turned to face Jhonig, who still held him by the inside of his shoulder, with tears rushing from his eyes.

"Mercy...please." The rebel leader pleaded as he starred up at Jhonig.

The spiritually assimilated youth only starred at Yemz with as much pity as he could spare. "You have ridiculed my family, and you have dishonored the gargoyle nation."

Using his power over the earth, Jhonig released Yemz from his grasp and summoned rocks from the ground to hold the rebel upright, in position for the final strike. As this happened, Jhonig flew across from the stone frame and conjured fire and water from his pores into a ball that hovered above his palm. Then, particles of wood and lightning followed by wind and metal sprouted out of Jhonig's hand, into the elemental ball. As the ball spun, the elements within it mixed together into a sphere composed of white light. This white ball of energy, derived from the earth itself, was the burden and suffering of every gargoyle who had ever died that was released in the afterlife as they deteriorated back into the earth. It was pain for the death of loved ones, pain for witnessing destruction and massacre of innocent life, pain that Yemz had never tried to comprehend or sympathize with.

When Jhonig was far enough away from Yemz, the white light fused with the young gargoyle's hand as he clenched his fist. Looking back at his opponent for the last time, Jhonig used his power over lightning to charge at the rebel leader faster than the blink of an eye and struck Yemz directly in his deformed stomach.

When Jhonig's fist was inches away from Yemz's torso, the radiance began to burn away at the rebel's mutated flesh, reverting him back into his original gargoyle form. The composed elements within Jhonig's fist, along with the weight of his nation's grief, shot into Yemz's genetic structure and tore away at his flesh, bones, atoms, down to the very last yoctometer of his being. Yemz roared in torment as the light burned away at the rest of his body, erasing his physical presence from the earth until he was no more, along with the rocks that held him in place. It was finally over, Jhonig had hit Yemz hard and fast enough that the turncoat blinked out of existence.

With his father's killer defeated, Jhonig took a deep breath and cracked his neck. The brightness in the gargoyle child's eyes dimmed as the master gargoyles flew over to him.

"Well done, Jhonig!" Tun-Taig said, patting the gargoyle child on the shoulder with a smile.

"There is no doubt about your destiny!" Xong-Zox continued after her brother.

"Excellent job, lad!" Aro said, "What was that last technique you did there?"

"I showed him mercy." Jhonig said glancing at the ground, "I gave him a few seconds of unbearable hell in exchange for an eternity of slow torment. I figured that since he was once a gargoyle, there was still room for a little sympathy. Trog told me that he won't be in paradise or damnation, he will just sleep forever, reflecting on his life in solitude."

This information took the masters by surprise, not only because the young gargoyle could speak directly to Trog, but also that he was capable of such power and mercy towards his enemies when necessary. With smiles on their faces, the master gargoyles congratulated Jhonig again as the clouds cleared, allowing the sun to shine on New York again. Ghin walked up to Jhonig and placed his hand on the child's shoulder.

"Tiogra would be very proud of you, Jhonig." Ghin said, remembering his best friend.

Jhonig smiled as he received the compliment and hugged his father's friend, happy that he was able to quell the anger he held inside of himself for Yemz. Just then, a team of reporters came out from behind destroyed buildings and ran towards the group of gargoyles, eager for information on what had just happened.

Noticing the reporters, Jhonig looked back at Ghin, who had just received a message from the grandmaster. He nodded his head to approve that now that the world knew about them, the grandmaster confirmed that it was safe for the gargoyles to come out of seclusion. Jhonig stepped forward, retracted his wings back behind his shoulder blades, and waited for the first reporter to ask a question. The reporters came running up with their camera crews as fast as they could.

"Hello, Mrs. Brandy, channel three news." Said one reporter, "The public would like to know… who are you people and how did you stop the attack on New York?"

"Where did you come from?" asked another reporter.

"Are you from outer space?" asked a third.

Jhonig smiled at the numerous questions being throw in his direction. "My name is Jhonig." He said, "These are the masters of my nation, and we are gargoyles."

The Final Dream

It was a year after the battle with Yemz and his followers that humans and gargoyles started to coexist in peace. Throughout that year, the gargoyles humbly helped repair the damage done to the human cities that were affected by the war and showed the human world leaders the customs of their nation as well as giving them a tour of their mountain in France. The gargoyles also told the human leaders about their nation's history, about Trog and how the prime gargoyle had become one with the earth. After seeing the amazingly large, environmentally efficient and awe inspiring caverns this ancient society of supernatural warriors dwelled in, along with learning that the earth was a living being, the human leaders asked the gargoyles to show them how to better their own civilizations so that they could benefit the earth as well. Hearing this, the grandmaster and the rest of the gargoyle nation happily agreed.

Bok and Tun-Taig showed human engineers and scientists how to modify the engines in their vehicles and machinery to run purely on water and electricity, with even more speed and power then they originally had. Mojhyn, Celan and Durin were able to build gargoyle institutions around the window makers located around the world with the permission of human governments. This also allowed Xong-Zox and the other gargoyles to teach humans about their methods of spiritual guidance and martial arts. After receiving a seat in the United Nations building as a representative for the gargoyle nation, Aro, along with a few other gargoyles, had helped the humans build weapons to help defend themselves against other threats that might occur in the future.

Along with these changes with the human populace, Boragen began to meditate on a regular basis in an attempt to find inner peace and the grandmaster remained in his prime form. The grandmaster had stated to his students that this was because now that he had stretched his body completely after centuries of keeping it diminished, it would be difficult to retract back into his smaller form. Plus, now that the gargoyles had made peace with the humans, there was no reason to be secretive anymore.

Even with all the changes taking place in the world, Jhonig was able to continue his training peacefully among his peers, but not without recognition for his fight with Yemz. Despite this peace, one day the grandmaster had received word that a vampire had come to the front door of the original gargoyle castle in France and had requested an audience with the prophesized gargoyle child. Jhonig overheard this message and responded by flying over to the front door from the castle's medical tower, with Mojhyn and Beihdah following behind. Looking towards the ground, Mojhyn immediately recognized the vampire from the gargoyle archives as Trang, standing in broad daylight. The vampire princess bowed at the sight of Jhonig as he flew down. Mojhyn instinctively stepped in front of Trang to shield her son from whatever tricks the vampire might have up her sleeve.

"Why are you here?" Mojhyn asked harshly.

Trang simply looked up at the gargoyle warrior from her bow, stood up straight and apologized for her presence.

"I know you are not happy with the way my father and grandfather treated your race." Trang said, "However, I am hoping I can set aside our differences and we can call a truce between our nations."

"Nations?" Jhonig asked, remembering how the vampire race was defeated over a year ago.

Trang waved her hand and behind her, twenty vampires dressed in ninja grabs and tinted goggles immediately rose up out of their hiding places, leapt behind their master and knelt at her feet. What surprised Jhonig the most was that these vampires did not completely turn to ash in the sun.

"What is this?" Jhonig asked.

"I have found a temporary cure for the skin condition my nation has." Trang said as she ordered her countrymen to pull back their hoods. The vampire's skin gently sizzled as they pulled their hoods back, leaving their flesh open to the sunlight. "It's not much, but their hereditary weakness to sunlight has been focused to their eyes. It should be enough to help us cope for the time being."

Jhonig nodded in understanding. "What does that have to do with you being here?" he asked.

"My hope is that we can see each other as friends from now on." Trang explained, "We could help each other. I could show your people my nation's sciences and you could help me find a cure to our weaknesses."

Jhonig nodded again as he heard the vampire princess's offer.

"Your father was an honorable man." Trang added, "He had discipline and courage in everything he did despite the stress that came with his responsibility. It would be an honor if your nation made peace with ours."

Jhonig stroked his chin, pondering how to respond to the offer.

"It's ok!" the grandmaster shouted from one of the towers, "You have my permission!"

Jhonig, Mojhyn and Beihdah laughed as they heard the grandmaster's voice and saw the other gargoyles above them, waiting for Jhonig's response to the treaty. Finally, the young gargoyle shook hands with Trang, and both gargoyles and vampires rejoiced. Later that day, Trang had received her place in the United Nations in the front row next to Aro.

The night that followed, Jhonig slept for the first time in weeks. A few hours into his sleep, he tossed and turned as he received another vision in his dreams.

In this dream, Jhonig saw the lycanthrope kingdom's army being led by a monstrosity that was cloaked in black mists, heading towards the human cities. This monster appeared to be strong enough to lift up sections of monorails with ease and tossed them like small stones. Jhonig saw his friends charge at the monster and were crushed beneath it's enormous fists. The battle was looking grim for the gargoyles until suddenly, an explosion erupted from behind the lycanthrope army and burned away at everyone caught within the blast. Children of all races cried and mothers and fathers wept as they were set ablaze by the devastating ignition. Among the burning remains of the scorched earth, a tall burning figure, neither human, lycanthrope, gargoyle or otherwise stood before Jhonig. As the young gargoyle stepped closer, he could see that the figure was wrapped in a cloak of fire and maggots. The figure sharply turned to face Jhonig as the gargoyle child approached it. It's face was nothing like Jhonig had ever seen. Two sharp, blue, shapeless eyes crawled across the figure's head as it grinned, revealing three rows of teeth that seemed to resemble fire that had taken solid form. Flesh was melting off of the many bones that the face's skull was composed of as it burned. Jhonig's fur stood on end as the figure called his name with a voice that sounded like burning flesh. As the figure spoke, numerous burning parasites poured out of it's jaw like mulch from a dump truck.

Jhonig jolted upright in his bed as he woke from the vision, gasping for breath. He leapt out of bed, put on his clothes and ran down the hall to the living room where Mojhyn was sitting on the couch, reading a book.

"Jhonig!" Mojhyn exclaimed, startled from seeing her son awake and breathing heavily, "What's wrong?"

Jhonig looked at his mother with his eyes as wide as they could be.

"Jhonig?" Mojhyn asked again.

"Mom…" Jhonig began in a calm tone of voice as he headed for the door, "We need to see the grandmaster."

"Wait." Mojhyn said, grabbing her son by the arm, "What's going on?"

"No time to explain, mom!" Jhonig exclaimed, "We need to hurry!"

Realizing that her son had received another vision, Mojhyn nodded and flew out the door with Jhonig, up to the castle level of the mountain.

Once the duo reached their destination, they ran down the halls of the castle to see the grandmaster, who was in the tavern enjoying a drink with the master gargoyles. When he saw Jhonig, the grandmaster stood up, ready to greet the youth who had saved the gargoyle nation from

Yemz's betrayal.

"Hey, Jhonig!" the grandmaster yelled, "How is it going?"

"Grandmaster!" Jhonig exclaimed, "I need to speak with you right away! There could be trouble very soon!"

The grandmaster stopped drinking and asked Jhonig and Mojhyn to walk with him into the hallway so they could speak in private. There, Jhonig told the grandmaster about the dream he had about the lycanthropes, about the monster, and about the burning figure he saw. Upon hearing this, the grandmaster rushed out of the hallway towards the communications tower and spoke into the alert system.

"Attention!" the grandmaster's voice exclaimed from the speakers, "Everyone, report to the courtyard for instructions! This is not a drill!"

As he watched the gargoyles fly towards the courtyard from the communications tower, the grandmaster slowly turned around to face Jhonig with a grave expression.

"Let's hope this prediction can be avoided, Jhonig." The grandmaster said, "Otherwise, it'll be hell on earth."

What is this new weapon Ulric is trying to create for the lycanthropes?

How long will this new peace between gargoyles and vampires last?

Will Jhonig be able to continue in his role as the savior of the gargoyles?

Find out in the next book of the "Stone Turmoil" series...

Hell
for
Company

www.ingramcontent.com/pod-product-compliance
Lightning Source LLC
Chambersburg PA
CBHW080901120626
46555CB00008B/2906